UNDONE

TINA BROOKS MCKINNEY

ISBN: 0-9821089-4-X
ISBN-13: 978-0-9821089-4-9

TABOO PUBLISHING

DEDICATION

This novel is NOT for everyone. Most of you will look at the characters and say "come on, nobody can be this stupid." Trust me when I say these situations and circumstances do exist. I actually know them. Don't judge lest you be judged. I dedicate this story to you, you know who you are.

ACKNOWLEDGMENTS

I am going to attempt to remember all the people that have touched my life during this writing period. As always, I know I am going to leave someone out. This time, I'm going to do something different and leave this blank space so you can help me out and fill in your own name if I missed you.

_____

To my best friend and husband, William McKinney, you show me every day the meaning of true love. My children Shannan and Estrell Young, my parents Ivor and Judy Brooks, you all are the fuel that keeps me going.

Once again my friend Theresa Gonsalves, has put her own work to the side and assisted me with getting this book together. She has truly been a great friend and I would not have made it through without her assistance. I love you Theresa. Together, we will make it!

My road dogs, Sharon Jordan, Joyce Dickerson, sisters from another mother, thanks for putting up with my crazy behind. My best friends Angela Simpson, Valerie Chapman, and Andrea Tanner, you already know. Barbara Morgan, Kim Moss Floyd, Patrice, Harlson, Muriel Bloomfield Murry, Detris and Candice Hamm, Marvin and Sabrina Meadows, Dee Ford, Stacy Tumbling, Tra Curry, Linda Coleman, Antionette Gates, Sheila Goss, Rose of Savvy Book Club, Ricardo Mosby, Princilla Johnson, Sydney Molare', Donna Johnson, Terrance Bethea, Sharon Russ, and the ladies of Words of Inspiration, the fuk dat crew: Lynn, Kim and Sharon, Bernice Bagley, Stephanie Heard, Mississippi Readers, Leona Romich, Wendy Darling, Leo Sullivan, all of you have touched my heart in one way or the other. Brittini Wiliams thanks for the beautiful book covers!

This year is about making my haters my motivators. Thanks Carl you made the top of the list!

1 GINA MEADOWS

On December 31st of every year, for as many years as I could remember, I always composed a list of promises to myself to do better. And every single year, I end up disappointed with my results. So for this New Year' day, I'm refusing to waste my time on preparing my list. Instead of thinking about all the grandiose things I wanted to do, I was going to pick one and do it. I and my good friend, Tabatha Fletcher, had signed up to take some real estate courses. The plan was to open our own business, selling residential housing and investment properties.

Starting a business was something that I wanted to do for a long time but my dreams were something I had always put on hold. I had promised myself that this year would be different. This time I wasn't going to let anyone or anything come between me and my dreams.

The first of my many problems had walked out my front door and I couldn't be more happy. Tiera, my boyfriend's daughter, finally moved into her own place so I could finally concentrate on getting my own stuff together. Dealing with Tiera had been rough. She was young, spoiled and hardheaded. Her own mother kicked her out for those very same reasons. But I hung in there for as long as I could in order to prove to my boyfriend, Ronald, that I was a better woman than his ex. It wasn't until Tiera got herself knocked up that I realized I didn't have a dog in that fight. It was hard enough trying to control Tiera, but with the new baby, it was next to impossible.

Ronald was part of the problem. He wouldn't let me discipline Tiera the entire time she stayed with me. How he could form his lips to blame me when Tiera got herself knocked up, was still a mystery to me. Personally, I felt as if she was crying out for some attention from her dad. That's all most girls wanted. I believed that if he had spent a little more time with her, and a lot less time running the streets, this might not have happened. Of course, this was just my opinion, and I could never say that shit in front of Ronald. He wouldn't like it. He thought that I was just as much a child as Tiera was. At least that is what he said when I complained about her behavior.

I wasn't home the day the shit hit the proverbial fan. Ronald was sleeping in the bedroom when he heard the crash. I had gotten up early to take Tiera's daughter to daycare since her momma failed to come home the night before. I got there just in time to see the tow truck hauling away Ronald's prized possession his 2002 Porsche. When I got in the house, Tiera was on the floor crying.

"Oh, my God. What happened?"

"That bitch has to go," Ronald shouted as he raised his hand to strike Tiera.

"Ronald! Wait," I yelled, as I ran over to the girl. I wasn't sure what had gone on but I couldn't stand by and allow him to beat up on a woman.

"Wait hell. She ran into my mother fucking car!"

I stepped back with my hands extended in surrender. Tiera looked up at me with tears streaming from her bloodshot eyes. Her look begged me to help her. She was on her own this time. For two years I had complained about Tiera's reckless behavior and Ronald wouldn't listen. I felt vindicated by what had happened.

"It was an accident," Tiera cried as she scooted out of the corner, trying to get away from her dad.

"I want her out of this house today," Ronald roared.

"Daddy, where will I go," Tiera cried.

"Frankly, I don't give a damn. I have done everything I could to help you. I'm done."

I couldn't believe the words coming out of Ronald's mouth. He hadn't done a darn thing to straighten that little girl out. The opportunity was there, he just never took advantage of it. None of that really mattered to me at the moment because the end result was that Tiera had moved out.

A week to the day after Tiera left, I picked up the phone and called Tabatha. She answered on the first ring.

"Hey, girl. I did it. I just registered for class."

"I don't believe you. I'm going to need to see the confirmation email or the receipt."

"Ha, ha. You trying to be funny?" I said laughing.

"Girl, if I spend my money and you're not in the class, I'm done with you. Going back to school is your idea. Don't have me sitting up there by myself."

"I swear to you, I've paid for it and nothing can change my mind. I'm in."

"Okay. I'm going to make my payment too. I just hope I don't live to regret it."

"You won't. Trust me. The only thing we need to do now is get our books and we're set."

"I know. I can't wait. I am so ready to meet a rich man who is willing to take care of me."

"Girl, please tell me you are not taking these classes just so you can get the hook up with a man and his money."

"Don't hate. I'm trying to find someone to help me pay these bills. I'm tired of doing this stuff by myself."

"Well I'm trying to make some money so I can pay my own damn bills." '

"You got your motivation and I've got mine. I filled out this form and I'm ready to submit it. I just have one more question. Have you told Ronald about your plans to go back to school?"

"No, I haven't gotten around to it yet. I will probably tell him this weekend."

"I think you need to tell him today, before I send in my money. You know how Ronald is. It's not like he encourages freedom of thought. I don't want any mess from him because you know this school doesn't give any refunds."

"Ronald is not going to be mad about my trying to better myself. Besides, if I'm making money, it will help us both out in the long run. A blind man could see that."

"I hear what you're saying, but I still want to be on the safe side. If you don't think it's going to be such a big deal, why are you hesitating to tell him?"

Tabatha had me there and I couldn't think of a witty response to her question. I was a little nervous about telling Ronald my decision. I wanted the timing to be perfect. That's why I didn't want to tell him over the phone. I wanted to wait until he came over to deliver the news to him face to face. I also wanted to make sure he was in a good mood before I brought it up.

"You still there?" Tabatha asked.

"Uh, I'm here. I was just thinking about something."

"What?"

"It's nothing girl. You know how I do. I go off in my own world sometimes."

"Yes, you do. Wait, I almost forgot. Has that little grown ass girl left yet?"

"Girl, yes. You should have seen the colossal mess she left behind her. I ain't even kidding when I say I wanted to kill her. I knew she was upset about having to leave, but damn. She gave me her ass to kiss with this one."

"I'm sorry but I would have locked the door and held her hostage until she cleaned up her mess. I swear, you let the child get away with murder over there. There is no way I would have let her run me in circles like that."

"I know what you mean. It was rough because not only did I have to deal with her and her little stank attitude, I had to deal with her daddy too. Every time I said something to her she didn't like, she would call him. Then I'd have to hear his mouth."

"I've said this before and I'll say it again ... you're a good one. There would have been no way in hell that I would have put up with the things you did in your own home. I don't care how much in love I was."

"You say that now. Just wait until you find that special person. You would be surprised what you are willing to do to keep them happy."

"I doubt that. I'm a firm believer that someone else's happiness cannot come at the expense of my own. Life is too hard as it is sometimes without me making myself miserable. That's just foolish to me."

"Who said anything about being miserable?"

"Oh, Lord. Here we go. Don't go getting all sensitive on me. I was just making a statement. I wasn't directing it at you."

"It's okay. I'm fine. I should be getting off this phone anyway. I just wanted to let you know I submitted my application. I am still working on that mess she left in the bedroom as well as some other house cleaning to do. If you feel like coming over here and helping, I sure would appreciate it."

"Oh, no you don't. You already know how I feel about that crap. I don't like cleaning up after myself. So you know I'm not cleaning up after another adult."

"I feel you there. I really wanted to help that girl too but Ronald really tied my hands with her. I am going to miss the baby, but I'm really glad that Tiera is gone."

"You should miss that baby too. Remember all those sleepless nights?"

"Yes I do! She almost cured me from wanting to have children of my own."

"She cured me child and I wasn't even staying at your house. If you ask me, something was wrong with that baby. It cried all the time. What's Tiera gonna do when she has to take care of her all by herself without you to fall back on?"

"I don't even know but, thankfully, that is not my problem anymore. I dealt with it for two years. She didn't act like she appreciated my help. So, I'm done."

"I hear you. Look I'm going to hit this submit button before the class fills up. Let me know what happens once you break the news to Ronald."

I sighed. Tabatha was a great friend but she knew the exact buttons to push when she wanted to get me going, especially when she started in on my relationship with Ronald. She wasn't my boyfriend's biggest fan. Then again, Ronald wasn't her biggest fan either. It was a delicate balance keeping both of them in my life.

It wasn't until I had hung up the phone and turned off the computer that I allowed my fears to catch up with me. Signing up for these classes was the only independent move I had made since losing my mother a few years before. I was pretty much reliant on Ronald for everything. I was grateful for his help, but there was nothing wrong with having my own. Ronald gave me money to cover most of the bills but there was barely anything left after I paid them. Often times, I did without. Even when he moved his daughter in, he didn't increase the amount of money he gave me, which really put a strain on all of us. I could only hope that he didn't misunderstand my reasons for doing this.

I was in the middle of emptying out the trash from Tiera's old bedroom when I heard the front door open. For a moment, I was scared. I wasn't expecting Ronald so soon and Tiera had left her key by the front door when she had left.

I tentatively crept over to the banister and looked down the stairs. I watched too many horror shows on television for me to rush down the stairs all helter skelter. If someone was down there, they would have to come up and get me.

"Hello?" It might have been my imagination, but it seemed like my voice bounced back at me off the walls. Those creepy movies had my imagination working in overdrive. I heard what sounded like another door open and I panicked. Someone or something was definitely in my house and I was completely defenseless.

"I've got a gun!" I shouted as I poked my head over the railing and snuck it back. My house was old, and my ears were trained to listen to its telltale creaks and groans. I could hear light foot fall in the hallway. I tiptoed back into Tiera's room so I could climb out the window. Although it was dangerous, it was the nearest exit. If I jumped, I would more than likely break a bone or two but I'd rather do that than sit around and wait to be attacked or killed.

My anxiety whipped into hyper drive when I heard distinct footsteps on the stairs. Whoever it was that was in the house was coming up the steps. I threw all caution to the wind and opened the window not caring if anyone heard the ruckus I was making. I had one foot out the window and was just about to stick my head out when Ronald stopped me.

"Woman, what in the hell are you doing?"

I froze. Feeling like a complete idiot, I pulled my leg back inside. "Um."

"Close that window. You are letting out all my heat." Ronald looked around the room and turned up his nose in apparent disgust.

Ronald hated mess and this room was still in a state of chaos. Papers, food containers, broken toys and discarded clothes littered the floor. I followed his eyes and cringed.

"I heard noises downstairs and I got scared."

"And this was your plan? Jump out of the window?"

I started to get defensive because all of this could have been avoided if he had answered me when I yelled down the steps. "What else was I supposed to do?"

"What about the baseball bat I left here? You could have knocked somebody out with that if you had too. Going out the window would have done nothing but gotten you hurt. Which would be another damn bill that I would be expected to pay."

Ronald had a way of making me feel stupid. "The bat is downstairs."

"Lot of good it's doing you down there. What's up with this room? You should have had this mess straightened up by now."

"Your daughter did this. She should be the one in here cleaning it." I knew I was stating the obvious. If the mess was bothering him so much, he should have volunteered to help me or force his kid to come back and do it herself.

"You should have made her clean up before she left."

"Are you kidding me? I couldn't make her do anything. That was part of the problem I had with her and you know it." I should have kept that last part to myself and I knew it before I said it, but I was angry. If Ronald would have come two seconds later, I would have been sprawled out on the front lawn.

Ronald grunted in a dismissive way. "Well, you need to clean this up. It ain't cute."

I could tell by his response that Ronald was in one of his pissy moods. When he got like this, there was no reasoning with him. So I did what I always did…I conceded.

"I will." I docilely replied even though I wanted to bash him upside the head for scaring the crap out of me. I didn't like Ronald when he was in this type of mood. The best way to get through it, was to keep agreeing with him until he shook off whatever he was going through. There were a lot of things about Ronald's life that I didn't know about that he kept from me. I didn't necessarily like it but, he said it was for the best.

"Fix your face and come on downstairs. I want to talk to you about something."

I drew back in surprise. As far as I knew, there was nothing wrong with my face, other than a frown that he put there. He could fix it himself if he were to smile at me, instead of barking orders like I was his child. Instead of telling him this, I simply said "I'll be down in a minute."

"Good."

I had no idea why I had to go downstairs to talk to him when we were both standing in the same room, but I was not about to argue with him. Ronald typically didn't do mid-day visits. Since he 'worked' mostly during the night, he normally slept during the day.

I went in the bathroom and grabbed a relatively clean washcloth and wiped my face. After I finished cleaning out Tiera's bedroom, I was going to have to scour the bathroom too. She might have been a pretty girl, but she was nasty as hell.

2 GINA MEADOWS

Ronald was playing around with his phone when I walked into the room. His handsome face was still twisted up in a frown which caused my heart to sink. If he was in such a foul mood, he should have stayed at his house. I didn't really need him coming over to ruin my day too. As usual, I kept my thoughts to myself as I stood in the foyer waiting for him to finish whatever he was doing.

Over the years, I had learned the hard way, not to question him. In due time, he would tell me everything I needed to know. After a few more seconds, he slipped his phone in his pocket. "Come over here," Ronald said.

I was about to walk over to him until I realized that he wasn't talking to me. I staggered back as two little boys got up off the sofa and came to stand next to Ronald. In my head, I tried to calculate their ages against the number of years Ronald and I have been together. Tiny bells started going off inside my brain. Unless these children were dwarfs, they were born after Ronald and I had started dating. I tried to keep my emotions in check while I silently seethed. *Here we go again.*

"Say hello to Gina," Ronald instructed the boys.

"Hello," they said collectively.

I couldn't speak because I was fifty shades of pissed. He had concealed these children from me all these years, why was he bringing them by my house now? Regardless of how I was feeling, I couldn't take it out on the children. I wasn't wired that way. Children had a special place in my heart. "Aren't you two adorable. How are you?" I chanted.

"Fine," they replied. They were mirrored images of each other and so cute. I could have walked over to them and pinched their cheeks. I might have too if I wasn't so pissed off at their father. I couldn't even look at Ronald, I was so angry.

Ronald was smiling. "These are my boys, Merlin and Gavin."

"Nice to meet you," I said between parched lips. It felt like I had a small fire going in the pit of my stomach. Ronald couldn't have hurt me more if he had punched me in the face. During the last five years that we had been dating, I had been nagging him for a child. He always said the timing wasn't right which I never could understand. Seeing these kids, I finally understood why.

Ronald was beaming as he patted his hand on the sofa. I looked at him questioningly. I wasn't sure who his gesture was intended for, me or his children.

"Come over here," he said looking right at me.

I swallowed the rather large lump that had formed in my throat. I wasn't sure what Ronald was trying to prove and I didn't know how much longer I would be able to put on this fake front. I walked over and sat down on the corner of the sofa. I still didn't want to look at him.

"Boys, go ahead and sit back down. You can turn on the television if you want."

The twins took off running for the remote that was sitting on the coffee table. Almost immediately, I could spot the aggressive twin. He simply pushed his brother out of the way causing him to fall down. The child looked to his dad but Ronald seemed oblivious to the aggressive act.

"Don't make me take off my belt. Now, get your clumsy brother up off the floor." Ronald said in a menacing voice. I was a little surprised to hear this stern tone in his voice. He didn't talk to his daughter that way when she was running buck wild.

The aggressive twin reluctantly helped his brother off the floor as they sat in front of the television. He surfed through the channels until he found the Cartoon Network. Even though he stopped surfing the channels, he did not give up the remote.

"They look just like I did when I was little," Ronald bragged. He didn't have any shame in his game and I surmised he didn't expect me to do anything but welcome them into my life.

"They look—young. How old are they?"

Ronald narrowed his eyes at me. "Shoot, girl, I can't remember. Six, maybe seven. Hey, boys, how old are you?"

The twins acted like they didn't even hear Ronald talking to them. He could say what he wanted to say but I know good and damn well, those boys were not that old. "Why aren't they in school, they sick or something?"

"They ain't in school, damn it. Why you asking all these questions?"

If he didn't like my first question, he really wasn't going to like my next one. "What are they doing here?"

"They're with me. You got a problem with it?"

This was one of those damned if you do or damned if you don't situations. Either way it went, I felt like I was about to get the short end of the stick. "Can we not discuss this in front of the children?" I hissed.

"Fuck them. If you got something to say, I want you to say it."

Ronald was being an ass. I was thinking more about his children than he was. "I will not have this conversation with you in front of them." He could be mad all he wanted, I just wouldn't do it.

"As long as those cartoons are on, they aren't listening. You can believe that. The only thing that will get them away from that show is if I shut off the power."

I was not amused. "Fine. I want to know why you are bringing these children over my house now? You've been keeping them a secret why are you showing them to me now?"

"Secret? I'm not hiding anything from you or anyone else. You have never asked me if I had any other children."

I could not believe he said that to me as if that would make it okay. "I do believe I did ask you about whether you had any other children when you brought your daughter over here."

"Well, I don't remember that. Besides, that was over two years ago. How do you expect me to remember some shit that happened that long ago?"

"I think you would remember if you had some other children out there or not. I know I would."

"You should. Women can't do like men do. Besides, you wouldn't do anything but clown if I did tell you. At the time, it wasn't necessary for you to know."

He had me all fucked up. "So, what are you saying to me? It's okay for you to lie to me because you don't want me to clown?" I got up from the sofa. I couldn't stand being next to him right now. Ronald yanked me back down to the chair.

"Don't you walk away from me girl. We ain't finished talking yet."

I snatched my arm back from him and rubbed it. Ronald hardly ever put his hands on me in anger. I tolerated his bullshit because I loved him but I wasn't a fool. I wasn't going to let him put his hands on me any kind of way.

"If it doesn't make a difference what I have to say about it, then why do I have to sit here and listen? I have got some cleaning to do. Don't you remember?"

"You can clean the damn room when we're finished talking. Now, listen here, the boys' momma is bugging. I'm going to need for you to keep them here with you until I can get her straightened out."

"Like hell I will. I'm not getting ready to do that Ronald. I don't even know these children." I stole a look at his kids to see if they were listening to our conversation but their eyes were glued to the set. Even still, I knew it was a chance that they were only pretending to watch television to keep from getting into trouble.

"That's why I brought them over here so y'all could get to know each other. Now, baby, you know that I don't ask you for much. I don't see how it will hurt you to do this small favor for me."

"Favor? A favor is when you ask someone to give you a lift to the bus stop or to loan them twenty dollars." I could not believe we were having this conversation. This should have been the point where I was scratching his eyes out. Were it not for his children being present, it might have gone down that way.

"Then it's not a favor. The boys will be staying with you for a while. End of discussion. How do you like them apples?"

"I'm sorry, but I don't want to do this. Therefore, I ain't."

"You have always been talking about how you want to be somebody's mother. This is your chance to show me what you are working with."

"Are you being for real? I said I wanted to be the mother of my own children, not your side bitch!"

"My momma ain't nobody's bitch!" The aggressive twin shouted as he jumped to his feet.

So much for the children not listening. But if Ronald didn't care about what they were hearing then it was not my problem. He had me all twisted by his audacity.

"Boy shut up. Your momma is a bitch and you don't even know what that is."

"And she said you are a bitch too!" The little one answered back.

If the little boy wasn't as wrong as two left shoes, I would have been dying laughing on the floor.

"What did I tell you about getting in grown folks conversations?"

"Then you shouldn't be calling her no bitch."

I couldn't decide whether the boy was fearless or foolish. This was better than a movie and if Ronald thought I was going to deal with this, he had another thing coming. This little boy had man sized nuts, which could be a good thing or a bad, depending on how you looked at it.

"Merlin you had better tell your brother to shut his mouth if he knows what's good for him."

Merlin yanked his brother's arm and pulled him to the floor where they tussled around for a few second before Ronald walked over and slapped both of them upside the head. He came back and sat down gruffly on the sofa facing me.

"Do you see what you have started?" The boys were crying softly.

"Me? How can you blame this on me?" I was still trying to wrap my arms around the fact that Ronald had slept with someone else and showed absolutely no remorse about it. I couldn't believe it.

"You had no right to call that woman out of her name in front of my children."

"You hypocrite! You called her out her name too. Besides, I asked you to have this conversation alone and you said no. I can't believe you brought them to my house." I kept waiting for Ronald to tell me that this was some kind of joke but he remained steadfast.

"It's only going to be for a little while Gina. Why are you being so difficult about this?"

"Are you serious right now? I won't do it. I can't." I folded my arms across my chest and shook my head vehemently from side to side.

"What do you mean you won't do it? I thought you were going to prove to me that you were ready to be my wife and have my children?"

"I've already proven myself to you. I've done everything you've asked me to do, including raising one of your children."

"Well, we know how that turned out. I now have a grandchild thanks to you."

"You are going to blame that shit on me too? Your daughter was hell on wheels and you refused to let me correct her. She made my life a living hell and I never complained once."

"You didn't have to complain. She told me all about it."

I opened my mouth to say something and I had to close. I didn't give two shits what little Miss Tiera said about me. What she really needed was a swift kick in her behind. I tried my best to do right by her and her baby.

"Like I was saying, it's only for a short time. It would really mean a lot to me if you would do it."

I took a deep breath before I spoke. "Ronald I signed up for school. I don't have time to take care of these kids."

"School? What kind of school?"

"I'm going to take a few real estate courses."

"Let me guess, your girl Tabatha, talked you into this shit."

I immediately got offended. "Why does it have to be shit? How come you can't say you are excited for me or congratulate me for having the drive and ambition to want better?"

"Maybe I would congratulate you if I thought this was something that you came up with on your own. But I know good and damn well you didn't."

"As a matter of fact, I did come up with the idea. But it doesn't really matter who thought of what. What matters is that I'm doing it." I was glad that my secret was finally out in the open. Although this wasn't the way that I wanted to tell it. At least he knew about it and I could call Tabatha in the morning and put her mind at rest.

"It matters to me. I have told you about a million times how I feel about you hanging out with that girl. She ain't nothing but trouble."

"You don't even know who she is. You don't know anything about her other than the fact that she's my friend."

"I know enough about her to know that I don't want you fooling around with her. Every time y'all get together, you start acting brand new."

I was not about to have this conversation with him again. He was just trying to get me to change the subject so he could get his way. "What makes you think these kids mother is going to let them stay with me? They don't even know me."

"Don't you worry about their mother. I got this."

"Really? Well, like I said before. I can't watch those children with my school and all. Why can't they stay with you?"

The television might have been put on mute, that's how quiet it was in the living room as I asked that question.

Ronald clearly was not expecting it based on the expression on his face. Gavin and Merlin had both turned around watching for their dad's reaction.

"Don't be ridiculous. You know what kind of hours I keep. I can't have any babies hanging out at the crib."

I nodded my head like I was even thinking about his preposterous idea. He didn't want his kids to interrupt his life but it was perfectly okay if they came over to my house and disrupt mine. I turned my head away from the look on the children's faces. For a brief moment, I actually felt sorry for them but not sorry enough to change my mind.

Ronald stood up. "I guess you aren't really the woman I thought you were. I'm just glad that I'm finding this out now, before I married you." Ronald walked over to the boys and pulled them away from the television. He got their coats from the closet and slowly put on each boy's coat. It was difficult for me to watch his parental display.

I felt like everything I had worked for during the last six years was walking out the door. I felt like I had sacrificed too much for me not to be Ronald's wife.

"How long did you say they would be staying?"

3 GINA MEADOWS

When Ronald first mentioned my watching his kids, I thought he was preparing me for something that was going to happen in the near future. I had no idea he meant for it to begin immediately. I was still a little stunned at how quickly it had all gone down. Ronald gave me his panty dropping smile and it was a wrap.

"Give Gina your coat boys and be good. Don't let me hear that you've been over here showing your asses." Ronald had his hand on the door knob.

"Wait, you mean this is happening now?" My mind had just caught up with my mouth.

Ronald snickered. "When did you think it was going to happen?"

"I thought you would give them a chance to get used to me. What about clothes? Where will they sleep? What do they like to eat?" All of these questions were spilling rapid fire like out of my mouth.

"Gina, parenthood doesn't come with an instruction manual. Some things you have to figure out for yourself. They got some clothes in the bags in the other room. I'll check on you later."

Ronald left without another word leaving me standing in the middle of my living room in a state of total shock.

"What just happened?" I kept staring at the door waiting for Ronald to say it was all in fun. But, after a minute or two, I realized that the joke was on me. I was dumbfounded. I could not believe I allowed Ronald to punk me. He wanted me to figure this mess out but I didn't even know where to begin.

"This is some straight up bullshit," I mumbled.

The twins were still standing by the door with their coats on. If they were upset by their father's sudden departure, they did not show it. Obviously, they were used to this bizarre behavior. "Take off your coats," I said as I turned the television back on. I needed some time to regroup and think.

The boys unbuttoned their coats and handed them to me. I could not imagine what was going through their minds. I couldn't help but feel sorry for them. They settled in front of the television while I hung up their coats. I had to give it to Ronald, he was smooth. He got out of my house before I could even go in on him for cheating on me.

When I walked into the kitchen to figure out what I was going to fix for dinner, I saw the bags Ronald had mentioned. Two white trash bags sitting in the middle of the damn floor.

"Who does this?" I asked in amazement.

He didn't even have the decency to put their things into an actual suitcase. I dragged the bags over to the kitchen table and had a seat. Since the children looked so much alike, I was going to have to find a way to tell them apart. I hoped that something in those bags which would help me to do it.

The first bag was filled with dirty clothes. I pushed it away from me in disgust. I grabbed the second bag hoping for better results but it was also filled with dirty clothes. This was some bullshit. The smell of urine filled the kitchen. I grabbed both bags and carried them over to the washing machine. If nothing else, they would have clean clothes. As I sorted through the clothing, I was practicing what I was going to say to Ronald when I spoke to him. I was furious.

I had just placed the first load of clothing in the washing machine when one of the boys walked into the kitchen. It was sad because I couldn't even remember their names.

"We're hungry," he said.

"Which one are you?"

"I'm Merlin. My brother is Gavin."

"You two look so much alike, I don't know how I'm going to tell you apart."

"That's easy." He held up his wrist for me to see.

"What's this?"

"The other lady made us wear these things. Mine is green, Gavin's is blue."

It was a good thing that I was sitting down because I would have probably fallen over. "The other lady?"

Merlin nodded his head. His dark brown eyes looked troubled or sad. "The one we used to stay with before."

I had this sinking feeling in my stomach. These poor babies must have been through a lot. "Honey, how old are you?"

Merlin held up his hand in front of his face. "These many!" He seemed very proud of himself when he held up five fingers.

"Do you go to school?"

He shook his head from left to right. I wasn't surprised. Given the deplorable condition of their clothes, it was understandable why they weren't in school. I felt sick to my stomach.

"What do you like to eat?"

Merlin puffed out his chest. "I can make grilled cheese."

He was so little, I couldn't even fathom his using the stove. "Is that what you like?"

Merlin nodded his head up and down.

"What about your brother? Does he like grilled cheese too?" I could not shake the incredible sadness I felt inside.

"Sometimes. He don't like for me to cook his food."

"I'm going to cook it, sweetheart, for both of you. I just want to know what you liked before I did."

"Goody," he said clapping his hands and jumping up and down. Merlin turned around to go back in the living room. I followed him to where Gavin was still glued to the television set. He was sitting in a yellow puddle of urine. The sad part about it was that he didn't even appear to notice.

"Merlin, do you need to go to the bathroom?"

He looked down at his brother as his eyes widened with what looked like fear. He stepped in front of his brother and said, "Don't hit him. I'll clean it up."

I felt a rush of sorrow come over me like a blanket. As angry as I was at their father, I would not take it out on those kids. "Honey, I'm not going to hit anyone. It's my fault, I should have told you both where the bathroom was. Come on Gavin, let's get you cleaned up."

Merlin continued to stare at me for several seconds before he stepped to the side. I thought he was sizing me up. For someone so young, he had old eyes. I pulled Gavin to his feet and walked him upstairs for a bath in my bathroom. Merlin was fast on our heels.

"Do I need to help you get undressed?" I asked after I finished running a shallow bath.

"I can do it myself," Gavin said. These were the first words he'd said to me since his father had left. It was already clear to me that Merlin was very protective of his brother. He was sitting on the toilet seat watching me like a hawk.

"Very well, I'm going to see if I can find you something to put on while your clothes are washing." I left them in the bathroom with the door slightly open. I couldn't wait for Ronald to come back so I could give him a piece of my mind. At the very least, he should have warned me about this before he left those children with me.

I cleaned up the mess on the floor and found one pair of jeans that didn't reek of urine and took it back upstairs for Gavin. I passed them through the door.

"Gavin, you can put these on for now."

Merlin pushed open the door. "Those are mine," Merlin said.

I wasn't sure how he could tell but it didn't matter to me. It was the best pair that I could find. "It's okay Merlin. He's just going to wear them until I wash all of your clothes. When he's finished, I'll wash them too. Is that okay?"

He nodded his head yes. "Are you still going to fix us some grilled cheese?"

"I sure will. I'm going to do it right now."

I gave up the waiting for Ronald to come back shortly after two in the morning and fell asleep on the couch. The children were fast asleep in my bed. I was a little worried about them wetting my bed, but I couldn't see myself making them sleep on the sofa. The children were innocent in all of this. Never once did they question who I was and why they were with me. Nor did they ask for their mother. I think that is what surprised me the most. It was almost as if she didn't exist. Considering how strange the day had been, the night hadn't gone that badly. The incident on the floor was the worst of it.

Before I put the kids to bed, I made sure they both went to the bathroom several times and I limited the amount of

Kool-Aid they each had with their supper. I could only pray that my mattress would be safe.

When I woke up, Gavin was sitting in front of the television with the sound down low. Merlin was sitting on the floor right next to me. "Is everything okay?" I asked as I sat up stretching my arms over my head.

"We're hungry," Merlin said in the softest voice.

"Oh, okay. Let me see what I have. I haven't been to the store yet. We're going to have to make up a list. Do either of you have to go to the bathroom."

"I went already," Merlin said.

"Gavin, do you need to go to the bathroom?" He didn't look up from the television until I went and stood in front of it.

"Huh?"

"Bathroom? Do you need to go?"

"No, I went already too."

"Good. Don't get too wrapped up in this television that you forget to go, okay?"

"Oooo-kay." Gavin peeked his head around my legs so he could still watch the television.

I stepped in front of the set again. "I'm gonna fix something for breakfast. What do you like?"

"Grilled cheese."

"You can't eat grilled cheese all the time. What else do you like?"

"French fries," Merlin shouted.

"With lots of ketchup," Gavin added.

"Guys, that's not breakfast. What about some bacon and eggs? Or some grits or oatmeal?"

"Eww." They said it at the same time. I didn't know if they were objecting to some of it or all of it but we would find out when we were at the store.

"Well, I'll fix grilled cheese this last time but we're going to the store when we finish eating. Like it or not, you two are going to have to eat some vegetables and drink some milk."

I called Ronald as I was fixing their sandwiches. I wanted to find out how much longer the boys would be with me, before I went out and spent money I didn't really have, on food for them. Instead of speaking with him, I got his voicemail.

"Ronald, I think you owe me an explanation. You need to call me as soon as you get this message."

Since the phone went straight to voicemail, I was pretty sure Ronald had either turned his phone off, or was ignoring the crap out of me. Either way, it didn't make me feel good. If something were to happen to these boys I wouldn't know what to do about it. He left us at a terrible disadvantage.

Even though I didn't think it could happen so fast, I was becoming emotionally attached to these little tikes. It was a tricky situation to be in that could potentially end with my getting hurt. Ronald knew how much I wanted children and I assumed that was why he brought them to me. However, it wasn't enough for me to mother someone else's kids. I wanted to feel life growing inside of my own body. Somehow or another, I was going to have to explain it to him so that he would understand how I felt.

In the meantime, I vowed to protect these children as best I could. They deserved that much even if I wasn't the one that owed it to them.

It wasn't until we had gotten ready to go to the store that I realized I couldn't take them anywhere. I didn't have car seats for them. It would be just my luck to get stopped by the police and hauled off to jail while trying to do the right thing.

"Sorry guys, we are going to have to postpone our trip until I can get your dad to bring me your car seats."

"Why your car don't have no seats?" Merlin asked.

"I have seats for grownups, but we need special seats just for you two."

"My daddy don't got no car seats. We sit in the same seat he does."

Gavin said, "I want a special seat."

"Me too," says Merlin.

I couldn't help smiling. Their naivety was so cute. "Since we've got our coats on, do you want to walk over to the park?"

"For what?" Gavin was already taking off his coat.

"Yeah, for what?" Merlin had his coat off too.

"To play. Don't you want to get on the swings or climb on the jungle gym? They might even have a sliding board."

"No thank you," Merlin said as he handed me his coat. Gavin threw his on the floor and went back to grab the remote.

I went into the kitchen and phoned Ronald again. "I know you are ignoring me but I need to get some food in this house. I can't go anywhere without car seats for the twins. So you need to call me back."

4 TABETHA FLETCHER

I had called Gina several times over the last couple of days but she wasn't answering my calls. Periodically this would happen and this time I had my suspicions why. Ronald. My guess was that he said no to the school and she didn't know how to tell me. I would not have been surprised if that were the case. That's why I wanted to make sure she told him before I enrolled. If she decided to back out, that was going to be on her. No matter what she did, I was going forward with it. I wasn't about to let Gina waste my money and I was ready to drive over to Gina's house and tell her so.

I snatched up my phone off the end table. "If you don't call me back, in the next ten minutes I'm going to be at your front door." The only thing that was stopping me from just doing a drive by was her funky-ass boyfriend. For some reason, which had never been explained to me, he didn't like me. It would have been different if he and I met and had words, but we hadn't. He told Gina it was because I was single. Or at least that was the excuse she gave me. I couldn't help it if I didn't have a man. It was not like I wasn't out there accepting applications. I couldn't help it if motherfuckers kept failing the test. So, until I found the right one, I would continue taking applications.

Frankly, I didn't believe that was the issue at all. Gina didn't have to say her man was controlling, because all of the signs suggested to me that he was. As much as I loved Gina, I knew better than to say anything negative about her man. I understood how it was with first loves. I had been down that road myself. And the only cure for those types of relationships was an ass whipping. Although Gina had gotten her hands slapped several times, she hadn't had that ass stomped yet. I wasn't talking about an actual slap. I was referring to the mental whipping. Those were the ones that left permanent scars. I called those types of beatings, motivators. They would propel your ass to change your way of thinking. Until that time came, the only thing I could do was lend a supportive shoulder to cry on and an ear for her to ventilate.

I called Gina one more time as I walked out to the mailbox to get my mail. This time, she answered. "It's about time you answered that phone. I was about to be like the police and come a knock, knock, knocking on your door," I said laughing.

"I know girl. I saw that you had called but I've been a little busy." Something about Gina's voice didn't sound right to me. I could always tell when something was going on just by hearing her speak.

"You sure you're okay? I could be there in about ten minutes. Fifteen minutes if I stop at red lights."

"If you stop for red lights? Or do you mean if you catch a red light?"

"I've run lights before. This won't be the first time."

"Well, you had better quit. You never know where they have those red light cameras installed. You'll get one of those big ass tickets and then be pissed at me."

"My GPS warns me when I get within five hundred feet of one of those things. Then, I would have to stop."

"I'm glad I know you are just talking out your head otherwise, I would be scared for you."

"Ain't no need to be scared for me. It's those other drivers that you need to be scared for because me and my Oldsmobile will make out just fine. They don't make cars like this one anymore." Tabatha had a dinosaur for a car. It was probably one of the last vehicles made from steel.

"That's because they stopped making cars by hand. That thing doesn't belong on the road, it belongs in a museum."

"I know you are not clowning on my car! If my memory serves me correctly, who did you call last winter when your car wouldn't start?"

"Big Red."

"That's right, you better recognize. You never know when you are going to need her again so I suggest you watch what you say about her. She's sensitive."

"I know, you're right."

"So, what have you been up to since you all busy and stuff? I can tell you ain't in that talkative mood. Is Ronald there or something?"

"Naw, he ain't here."

'Is that it? You ain't gonna offer an explanation or say no more about it? What, you mad or something?" She was starting to get on my nerves. I was concerned but not enough to drag the information out of her piece by piece.

"I'm just tired, that's all. I'll be all right."

"Did you tell Ronald about going to school yet?"

"Yeah, I told him."

"Good, what did he say?"

"Actually, he didn't really say too much about it."

"All right then. I'll talk to you later." I was ready to hang up when I heard some yelling in the background.

"Stop it before you break something," Gina said angrily.

I heard the sound of glass breaking.

"Shit, hold on. Don't move." Gina moaned.

"Who is that? What's that noise?" I was ready to get in the car and find out for myself.

"Tabatha I got to call you back."

"Girl, if you hang up this phone, I'm coming over there."

Gina sighed. "Fine. Hold on."

I distinctively heard the sound of little children but for the life of me I couldn't figure out whose children it could be. The only child that I knew of, would be Tiera's daughter but I strongly doubted she would be visiting so soon. Especially since their parting was less than amicable. Gina returned to the phone a few minutes later.

"I'm back." She sounded a little annoyed.

I waited for her to answer my questions but she didn't seem like she wanted to offer any information. "When you are ready to talk about it, give me a call." I wasn't going to play that game with Gina. If she needed me, she knew where to find me.

"Hold on a second. I had to go in the other room. I'm doing a little babysitting and things kind of got out of hand."

"I kind of figured that out. I'm just curious who are you babysitting for?"

Gina sighed again only louder. "I think you already know the answer to that question."

"Shut the fuck up. He did not drop a kid off and ask you to baby sit it."

"It wasn't one kid, it was two."

"Dead. That niggah would be d-e-a-d."

"I'm not saying that the thought didn't cross my mind. I was twisted for a minute."

"I guess so. How old are the children?" '

"Five, and before you say ask the next question, I did the math, and yes he cheated on me."

"I wasn't going to saying that."

"You are lying through your teeth."

"No, I'm not. I was going to ask how the hell he talked you into babysitting given the fact that he cheated on you."

"I'm still trying to figure that out my damn self."

"Like I said, that niggah would be dead to the world. If I didn't kill him, he would be out my life for good."

"I know what you mean. Believe me, I thought about it. But I have so much invested in this man I'm not ready to throw him off to the next chick."

"It don't look like you have to. Y'all are teammates, sharing him. You are just waiting for the next one to pass the ball."

"See, this is why I wasn't going to tell you anything. It's bad enough that I'm hurt behind this mess but you want to make jokes about it. That's not what I need from you right now."

"Fine, what is it that you need from me?" If she asked me to babysit them I was going to straight hang up the phone. I wasn't going to be one of her teammates.

"Can you go by the store and pick up a few things for me? We've been living off of grilled cheese sandwiches and I can't take it anymore."

"Something a matter with your car?"

"No, Ronald forgot to leave me their car seats so I can't take them anywhere."

"Humph. Why don't you have him bring the chairs over the house then. That seems like it would be the simplest thing to do. Then you won't be chained to the house."

"Don't you think I thought of that? He's not answering his damn phone."

"Ooh, girl, you are a good one. It would not be me." '

"Are you going to run to the store for me or not?"

"How long do you have to watch them?"

"Uh,"

"Humph. Text me your list and I'll be there as soon as I'm done. And have my money ready too because I'm not about to pay a dime for somebody else's kids."

"Thanks Tabatha. I really do appreciate it. I know you don't understand it and all. I wish I could explain it to you."

"Honey, I wish you could explain it to me too. Send me that list. I'll see you in a few."

Gina and I knew of each other in high school, but we didn't become good friends until after we had graduated. We didn't exactly travel in the same circles. She was a bit of a nerd and I didn't have time for that. I transferred out in my sophomore year but came back just in time for graduation. By that time, Gina had blossomed and we became fast friends.

The only bone of contention between us has always been her boyfriend, Ronald. He never let her do anything fun. When I told her she was too young for all that, she wasn't trying to hear it. I could only pray that this latest stunt would be the straw that broke the camel's back and she would finally see the light.

5 GINA MILLS

Ronald was a street nigga. I knew that when we met. He wasn't happy staying in the house for long periods of time. He always had someplace to go or something he needed to see to. When I met him, he was the largest weed dealer at my school. It was part of my attraction to him. He kept a wad of cash in his pocket and he exuded confidence which was something most of the other boys in my school lacked. The other part of my attraction was his looks. Ronald was the type of man women drooled about. I dreamt of his smooth brown complexion, bald head and tight ass many a nights before he noticed me.

Back when I was in high school, I had the biggest crush on him. He was older and he didn't go to my school, but he was there so much it would have been easy to think that he did. He supplied drugs to all the kids, so it was normal to see him walking around the parking lot or across the street from the school. He was smooth and all the girls loved him.

In my junior year, he started flirting with me. That was the year my boobs and ass developed. Up until then, I was flatter than a pancake. All the boys were trying to get at me, but I only had eyes for Ronald. I wasn't dumb enough to believe I was the only one vying for Ronald's eye, but I reveled in the attention he poured on me. At the time he seemed to sincerely want me and only me.

In the beginning, he would be waiting outside my school, parked right next to my bus. Every day he would ask me if I wanted a ride home. I would always say no until one rainy afternoon my girlfriends persuaded me to take him up on his offer. From that day forward, I was hooked.

Of course, our relationship wasn't without its share of problems. Ronald was a handsome and charismatic man. He also loved the ladies and they apparently loved him back. Although I knew this, it didn't deter me from wanting him. I thought I was going to be the one to tame his whoreish ways. I believed if I loved him enough, we would eventually be together. But it was hard. Each time I thought I had had enough, he would do something to draw me back in.

That lifestyle lost all of its appeal when Ronald got locked up. Those charges were eventually dropped but it was an eye opener for me. After his release, Ronald tried to convince me that he was giving up weed selling. I might have been naïve, but I wasn't stupid. He was a born hustler, but had toned his game down somewhat when he got a real job working at the GM Plant in Doraville.

As difficult as things were between us, I never doubted my place in his life until now. This time was different from all those other times I suspected him of being unfaithful. He had never openly disrespected me like he was doing now. He had dropped his kids off at my house and had vanished. I didn't think I had enough love in my heart to fix this mess that he had created.

Ronald came in the house looking like a crack head. His clothes were disheveled and he smelt like he had been drinking excessively. Not only was it on his breath, it was in his pores.

"Gosh, you stink," I said as I tried to push away from him. I was still sleep when he came in and my brain wasn't functioning on all cylinders.

"Shit. I knew I shouldn't have come here."

For a moment I felt the same blind panic I got every time he suggested that being with me was wrong. I knew Ronald was playing me.

"I can't do it Ronald. I just can't." I held my head in my hands. I didn't even want to look at him. I knew what he was going to say even before he said it. He hadn't come over to pick up his children, he was going to try to get me to keep them indefinitely.

"What do you mean you can't? I haven't asked you to do anything yet."

"Not yet, but it's coming. Isn't it?"

"Well, yeah. But it isn't what you are thinking. All I want you to do is take care of my boys until I can fix things."

"Things? What things? You want me to keep them while you patch things up with their mother? Is that it?" That was one of the scenarios rushing through my head.

"Don't be stupid. I told you not to worry about her."

"Ronald, you left me here stuck with those boys for a week and didn't have the decency to check up on them, or me for that matter. I didn't know if you were dead or alive. I left you about a million messages and I got nothing from you."

"I'm sorry about that. I really am."

"Did you even look at the clothes you brought over here? They were filthy and half of them don't even fit."

"You figured it out didn't you? I knew you could do it."

His condescending tone was highly irritating.

"Well, I've been sleeping on the sofa and trapped in this damn house with two strangers. This is some bullshit Ronald. Some straight up bullshit."

"I thought you said the boys were adjusting well." Ronald stood up and started pacing in front of the sofa.

"They are children Ronald. They have no choice but to adjust. But that doesn't make it right. Where is their mother for Christ sake? You got me thinking that you snatched them from her. Is she looking for them as we speak? I'm afraid to turn on the news for fear of seeing a bulletin with their faces on it."

"I told you not to worry about that. I have that under control."

"Just like you got me under control?"

"I didn't say that."

"Your actions imply differently."

"I got this."

Well, maybe that is not enough for me. Those kids deserve more than that. I deserve more than that too."

"Why do you think I brought them here to you? Don't you think that I know their lives have been less than perfect? Or are you only thinking about yourself again? Everything ain't about you Gina," Ronald said angrily.

"Keep your voice down," I hissed. I couldn't believe he was getting mad at me after what he had done.

"Can you stop your bitching for five fucking seconds and listen to me? I know I was wrong for not calling you but things have been crazy. Someone broke into my place and trashed my crib. They stole some money that didn't belong to me."

My blood felt like it had turned cold. Never once did I consider that something had seriously happened to Ronald. I just assumed he was fucking off. "Are you okay?" Now I understood his frantic looks and his disheveled appearance.

"No. I've got to get out of town for a while until the dust settles and I can get back the money that was taken."

I felt the hair rise at the nape of my neck. "And what are we supposed to do while you figure this out? I can't be stuck in this house with these children. What about my school? Classes start next week."

"Is that what this is about? That God damn school? I could care less about that. Didn't you know we were in a recession? You're not gonna make any money selling houses. Not now anyway. That's just a waste of damn time. Besides, you are too damn shy and you don't have the personality for it anyway. You have to be sharp to sell real estate."

Ronald's words cut threw me like a knife. If he thought I was such a loser, why was he with me in the first place? Why did he entrust his children to my care? "Ronald, I've already paid for the classes. They won't give me my money back."

"Is that what this is about? Money? You want money?" Ronald pulled a huge knot of bills out of his pants pocket. He counted out two thousand dollars and threw the bills down on the table like it wasn't nothing.

"It's not just the money Ronald. What if the boys get sick? What am I supposed to do then?"

"Then you take them to the damned doctor, that's what."

"And tell them what? I'm going to have to fill out paperwork and I don't know a damn thing about them. What am I supposed to say when they ask me who I am?"

Ronald pulled out his wallet and placed a card on the table next to the money. "Tell them you are my wife. The boys are covered under my insurance."

"But I'm not your wife."

"You will be. When this is over and I come back, we can get married. That's what you want isn't it? You still want to marry me don't you?"

"Well, yes. That's what I want."

"When I get back, we'll get married. Are you happy now?"

"I still don't understand why we can't go with you."

Ronald exhaled loudly. "The job in Ohio is only a temporary transfer. Just till I get my money right. It doesn't make sense to uproot all of you for a temporary situation. I'll be back before you know it."

"We don't mind temporary."

"Lord, woman, you are trying to complicate this. If I take you and the boys with me then I won't be able to work as much as I need to. I won't have time to worry about you. You know you hate to drive in the snow and if I left you in the house you would be bored in a strange city. Besides, what about your house? You think you can just up and leave your house and think nothing is going to happen to it. Believe me, I have thought this whole thing through and the only way it is going to work is if y'all stay here and let me do what I got to do."

He was making some sense but I still wasn't convinced. "How long is this going to take?"

"Damn, I don't know. Six months, maybe a year tops."

"That's a long time Ronald. These kids will need to get in school. How am I going to do that? I am going to have to register them and I will need more than just your insurance card to do it. They will need their birth certificates and their immunization records."

"Shit, Gina. I will be back before all that happens. If I'm not, I'll make sure you have everything you need. When I get situated, you all can come for a visit."

"I don't know Ronald. I just don't know that I can do it."

"Honey, let's not fight. You know I don't like it when we fight." Ronald sat on the sofa next to me and began kissing me on my neck and around my shoulders. I threw back my head as I allowed myself to feel the warmth of his lips. He felt so good to me, I could not stop the moan that escaped my lips. He pulled me onto his lap. I felt the imprint of his dick pushing against my ass. I gently rocked on it. I could almost feel the heat.

"Do you like that baby?" Ronald whispered in my ear.

"Yes, I do." The words oozed out of my mouth. It had been a few weeks since Ronald had taken the time to feel me and my body missed his touch.

"I like it too. I haven't been giving you enough attention. I am going to have to fix that soon. I know you have needs, I have needs too."

"It's been so long," I moaned. I wanted him to squeeze me. Take me in his arms and tell me how much he loved me. He hadn't said that in a while and I missed it. I needed him to reassure me especially since he was talking about going away for an extended period of time.

"I know baby. And if the kids weren't upstairs, in your bed, I'd show you how much I missed you." He punctuated each word with a kiss.

I paused as I realized that Ronald wasn't going to make love to me. He almost had me fooled. Ronald was playing a game but two could play that same game. Having his children would always keep me connected to him. "Speaking of beds, if they are going to stay here they are going to need somewhere to sleep. Gavin wets the bed. I can't have him messing up my mattress."

Ronald still had a sizeable knot in his pocket so I didn't feel bad as he peeled a few more hundreds off the stack and added them to the pile on the table.

"You should be able to get something for them with that. I'll be back to check on them soon." Ronald pushed me off his lap and stood up. I followed him with my eyes as he walked to the door.

"How will I know where you are?" I felt as if my heart was breaking. I didn't understand how things had changed so quickly. The twins, the alleged robbery, the job, the move, it was all happening so fast I couldn't make sense of it all.

"I'll call you when I get settled."

I called out to Ronald before he was able to close the door. "Do you still love me?"

"You know I do. I don't even know why you asked me such a dumb question. I will catch you later." He shut the door firmly behind him.

6 TABATHA FLETCHER

I got back in my car and pulled out my phone to call Gina. "Girl, what are you doing? I stopped by your house and you aren't here."

"Hey girl. Long time no hear. What's good with you?"

"I asked you first. Where are you?"

"Me and the boys are doing a little shopping."

"Shopping? And you didn't call me? You know I love to shop."

"I would have boo, but I'm not shopping for me. I didn't think you would want to tag along on this trip. I am so sorry I missed you. I haven't seen you in like forever."

"I know girl. It has been too long. Where are you shopping at? Are you nearby? I brought some donuts."

"We're actually finished. We, um, had to cut this little outing short. We're not that far away. If you can hang tight, we should be there in about ten minutes."

"Cool. I'll just sit here until you get here."

"Okay, see you in a few."

I turned off the car and turned up the radio. It was a good day to be out in Atlanta. The sun was shining and the thermostat was trying to break free of the abnormally cold weather we had been having. It would have been a good day to have gone shopping, trying on new spring fashions. I missed spending time with my friend. Just as I was about to get restless, Gina turned the corner and pulled up in front of me.

I watched as Gina and the twins got out of the car loaded down with bags. She didn't appear to be happy at all. I waited until they had gotten onto the porch before I got out of the car.

"You need some help," I asked. I reached over to the passenger seat and grabbed the donuts that I had brought. "Very funny. I could have used some help before I got them up on the porch."

"Who peed in your coffee?" I said smiling. Gina did not return my smile.

Gina got the door open and the twins quickly went inside leaving Gina standing on the porch. "Girl, motherhood."

Something inside me twitched involuntarily. I couldn't put into words what I was feeling, but I didn't really like it. "It's good to see you." I gave Gina a one handed hug.

"It's good to see you too. I missed you."

We walked inside and Gina shut and locked the door behind us.

"Where are the twins, they got ghost?"

"They know they are in trouble that's why. They are probably upstairs in their room."

I laughed again. "What did they do? Showed their asses in the store?"

"You know it. I thought I was going to catch a case I was so mad."

"But you survived, right?"

"Barely, it was a good thing there were witnesses or it would not have been cute."

"So, I take it the honeymoon phase is over and they are showing you who they are."

"The honeymoon phase has been over for three or four months. I haven't seen your ass since that day you came over and went to the market for me."

"I know, I'm sorry. That school has been kicking my ass. I honestly didn't think it would be this hard to go to school and work full time." I was still holding the donuts in my hand so I held them up as a peace offering.

"Thanks for the treats but what I really need is some scotch or some whiskey!"

"Not the brown liquor. Has it been that bad?"

"In one word, yes."

"Fine, put your stuff away and I'll run down to the store and get us some libations. I'll be right back."

"You'd do that?"

"Hush. I'll be right back." I grabbed my purse and rushed out the house. I didn't like what I saw in Gina's eyes and I couldn't wait to get back to find out what was really going on with her. For a moment, I felt a twinge of guilt for staying away so long. Although school was kicking my ass, it wasn't as bad as I led her to believe. I did have some free time. I just didn't want to spend it with kids. I wasn't like some of the other women that I knew. I don't think I had a maternal bone in my body. So, I stayed away. I could only hope that I made the right decision.

♥♥♥

"I can't tell you how good it is to see you. I feel like I have been starved for adult conversation."

I lifted my glass and clinked it against Gina's. "Truth?"

Gina nodded her head, "Always."

"I got to feeling like a scum bag. I was afraid you were going to ask me to babysit, so I stayed away." The booze was already talking for me. I had no intention of admitting that to Gina.

"Brown liquor, it will do it every time," Gina said laughing.

I thought she was going to be mad but she didn't act like she was. I was relieved. It was better that I placed my cards on the table anyway. That way I didn't have to hide out like I had been doing.

"Yeah, the best truth serum in the world. You want to tell me what's been going on? I don't mean any harm. You don't look so hot."

"Thanks," Gina dryly replied.

"I'm just being honest. You look like you've picked up a few pounds and your hair could use some attention. Maybe, something simple, like a comb?"

"I hope you didn't come over here to insult me. Because if you did, you can leave by the same door that you came in. But, could you leave the bottle please? I really want to self-medicate."

"Honey, hush. You told me to be honest. If I said girl you looking good, then you would know I was lying. Right?"

"I guess so. I'm just tired. I could really use a perm but I just don't have the desire to do it."

"Since when do you do your own perms?"

"Since I had two children who require more things than me."

I cringed again. Gina talked liked those kids were actually hers and it bothered me. What was she going to do when she had to give them up? "I imagine kids are expensive. Isn't Ronald helping you out?"

Gina squirmed around in her seat, avoiding my eyes.

"Truth, remember?"

"He sends me what he can. It's not nearly enough though."

I felt myself getting angry. I didn't know much about Ronald, but what I did know wasn't that flattering. I thought him to be a selfish prick. "What does that mean?"

"He said he can't get the hours that he thought he was going to get when he transferred. And since he's not doing the extra hustle that he did down here, things are a little tight."

"Wait, what the what? Transferred? Where is he at?" I was more than a little confused and I couldn't blame it on the alcohol.

"Girl, a lot has happened since I last saw you. What, six months ago?"

I felt that flicker of shame again. I knew I hadn't been much of a friend. "It hasn't been that long and you know it."

"You're right, it just feels that long. About a week after he left the kids here, Ronald came over and told me that his place got broken into. He said whoever did it took some money that didn't belong to him. He had to leave town supposedly to buy himself some time to recoup the money. He had his job transfer him to the GM plant in Ohio. It was only supposed to be for a few months but it's taking longer."

"I call bullshit." Gina was so gullible when it came to Ronald it was sickening to me. He could tell her just about anything and she would believe him. I couldn't understand how someone who was so sensible in other areas could be so stupid when it came to her man.

"How are you going to call bullshit when you don't even know Ronald? You just don't like him, that's all."

"You're right about one thing. I don't like him. But that is not why I'm calling bullshit. It's all too convenient to me. For all you know, that niggah could be living right here in Decatur or somewhere else in Atlanta. He would have to show me is all I'm saying, especially given his track record."

"And just how is he supposed to prove it to me little miss I'm so full of bright ideas?"

"Getting smart with me ain't going to change a damn thing. I just don't think you should believe everything he tells you. I'm not talking about just this either. I mean damn. If that man told you the sky was purple, I think you would believe him even though you can see for yourself it wasn't."

"I'm not that naïve, Tabatha. I would have to call bullshit if he said that to me."

"Then you should call bullshit on this one too. How long does he expect you to hold on like this?"

"Uh,"

"Exactly."

"What am I supposed to do then?" Gina picked up the bottle and poured herself another drink.

"Take your ass to Ohio and see for yourself. That's what you do."

"Yeah, right. What am I supposed to do with the kids? Stuff them in my suitcase? I can't afford to take them with me. They charge an arm and a leg for tickets. I'd have to sell my whole damn body to afford that."

I had set myself up and didn't even realize it until it was too late. Now I was going to have to put up or shut up. It was one thing for me to tell her what she should be doing but as her friend, I needed to help her do it or leave it alone. "Fine, I'll watch the kids while you go up there for a few days. And I do mean a few days too. You can go up there on a Friday and come back Sunday night so I won't miss my class on Monday."

Gina's eyes grew wide as she waved her hands excitedly. "You would do that for me?"

I held up my glass. "Brown liquor, it will make you do some things even if it's against your better judgment."

The fire went out in Gina's eyes just as quickly as it appeared. "Thanks, but no thanks. I can't do that to you or them for that matter. They might get on my nerves sometimes but I don't hate them."

"Just because I'm a little apprehensive about it doesn't mean I'm going to abuse those children. I can manage to be nice for two and one-half days."

"I'm not saying you would abuse them, but those kids have been through so much. It just breaks my heart sometimes when I think about it. They really are cute kids."

"Now they are cute, but a half hour ago I thought you wanted to stomp a hole in them."

"That's because I caught them in a lie. I haven't whipped their asses about it yet, but that don't mean I'm not going to do it."

"Oh, my. What did they lie about?" I reached for the bottle and poured myself another drink. This was the Gina that I missed hanging out with.

"We went to Walmart to get some pants for them. They are growing so fast. I can't have them walking around representing me with short ass pants on. Anyway, I told them before we went into the store, don't ask me for nothing."

"Okay, that sounds right. My momma used to say that to me too." I said as I remembered how it used to be back in the day. It was her mantra, look but don't touch.

"So, Gavin decides to take what he wanted. That boy had all kinds of shit sticking out his tight ass pants. We go to the bathroom and I pull down his pants and all this shit falls on the floor. His smart ass, blames his brother who is standing there and not saying nothing. I was so pissed girl, I didn't know what to do but pay for the shit I already had and leave."

"Oh, wow. Stealing ain't cool. You did the right thing."

"Yeah, but what pisses me off more than anything, was the fact that Merlin didn't speak up for himself. I know good and damn well, he didn't have anything to do with trying to steal that stuff. Hell, I stole shit when I was a kid too."

"Yeah, we all did."

"Not saying that it's okay. But I understand it. I just don't like the way that Merlin doesn't take up for himself. So, I had to punish them both to teach them a lesson."

"What's their punishment? Going to bed without supper?"

"Hell no. Those little niggers will be down here raiding the refrigerator as soon as I closed my eyes. They are very resourceful when it comes to food. I had to hit them where it hurt. No television. Gets them every time."

"Ouch. Oh, well. I'm glad you are taking a more active role in disciplining them than you did with Tiera. That girl was a hot mess."

"With her, there was nothing I could do. She was already spoiled rotten when she got here. Her daddy made sure of that. With the boys, it's different. I don't see where Ronald or their mother, had much influence in their lives. They don't even ask about them."

"That's the problem with a lot of parents. They are so busy trying to be friends with their children that they forget to discipline them. Children need it and some adults do too."

"I know. I completely agree."

"Are you going to go to Ohio and check out Ronald's story?" Our conversation had gotten a little off track.

I saw the doubt written all over Gina's face. She was afraid, a blind man could see it. "I can't afford plane tickets. Ronald had me apply for public assistance. He sent me a limited power of attorney for the children so that I would be eligible for food stamps and shit."

"Oh, wee. I know you hate that shit. It is so degrading to me." I opened the box of donuts and took one of the chocolate ones before I passed the box to Gina.

"Honestly, it's not as bad as I thought it would be. They give you a debit card that looks just like a bank or credit card. I hide the front of the card and swipe it really quick. What is more embarrassing to me is going to the store and not having enough money to buy what I need. Then you have to start putting shit back, holding up the lines. That's degrading."

"I feel you." I pulled out my phone and started playing around with it while Gina helped herself to a donut. I was still feeling a little guilty for abandoning her when she really needed my help.

"What are you doing?"

"Southwest Airlines has a special going on. Round trip tickets will cost a little over one hundred and twenty-five bucks."

"The only way I could afford to go was if it were free. The kids will be going to school in a few weeks. I need to get their school supplies and stuff."

"Consider this an early birthday present. You leave in two weeks so you'd better get your shit in order." I confirmed my purchase and put my phone back in my pocket.

"Are you serious? My birthday isn't for two months."

"I said it was early. Now don't you forget that I did this shit and look at me all crazy when your birthday actually comes around."

"Are you kidding me? I will never forget this as long as I live! I really do need the break."

"I'm not sending you on vacation nigga. I want you to go up there and find out what is going on with Ronald. Are those little niggahs gonna tear my house up or do I need to stay over here and let them tear up yours?"

"They aren't puppies. They do have home training Tabatha. As long as you have the cartoon network, they will be fine. If they act up, you have my permission to tear their behinds up."

"Believe that. And we won't be going to any stores while you are gone."

"Ronald is going to freak when I tell him!"

"I wouldn't tell him until I was at the airport in Ohio. If you want to find out what is really going on, the best way to do it is by surprise."

"What happens if I get to Ohio and he doesn't answer my calls? Then I will be stuck like Chuck."

"Does he normally not answer your calls?"

"He can get missing sometimes."

I shook my head. "Then you might have to resort to some sneaky tactics to get him to answer the phone. Send him a text before you get on the plane and turn your phone off. Lie if you have to but by all means, don't tell him you're coming until he can't do anything about it."

"What if he leaves my ass at the airport?"

"Excuse me, is that your man or what? You always telling me how much in love you two are. Seems to me he would be pining for that pussy as much as you're aching for that dick. Sniff that shit out. Then fuck that niggah like you are trying to pay some bills and have his ass racing to come back home." I reached over and snatched the last bite of donut from Gina's hand.

"Hey, I was eating that."

"Trust me, you don't need it." I popped the donut in my mouth instead. I could stand to gain a few pounds but right now, Gina could not.

"That little bit of donut was not going to make a difference. But I get what you are saying. I'm going on a liquid diet until my trip. I got to get my ass back in those skinny jeans. Thanks girl, I really do appreciate what you're doing for me."

"I just hope I don't live to regret it."

7 GINA MEADOWS

I did exactly what Tabatha suggested and sent Ronald a text saying I was at the hospital right before I got on the plane. By the time I landed, he had called me three times. Rather than answer his calls, I sent him another text telling him that the hospital needed a secondary address for him. Ronald immediately texted me his address in Ohio. I put him on radio silence again as I took some of the money I got back from my taxes and rented a car. '

I wasn't normally a deceitful person, but Tabatha was right, Ronald had some explaining to do. She said to catch a crook you had to act like a crook.

I called Tabatha to check on the boys after I had put Ronald's address in the car's GPS. This was the first time that I had ever traveled anywhere by myself. I would have loved to have been able to take in the sights, but I was on a mission.

"Everything all right on your end?"

"We are fine. I brought the boys home with me and they are chilling. They are watching television while I study."

I felt a pang of guilt for leaving them, even if it was only for a short amount of time. While I was happy that they were doing okay without me, it would have been nice if they at least said they missed me.

"Cool. It's colder than a witches' tit here. It's a good thing you made me bring this ugly coat. It might not look like much but at least it's warm."

"Right. You can save the cuteness till you get inside his apartment. Speaking of which, does he know that you're there yet?"

"No, not yet. He just sent me his address and I'm headed over to his house now. GPS says I will be there in about fifteen minutes."

"That motherfucker is going to shit a brick."

I cringed. "Tabatha, please watch your language around the children. Gavin is like a sponge. You might not think he is listening, but he hears everything you say and he will repeat it."

"Okay, my bad. I will do my best to keep my mouth under control. You have to remember I have absolutely no experience with children."

"I know. Just remember, don't let them eat grill cheese for every meal. Try to feed them at least two vegetables while they are there."

"Okay, I promise. Be careful and make sure you check in with me and let me know how things are going. Even if the only thing you can do is send me a text."

"I sure will. Call me if you need me. I will be keeping my phone on in case of an emergency."

"Relax, I got this. Handle your business."

"Thanks. Wish me luck."

"You know I do."

My expectations for Ronald's apartment were not high. I expected to see that the struggle was real and for him to be living in an apartment similar to the one that he had in

Atlanta. A no-frills building in a non-descript neighborhood. So I wasn't prepared for the chic glass towering skyscraper that I stopped in front of. In the heart of what I assumed to be the city, this modern building boasted of many amenities.

My hands were shaking when I pulled out my phone. Ronald answered on the first ring.

"What's going on? Why are you at the hospital?"

"It's fine now. Everything is just fine."

"What do you mean it's fine? I've been calling your ass for two hours and you are just calling me back?" Ronald screamed at me.

I could understand why he was so upset. I would have felt the same way if he'd called me from the hospital and didn't tell me why he was there. But it was also payback for all the times when I called him and he didn't answer. "I'm sorry. I had to turn my phone off for my flight."

"Flight? Fuck you talking about Gina. Where are you?"

"I'm downstairs of your building. I'll be up in a second." For a moment or two there was complete silence on Ronald's end as I exited the car and started walking to his building. If he had someone in his place, he had a short time to get rid of them. I really tried not to get much thought to what I would do if that happened.

"You need to stop playing. It's too damn early in the morning for jokes."

"I'm not joking. I'll be there in a minute." I tried to sound more confident than I felt. I had never done anything like this before. Even when he was staying in Atlanta, I never once showed up on his doorstep. The knowledge that he wasn't living just as bad or worse than me drove me on.

Ronald was standing in the hallway when I got off the elevator with a surprised look on his face. Even though my mind was pissed as hell at him, my body didn't know it. My cat was practically purring at the sight of him.

"What are you doing here, Gina?" Ronald demanded. His handsome face marred with a menacing grimace.

"What? I don't get no hello?" I walked up to him and stopped short of touching him. I was trembling on the inside but remained rigid on the outside.

"Hello my ass. What do you think you are doing here?"

"I'm coming to see my man. Are you going to invite me in or are we going to stand here in the hallway and have this conversation?" I knew Ronald was tripping. He must have thought I had lost my ever loving mind.

Ronald reluctantly opened the door. My eyes practically jumped out of their sockets when I saw the inside of Ronald's apartment. The motherfucker was living large. If he was struggling to make ends meet, I could understand why. His apartment and it's furnishings had to cost a small fortune.

"Nice place. Funny, it's a lot nicer than you led me to believe." I said sarcastically. I was heated. He might as well have been living in the White House compared to where I lived. I didn't see a single thing that had come from his old place.

"Thanks. Are you ready to tell me what you are doing here?" Ronald made no attempt to make me feel either welcomed or comfortable.

"Did I interrupt you? Do you have company or something?" If he did, I wouldn't have been the least bit surprised. Pissed maybe, but surprised, not a chance.

"Where are the boys?" Ronald walked over to his sixty inch flat screen and turned it off." The set almost took up the entire wall.

"You think that thing is big enough? Bet it catches all the action, don't it?" I wanted to take off my shoe and throw it at the screen.

"It's all right. I'm holding it for a friend."

"And you bolted it to your wall? Some friend. Who is she?" I was surprising myself with how calm I was acting. In spite of my anger, I still had to find a way to get through the next two days.

"Who said it was a woman? And yes, I bolted it to the wall. What else was I going to do with it? Sit it in the corner?"

"I don't know why you are throwing all this shade at me. I thought you would be happy to see me. I mean, I am your girl right? Ain't that what you be telling me over the phone?"

"Of course you are my girl. You just surprised me, that's all." I could almost hear the wheels turning inside his head.

"I could use something to drink." I walked over to his white leather sofa and ran my hand across the soft leather. I took off my ugly coat and tossed it to the side. I would have put my feet up on his coffee table but that would have been pushing it.

"What do you want? I might have some iced tea in the refrigerator."

"That's not what I had in mind. I could really use a drink. The flight still has me on edge. I'm not much of a flyer." I didn't wait for Ronald to tell me it was okay for me to fix myself drink. His huge bar seemed to be well stocked. I walked over and chose the first brown bottle I got my hands on. I planned on drinking till I felt better about this situation.

Ronald didn't say anything until I had fixed my drink and was sitting on the loveseat across from him. "Comfy?"

"Very." I raised my glass to my lips to keep from saying anything negative. This apartment explained a lot to me. Evidently, Ronald has his priorities all fucked up.

"Let me guess. Tabatha put you up to this shit? Didn't she?" He practically spit out Tabatha's name.

"She didn't put me up to anything. The only thing that she did was agree to watch your children while I came to visit you since you seem to have forgotten the way."

"I don't want that bitch around my children. You know I don't like that ho."

"You don't get to say who I get to watch your kids. I needed a break and she was nice enough to give me one. I didn't sign up to be a full time mom, you appointed me."

"For the past six years you have been telling me you wanted to be a mom. Isn't this what you said, over and over again? Make up your mind Gina." Ronald fixed himself a drink. His anger was written all over his face.

"I wanted a family with you in it. Not me, your kids and six thousand miles between."

"Give me a break Gina. I told you this here was temporary. You have got to give me some time to fix this shit."

"This don't look all that temporary to me. Hell, I'd trade places with you in a heartbeat. Are you going to show me around?" I was beginning to see who Ronald really was. His apartment, lavish lifestyle and his sports car painted a vivid picture and none of those visuals included me. It was a bitter pill for me to swallow. As much as it pained me to do it, I was going to have to severe my relationship with Ronald so I could get on with my life. He was doing nothing but holding me back.

"I have been doing a lot of thinking and soul searching and this isn't working for me Ronald. When I get home we are going to have to make some other arrangements."

Ronald slammed his glass down on the granite counter. "What do you mean other arrangements?" His voice was low and menacing.

"I mean, I don't want to be in a long distance relationship and I'm tired of taking care of your children by myself."

"So, you are going to throw my babies out on the street? What kind of mother are you?"

If he had of slapped me it would not have hurt worse. "I'm a damn good mother, but you wouldn't know anything about that because you are not around to see it."

"What has gotten into you? I don't even know who you are."

I emptied my drink. "And I don't know who you are either! You want to know why I'm here. Well, I'll tell you. I came here to see if there was anything left in this relationship worth salvaging. Unfortunately, I don't think there is."

"Gina, wait. You just surprised me, that's all. How long are you here for? We can start all over."

I looked at him skeptically. More than anything, I wanted him to prove to me that coming there wasn't a mistake. "My flight leaves Sunday."

"Good. Come over here and give me a kiss."

I placed my glass down on a magazine on the table and slowly walked over to Ronald. In spite of the circumstances, I couldn't help but feel a tingle between my thighs. Ronald always had a way with him.

"Are you warm enough," he asked as he started to work the buttons down the front of my blouse."

"I'm good." I followed his fingers with my eyes, like I was in a trance. I truly believed we could take a break from our anger for a little recreational procreation.

"Did you miss big daddy?"

"I sure did." I was so eager, I was dripping.

Ronald pushed me onto my knees. "Show big daddy how much you missed him."

I really did miss him but I wasn't sure if I wanted to put my mouth on his dick. I hadn't seen him in six months. Only the Lord knew what he had stuck his dick into in all that time. I couldn't even get on my knees right before he had his junk stuck in my mouth. He rammed it in so hard, I thought he was trying to choke me. It took a few moments for my throat to relax and accept his girth without gagging.

Ronald was like my puppet master, but I pulled a Pinocchio on his ass. I came to life and started working his dick like I was playing with a game boy. By the time I was finished with him, he was whimpering like a puppy.

I slowly rose to my feet with a satisfied smile on my face as Ronald staggered back against the wall. I don't know why he looked so surprised at how quickly I was able to suck him off. He taught me everything that I knew about sucking a dick. Where he might have intended to put me in my place by pushing me to my knees, it backfired on him because I actually liked sucking dick so it wasn't a punishment to me.

"Damn, girl. You sure got some skills. You sure you haven't been practicing while I've been gone?"

The puppet master struck again wiping the smile right off my face. "Damn, why did you have to ruin it? Are you trying to make sure I don't have a good time so I don't come back?"

Ronald laughed nervously. "I was just kidding with you girl. Stop being so sensitive."

I didn't feel like I was being overly sensitive. There wasn't anything about this visit that made me feel remotely warm and fuzzy inside. I started to button up my shirt.

"Wait, what are you doing?" Ronald had regained his second wind.

"I thought you were done." My pulse rate quickened as my booty got to bouncing.

"You should know me better than that. Get those pants off and back that ass up to me like you missed it." He pointed down at his dick which was pointed back at me.

My thirsty ass could not get my shoes off fast enough. I had been feigning for his dick for months and now he was about to give it to me. I was so excited, it didn't even bother me that we were doing it in the living room with the drapes wide open. Ronald's dick was peeping at me through the zipper of his jeans. I bent over and watched him through my legs. My breath caught in my throat when he entered me roughly from behind. It was a good thing he was holding me or I would have bumped my head on the wall.

"You flew all the way over here to get this dick, you'd better take—it."

"I'm taking it."

"No you're not. Why you running then?"

I couldn't even answer Ronald as he continued pounding between my thighs. The pain intermingled with the pleasure. Ronald was fucking my mind, body and soul but something was missing from our love making. Where was the love? He was so intent on giving it to me hard, the only thing I could do was take it. I just couldn't let this go down like that.

"Damn baby, you sure know how to give it to me good."

Ronald paused for split second. "Ain't my shit tight?"

"Yeah, it's tight."

Ronald slowly grinded his pelvis into my ass.

"Can't you tell I saved it for you daddy?"

"You saved this pussy for me?" He gently slapped my ass.

"I sure did daddy. You had my pussy dripping on the plane on the way over here. I couldn't wait to get to you."

"Ah," Ronald grunted as he came. His body stumbled forward pushing my head into the wall. He let me go and I fell to my knees. Instead of feeling sexually satisfied, I was ashamed of myself. I told Ronald the things that he wanted to hear to keep him from banging a hole in my uterus. It should not have been like that.

"Bathroom is down the hall," Ronald said after he caught his breath.

I gathered my clothes off the floor and went to the bathroom. I didn't allow my tears to fall until after I had turned on the shower and closed the door. I refused to let Ronald see me cry. Not this time. This time would be different. He didn't act like he loved me now but, I still had time to fix it.

Before I got into the shower, I sent Tabatha a text letting her know I got there okay. I would have called her but I knew I would not have been able to hold it together if she asked me how things were going.

8 TABATHA FLETCHER

I woke up early Saturday morning to fix some breakfast for the kids. This was a first for me since I didn't normally eat early in the day. My mornings consisted of a cup of coffee and a smoke. It suited me just fine. Gina told me that the children liked pancakes so I intended to fix them some with some bacon. What kid in their right mind could turn down bacon?

I was walking past the bedroom that they shared and I overhead them quietly talking. I crept closer to the door so I could hear what they were saying. I felt a little guilty about it but it didn't make me move away from the door. Thus far, the children hadn't said much to me.

"Do you think Gina is coming back?"

"Who cares? One cunt is as good as the next one."

"That's not nice Gavin. You shouldn't say that about Gina."

"Why? What are you going to do about it?"

"I, um. I'm just saying you shouldn't say bad things about her. She's been nice to us and I think she likes us."

"She's only being nice because she wants something from our daddy."

"Na, uh, I think she loves us."

"She might love you. She don't love me."

"That's not true Gavin. She loves us both. She does nice things for us all the time."

"You need to stop acting like a pussy."

I was caught between a rock and a hard place. Part of me wanted to march in the bedroom and interrupt their conversation, the other part of me said it was wiser to listen. I was appalled by Gavin's language and his attitude about women. He obviously learned to talk like that from someone because I knew Gina would not tolerate that kind of language in her house.

"I am not a pussy."

"You are too. You're a big baby pussy."

I could hear Merlin crying softly and it tore at my heart. I finally understood why Gina had fallen for these children. I knocked on the door and pushed it fully open.

"Who wants to help me make some pancakes?"

Merlin used the sheet and wiped his face dry from his tears. "I do."

Merlin threw back his covers and ran from the room as if the very devil were chasing him. I stood there for a second to see if Gavin was going to come as well but he turned over like he hadn't even heard me.

"Oh well, I'll call you when they are done." I shut the door quietly. Gina was going to have to find some way to get through his hard exterior or I feared that one would be headed for trouble.

"Merlin, why were you crying when I came into the bedroom?"

"I wasn't crying," he said pouting folding his arms across his chest.

"Oh, okay. I'm sorry. I thought you were sad about something. You know, it's okay to be sad every now and then don't you?"

Merlin didn't say anything for several seconds.

"Gavin says I'm a pussy."

"That's not a very nice word Merlin. You shouldn't say it anymore."

"I know. It makes me feel all yucky inside."

I stifled a laugh because I knew that in the not too distant future he wouldn't feel the same way about pussy. "Have you ever made pancakes before?"

Merlin shook his head no. "I can make grilled cheese." He announced proudly.

I took a large bowl out the cabinet and put it in the sink. I pulled a chair over to the sink for him to stand on and helped him up. Next I poured some pancake mix into the bowl. I measured out the water and handed it to Merlin. "You can make grilled cheese? That's a pretty grown up thing for such a little man like you."

Merlin's smile was priceless.

"You want me to pour this water in there?" His finger was already in the bowl poking the pancake mix. I shook my head. I had forgotten to tell him to wash his hands first.

"Yes, and while you pour the water, I'll stir the bowl."

"Can I stir the bowl?"

"Sure you can. But you have to make sure you do it slowly okay? We don't want to make a big mess."

"Okay, I'll do it slow." Merlin's stuck his tongue through his lips as he appeared to concentrate on stirring the mix.

"Who taught you how to make grilled cheese?"

"One of daddy's trick's."

His response caught me completely off guard. My better judgment told me to leave this line of questioning alone, but I was intrigued. "Does your daddy have a lot of tricks?"

Merlin had to learn that word from someone and I wanted to know who it was.

"What is a lot?" He had stop stirring the pancakes and was eyeing me closely.

"More than three?"

Merlin nodded his head yes. I emptied the rest of the water in the bowl as Merlin started stirring again.

"Honey, who taught you that word?"

Merlin stopped. "Is that a bad word too?" He looked as if he were about to start crying again.

"It's not a nice word. You don't want to hurt anybody's feelings do you?"

"No," he said between sniffles.

"It's okay, Merlin. You didn't know it wasn't a nice thing to say."

"I won't say it anymore."

"Good. Now how many pieces of bacon do you think you and your brother will eat?"

"Four!" Merlin said clapping his hands. I picked him up off the chair and put him on the floor.

"Thanks for your help. Go get washed up for breakfast. I will call you when it's ready."

"Okay." He started to run off but stopped and turned around.

"Is Gina a trick?"

I got down on one knee in front of him and looked Merlin right in the eye. "No, honey, she's not. Gina loves you very much."

"She does?" His eyes grew wide and a smile appeared on his face.

I nodded my head. If he didn't learn anything else from visiting me, he learned that someone loved him. Merlin threw his arms around my neck. "I knew she loved me." I patted his bottom and he ran out of the room. My downstairs neighbors were going to hate me.

We were sitting around the table having breakfast when Merlin blurted it out. "I told you Gina is coming back."

"Who told you that?" Gavin glared at me.

"She did," Merlin pointed at me with a piece of bacon in his hand.

"Why would you tell him that? You shouldn't have done that," he said as he jumped up from his chair.

"Gavin, sit down. Gina is coming back just like I said she would. She will be back tomorrow."

"We don't believe you," he said with tears running down his face.

"Sweetheart, it's true. She is coming back. I promise."

"Lies," Gavin said as he ran from the room.

Merlin continued to eat his breakfast as if nothing had happened. I was confused as to what to do. After several seconds of indecision, I called Gina.

"Hey girl, is everything okay?"

"Sort of kind of."

"What do you mean?"

"It's Gavin. He's upset and I think you should talk to him."

"Why, what's wrong?"

"Merlin asked me if you were coming back. I told him yes but Gavin seems to think I'm lying to him. I think you need to talk to him to reassure him."

"They seriously asked about me?"

The sentiment in Gina's voice was undeniable. "Yeah, girl. Y'all gonna make me start crying up in this bitch."

"Oh, you said a bad word," Merlin taunted.

"Watch your mouth, Tabatha."

"Oops."

I carried the phone to the bedroom and knocked on the door.

"Go away," Gavin shouted.

"Honey, I have someone on the phone that wants to talk to you."

"I said go away."

This little nigga was trying to make me put hands on him. I opened the door and put the phone on speaker.

"Talk to him, Gina, he can hear you."

"Gavin, are you being a good little man for me?"

Gavin didn't so much as look up.

"I got you two some hats and some airplane wings. Would you like that?"

Gavin raised his head. "From a real airplane?" He said as he wiped his face.

"It's made from a real plane. When I get back, I'm going to take you to see a real plane. Would you like that?"

"Yeah, when will you get home?"

"You can come pick me up tomorrow. Okay?"

"Okay, Gina. I'll see you tomorrow. Be good."

Gavin got out of the bed running into the kitchen leaving the phone on the bed. I took the phone back and took it off speaker.

"Whew, girl, thanks. He was having a serious meltdown."

"No, thank you. I didn't even know that they cared. I can't wait to get back so I can see them again."

"Is everything else going okay? Where's Ronald."

"We have had our moments. But it's alright, I can't really talk about it now."

"All right then. We'll see you tomorrow."

8 GINA MILLS

Two Months Later

Tabatha looked at me as if I was speaking a foreign language. The frown and squinted eyes told me she was disappointed in me. She walked the floor of her living room, while shaking her head in disgust.

"Gina, how many times have we talked about this before? Were you not listening? Do I have to spell it out for you?"

"I don't want to hear it, Tabatha. As far as I'm concerned, that's my husband and I'm sticking with him."

"He is not your husband. That is some sort of fantasy you whipped up in your head. Did you two run off somewhere and get hitched and didn't tell me? No, I don't think so. To those of us in the real world, you are perpetuating a fraud."

"That's a matter of opinion."

Tabatha was starting to really piss me off. She was so opinionated. I didn't ask her for any advice nor did I need her to enumerate all the problems with my relationship. I was well aware of them.

"And we know he didn't promise to forsake all others. Otherwise you wouldn't be in the situation you're in now." Tabatha walked over to the other side of the room, as if she were suddenly interested in whatever was happening outside her window.

I was hurt. "Why must you always take it there? I don't need you throwing this back in my face all the time. It's over with now, deal with it." She knew how attached I was to Ronald's children and I didn't appreciate her throwing them into our argument.

Tabatha's anger was etched on her honey-brown face. "Because someone needs to take you there because it appears as if you've forgotten the gritty details. You keep looking at your situation through rose-colored glasses. Gina, it's time to take off the shades and see shit the way it really is."

"And what way is that?" I could feel the blood rushing through my veins as I struggled to hold in my anger.

A look I didn't immediately recognize came over Tabatha's face. "Uh—"

"Don't get to stuttering now. If you have something to say, say it." I was trying real hard not to call Tabatha out her name. She could be so judgmental sometimes.

"Fine, I'll say it. It's all jacked up and I think you are a fucking fool to continue on with this farce you call a relationship." Tabatha stuck out her chin. Her look was defiant, as if she dared me to challenge her.

"What…I…" So many words struggled to get out of my mouth at the same time, I couldn't get any of them out. I felt like she had attacked me. There were some positive things about my life with Ronald that Tabatha didn't see. She only saw the negatives.

"Who's stuttering now, Gina?" Tabatha taunted. She reached for my hand and I snatched it back.

"Girl, you know I wouldn't say that shit to you if I didn't love your stinking' drawers."

In my heart, I knew that she did, but it still hurt to hear her say negative things about my choice in life.

"Tabatha, regardless of whether you approve of Ronald, I can't help who I love. Just because we didn't practice the traditional rhetoric to profess our commitment to each other doesn't mean it's less real. In my heart, we are married. Anyone who can't respect it can kiss my natural black ass. This includes you."

"I hear what you're saying and I feel where you are coming from. In the eyes of the law, he's not considered your common-law partner, and what he's asking you to do is a felony."

"It's only a felony if we get caught."

"Girl, there are two things you shouldn't play with. The police and the IRS. I'm telling you Gina, I don't understand what has gotten into you. Filing a false tax return is huge. You just can't claim someone else's children even if they are living with you. You haven't talked to the children's mother so you don't know what her story is. She might have a good reason why the children aren't living with her."

"What kind of reason could she possibly have to keep her away for almost a year?"

"She could be ill, in reform or in jail. The only person that knows ain't talking. I'm scared of what will happen if she claims them too. When they catch your ass, they are going to fry you and my fear is that man of yours won't be around to save you."

"What are you talking about, Tabatha?"

"Don't make me spell it out for you 'cause you already know."

"No, I have no idea what you are going on about."

"Okay, you asked for it. You are setting yourself up for failure. This man you claim as your husband is going to go away and leave you sitting in the same spot, looking stupid.

If he was going to actually marry you he would have done it already. And, since I'm being honest, if everything was on the up and up with these children, why isn't Ronald claiming them?"

"He is letting me do it because I could really use the money."

"Humph, I find that hard to believe."

I was determined not to let Tabatha's negative attitude bother me. "Do I detect a little hater-ade?"

"Child, please. What is there to hate on?"

"Maybe you're hating because I have a man and you don't."

"If I thought you really meant that I would kick your ass right out of my apartment. If all I wanted was a booty call, I could get that twenty-four hours of the day. Believe that."

"Wait. That was uncalled for. I'm sorry."

Tabatha waived off my apology. "Just remember, you heard it from me first. That man is fucking you doggy style and riding bareback while doing it."

Tabatha's words cut deep, but I refused to let her know it. I was tired of people sticking their noses in my business. I loved Tabatha like a sister, but I would cut her from my life if I had to.

"He might be riding it doggy-style but it's just the way I like it."

"Whatever, I'm done. It's your life and I'm going to let you live it. Don't say you haven't been warned."

"I got it. If, and I stress the word *if*, something does happen, I promise not to call you. I'll call someone else that has my back."

"Girl, you are just bugging. I didn't say I wouldn't have your back if you needed me. I just wanted you to know I will be saying I told you so about three hundred million times."

"Do you think we could crash here for the night? The boys are already passed out and I'm not trying to carry them in the house. I'm so tired all the time now."

"Mi casa es su casa. Have you broke the news to Ronald yet?"

I bolted to the bathroom as my stomach and my intestines battled it out. It was only a matter of time before one of them won. My job was to ride it out until it was over. As I stumbled out of the bathroom, Tabatha was standing in my way.

"Move."

"Negro, please. You are in my house." Tabatha slipped her hand under my arm to help me over to the bed.

"I can make it by myself." Tabatha was pissing me off. I knew she was trying to help, but I couldn't take her condescending looks.

"How did you know I was pregnant?" Tabatha was good at reading me, but I didn't think she was that good.

"I didn't know for sure until now. I'm not psychic. Not only do I listen to the things that you say, I hear the things that you don't."

"Since you are going to be a godmother, how about writing me a check?"

"Now you wait one minute. I am the godmother to be, not an ATM machine. Don't get that twisted. I won't mind doing something every now and then but that will be by choice and not a requirement."

"I'll have you know, godmothers provide financial support and you haven't done anything for Merlin and Gavin."

Tabatha punched me in the shoulder.

"Hold the fuck up. Let's get this straight right now. Merlin and Gavin did not come from your pussy. So I'm not trying to be there for them like that. They are some cute kids but they aren't yours. Now the one that you are carrying, that's another story. Are you trying to say because I didn't financially support Merlin and Gavin, I can't be a godmother to this one? Because if this is what you are saying, let me know now."

"I want someone that is going to treat my baby as their own and spoil the crap out of them. If you're not the one, then I need to keep looking." I wasn't being completely serious but there was some element of truth in my confession.

"That's not fair, Gina and you know it. It would have been different if those were your children. To be honest, I never thought you would take total responsibility for kids you didn't have. Besides, money ain't everything. When you need me the most, don't I come through? You can't put a price tag on that?"

Tabatha made a good point. She was always around when I needed her and I didn't have to worry about my words coming back to me in the form of malicious gossip.

"You're right. I'm tripping. I value your friendship and I need to start acting like it."

"It's about time you recognized."

Tabatha was gloating as she should be. If she wasn't such an extraordinary friend, she would have drop-kicked my ass to the curb a longtime ago. I was the stupid one in this friendship, and I was woman enough to admit it.

"I hate to bring this up at a time like this but how are you going to manage with another mouth to feed?"

"Tabatha, you of all people know how long I've been wanting to have a child of my own. Every time I looked at a pregnant woman it went through me like a knife because it wasn't me. The pain I felt was changing me. I had become such a bitter person."

"You ain't even lied. But I don't think it's because of your not having a child. I blame it all on that man you are trying to hold onto."

I threw my hands up in the air in frustration. "Are we about to go through that again?"

"Hey, it is what it is. You have already opened your home to his two illegitimate children. Ronald isn't doing much to support them. How are you gonna take on these additional expenses? Cribs, strollers, diapers, and don't forget you are dealing with a double barrel nigger. What will you do if you're carrying twins too?"

"You are looking at this all wrong. This baby or babies might make Ronald change. If nothing else, it will link us together forever."

Tabatha knocked on my forehead. "Hello? What kind of drugs are you taking? Because you need to give me some. People, like animals, don't change their spots. They are what they are. You either accept them or leave them alone. What you don't do is add more to the plate."

"You're not psychic remember?"

"Hello, is he taking care of those boys out there or are you?"

"If he doesn't want to support us then fine, I don't need his help. This is my baby. I'm keeping it." I massaged my flat stomach hoping it would give me a feeling of peace and serenity.

"If everything is so perfect and there is nothing wrong in your world, why haven't you told Ronald about the baby?"

I didn't even want to look in Tabatha's direction for fear she would see bullshit written on my face. "He is coming home in a few weeks. I'm going to spring it on him then."

"Girl, you got some balls. You should tell him this news over the phone just in case it doesn't go the way you want it to. I have a bad feeling about this."

"Well I don't. He's been looking for a reason to move back to Atlanta. This is a perfect one. We can get married for real, and we can raise these children together."

Tabatha shook her head. The expression on her face was sad. "That sounds all good, Gina. However, Ronald's track record doesn't support what you're thinking. Do you even know how many baby mommas he has out there?"

"My situation is different. I have done the work that the other ones didn't. Now that I'm pregnant too, it has to count for something." I didn't know who I was trying to convince more, me or her.

"It would count in my book. But I'm not the one keeping the records. Ronald is the bookkeeper and like I've said before, his recordkeeping don't jive."

"You don't know everything about Ronald. To you he might not look like much, but he's there for me and that's what counts." I felt like this baby was the answer to all my prayers.

"If you ask me, Ronald only thinks about himself. He graces you with his presence when he feels like it. He hands you a little money, and you take it. I think you deserve more than that and ain't no baby going to fix it."

If I were truly honest with myself, I would admit that Tabatha was right. When I thought about how he was living in Ohio, it made my chest hurt. I actually wanted better, but I was prepared to play with the cards that I'd been dealt. I loved that man to the point of distraction.

"That is easy for you to say. I know you didn't approve of what I did when I took those twins in. But I changed their lives. Were it not for me, they would have more than likely wound up in the system or on the streets. I wouldn't have been able to live with myself if I turned my back on them too. I don't have any regrets about what I did with regards to those children."

"You don't deserve to be pregnant. You deserve a fucking medal. Wait, I have an idea. You know what you should do?"

"What?"

"You should make this whole thing into a business and help yourself for a change. Stop being a baby momma to your pimp. Take your expertise with children and make it work for you." Tabatha had completely loss me.

"First of all, Ronald is not a pimp. He's just fertile. It's not his fault he chose to lay down with worthless women." I was struggling to come up with excuses for Ronald's wayward dick.

"What are you saying? If it wasn't his fault, then whose fault was it? He did have a choice in the matter of who he was going to fuck."

"Damn, Tabatha. Why does every conversation with you lead back to this?"

"Because I'm speaking the truth! Something you should become familiar with, but you aren't."

"The truth according to you. I don't care what you say. Ronald loves me and he's going to love our baby."

"Gina, the man is a walking time bomb ready to self-destruct. He doesn't even think enough of himself—or you for that matter—to wrap his dick up when he's out there in those streets. Do you know how fortunate you are that he hasn't given you some type of disease. They got some shit out there now that there isn't a cure for? He's actually playing Russian Roulette with your life."

Her words hurt me more than I cared to admit. I had often thought about how careless Ronald was with my life, but at the end of the day, I still loved him. I didn't believe that he was deliberately being careless, I thought he just didn't think sometimes. Some days this was harder to accept than others. I used to believe I was a vibrant woman, but lately I felt like a piece of shit stuck on the bottom of someone's shoe. I began to feel better about myself when I found out I was pregnant.

"Are you even listening to me?"

"Yeah, I hear you but for the first time since he left, Ronald is actually talking about moving back home."

"Ah, now we're getting somewhere. You think if you tell him over the phone, he might change his mind about moving. I'm right aren't I?"

I didn't answer her. I didn't need to because she already knew the answer to that question.

Tabatha clapped her hands together slowly. "I've got to hand it to the brother, he's good. He's got your mind so messed up you can't even tell when he's pissing all over you."

I stepped back as if she had slapped me. She had gone too far. "You know what? I think I need to leave. Obviously, I have outstayed my welcome."

"Gina, no, I'm sorry. I shouldn't have said that. I just hate that you keep giving that man all your love while he continues to crap on you. I want you to wake the hell up and be aware. Do you know what Merlin told me when I asked him who taught him to make grill cheese?"

I was a little surprised by this change in conversation. "No, what did he say?"

"He said one of his daddy's tricks."

"Oh, my." I patted my hand against my chest. My heart had skipped a beat with that one.

"And then, I asked him if his daddy had a lot of tricks. And he wanted to know what I considered a lot. I told him three and he said yes."

I was stunned. Why didn't I think about asking the kids these types of questions? I guess it showed that I wasn't about that life. "I want you to understand and respect this, Tabatha. I love him. For all his faults and betrayals, I love that man. How he treats me is my business. Now, I love you too, but I can and will cut you from my life if I have to continue to defend my decisions to you."

"I hear what you're saying. I will try to keep my opinions to myself, but would you at least consider my idea? If you are going to take in wayward children, why not get compensated for it? You could apply for grants and give the kids the love that is in your heart while you get paid."

"Tabatha, you are missing the point. What I do for Ronald's kids, I do from my heart. I don't want to get paid for it." I felt like I was fighting a losing battle. I would never be able to make her understand how I feel. I needed to grab my kids and get the hell out of there.

"Doing from your heart is one thing but your purse is on empty. You need some help. How do you plan to support another mouth when you're barely making it as it is?"

"My husband will support me and the children."

"That's the thing, sweetie, he's not your husband and those twins are not yours. If Ronald decides tomorrow that he doesn't want to have a damn thing to do with you, there won't be anything you could do about it."

"Tabatha, I'm going to say bye before I say something that I can't take back."

"You do that. You can continue to delude yourself if you want to. Remember, I'm not going to say all the things you want to hear just to make you feel better. The things I say, I say them because I love and care about you. There is a difference."

"Gavin and Merlin tell Auntie Tabatha bye. We are going home." I gathered the rest of my belongings and headed out the door slamming it behind me. Tabatha opened it back up and yelled out to me.

"I hope you are not getting me emotionally invested in this one for nothing. You know what he made you do the last time."

It was moments such as this one, that made me wonder why we were still friends.

"Bye, Aunt Tabatha," Merlin shouted out the window.

9 GINA MILLS

The sound of Ronald's horn interrupted my thoughts. After changing clothes at least fifteen times, it was time to go. I got up and grabbed my shoulder wrap. For a minute, it was just like old times. Tabatha and I had made up and she agreed to keep the kids so that I could have a grown up night with Ronald. I patted my stomach and ran out to meet my man.

"Where we going?" I asked as I closed the door behind me. I leaned across the seat to give Ronald a kiss, but he waved me away. The smell of weed was cloying in the car, clinging to his clothes. He had told me he stopped smoking. Even though I was disappointed, I wasn't about to bring it up tonight. I didn't want to do anything to ruin our night together. I cracked the window so I could breathe.

"You already know what time it is, we're going to Copelands. You know how much you love the place," he said laughing.

I held in my sigh of frustration. Every time we went out to eat he took me to Copelands and I was sick of it. I knew what time it was alright. He had the munchies and he was ready to eat.

"Ah, aren't you sweet." I was so sick of Cajun cuisine from that restaurant, I could scream. Not to mention the fact that my baby didn't seem to care for any spicy foods. But once again, I held my tongue so I wouldn't piss Ronald off.

I was trying so hard to make this a pleasant visit, but it came with a price. Heart burn and indigestion were small prices to pay for a night out with the man I loved.

Ronald wasn't interested in what was going on in my life and I was struggling to find safe topics to talk about. I knew I had to tell him about the baby tonight and I wanted to keep the mood jovial. I had put off telling him long enough. He would have to step up to the plate and help me.

"Why are you being so quiet?" Ronald looked at me from the corner of his eye.

"Huh?" Whatever he said was completely lost on me. I was trying to decide how I was going to broach the news of our baby.

"You were like a million miles away. I guess you didn't miss me like you told me over the phone." He playfully pushed my leg. His touch excited my flesh and made me more nervous.

"I did miss you, baby. I was just thinking about the kids and how much they would enjoy eating out with you.."

"Damn, Gina. Must you bring them up right now on our night out? We're supposed to be enjoying ourselves. We can talk about those crumb snatchers later."

I didn't appreciate his calling the kids crumb snatchers. It was easy for him to be so dismissive of them because they weren't a part of his everyday life. Right now, he was on holiday and when he went home, it would be to peace and quiet, while I was left alone to raise his children. At times, I didn't mind their constant bickering and fighting. It kept me from dwelling about my loneliness. The situation was less than fair, and I deserved more. Once again, I didn't say any of the thoughts that I was thinking.

"You're right. This is our night. I'm so glad to have you home. Don't get me wrong, I like Ohio, but it's much too cold in the wintertime. I hate that you had to move there for a little while."

He said, "You ain't even lying. When I got back in Georgia, I just started peeling off my clothes. It feels like spring here but back home, it's still considered winter. It's going to be hard making the drive back."

Having him claim Ohio as his home stung. I wanted him to say that it would be hard for him to leave me and not the stinking weather. Home was supposed to be where his family was—we weren't in Ohio. For a moment, I started to see everything that Tabatha had been drilling in my head. It was like a light had finally turned on. Unfortunately, the timing was all wrong and I had to shoo those thoughts out of my head before it ruined my night. However, a snippet of doubt remained.

♥♥♥

In spite of my earlier trepidation, we had a very nice dinner. Ronald was charming and engaging, much like he was when we had first met. I allowed myself to lay back and relax for a change.

"I can't wait to get back to the house to make love to you," Ronald whispered in my ear while he toyed with the hem of my dress. We were sitting next to each other like young lovers who couldn't keep their hands off themselves.

"I hope you're ready, because you are going to have to put in work. I've got a lot of pent up sexual tension that I have been storing inside."

"Oh yeah? It's like that baby?"

I was flirting shamelessly with him, tugging on his dick and massaging his balls through his pants. My stomach was knotted with anticipation. It had been over two months since we had last made love and I was more than ready to stop the clock from ticking. "I can't wait for you to come home to stay. Do you know when that will be?"

I felt Ronald's body stiffen. Before he could answer me, the waiter came over.

"Would either of you like some dessert?"

Ronald pushed his plate away, knocking over his glass of water.

"I'd like the cheese cake," I said smiling. I wasn't paying attention to the sudden change in his persona.

Ronald pulled away from me. "I don't think you need it. You're getting a little fat."

My cheeks burned with shame. I closed my eyes to keep the tears that were stinging my eyes from falling.

"Very well then." The waiter quietly backed away from us after placing the check face down on the table.

"Excuse me." I got up from the table and rushed to the restroom. I refused to let Ronald see me cry. He could be a cruel bastard at times when he wanted to be. Attacking my weight was just one of the things he used to keep me in my place. It was my Achilles' heel and he knew it. I was not as razor thin as some of the other women he used to deal with. He made me feel self-conscious when I didn't need to be.

I went into an empty stall and threw up my dinner. It sat in my stomach like a rock. My blinders about Ronald were falling off. As long as I stayed in my lane, everything was good. The moment I crossed over the line, Ronald found a way to shut me down. This little glimpse of clarity didn't make me feel any better about my situation. Despite how I was feeling about Ronald right now, I still wanted my baby and I was determined to bring it into the world. I sat on the toilet for a few minutes before I was ready to leave the bathroom. Ronald was waiting for me by the door.

"I thought I was going to have to come in and get you. Let's get out of here," he said curtly.

I walked past Ronald without bothering to hold the door for him. It was a long, silent ride home. The tension in the car was undeniable. I just wanted to get home to take my shoes and stockings off.

Ronald parked the car and for a moment we just sat inside. Since he was still angry, I wasn't sure if he was going to come in or not. That's the other part about our relationship I didn't like. Ronald didn't always stay the night with me. He continued to maintain his old apartment and depending on where he was, he often claimed to stay there.

I waited until he opened his door before I got out of the car. It was late so I was glad he decided to stay with me, instead of going heaven only knew where else. My hands shook as I tried to insert my key in the lock. Frustrated, Ronald took the keys from me and opened the door. I was feeling self-conscious and afraid. Feelings I didn't like one bit.

Ronald plopped down on the sofa in the living room and turned on the television. I wanted to get us back on an even keel, but I was still hurt from his earlier remark. I left him in the living room while I went to take a shower. I felt dirty and I needed to wash away the filth of dejection. I locked the door behind me. As the warm water rained down on me, I cried. Inside my shower stall, I allowed all my fears to show. I gave myself a fifteen minute pass to wallow in self-pity. I stayed in the shower until the water ran cold. Shivering, I left the discomfort of the stall and dried off. I could not bring myself to look at my reflection in the mirror.

Ronald was in the bed when I came out of the bathroom as if nothing was wrong. I paused. I was self-conscious about my nakedness. I didn't want him to see me. He had called me fat not more than an hour before.

"What are you waiting on? Get in the bed. The house is chilly."

He was right. The house was chilly and that was another reason for Ronald to come home to me and his children. My mother had left me the house when she passed away a few years ago. I wanted to sell the place, but Ronald talked me out of it. He said he was going to fix it up but thus far that hadn't happened. The windows needed to be replaced. The rooms were cramped and the plumbing sucked. In the wintertime, we practically froze. In the summertime, we damn near died of heat strokes. The only consolation was that it was paid for. This was the argument that ended all discussions about selling my house.

Pulling back the covers, I slipped into my full-sized bed. I stayed on my side because I was not ready to allow Ronald to touch me. I could hear the television playing in the other room. I was so cold, I didn't feel like getting up and turning it off. "Why did you leave the television on?"

He nonchalantly said, "I didn't know if you wanted me in here with you."

I turned to face him. In all the years that we'd been together, I had never said no to him. "What do you mean?" He had me totally confused. *Was saying no to him an option?*

"I know I hurt your feelings back at the restaurant. I didn't mean to."

Whoa, who was this stranger? I couldn't remember a single time when Ronald had acknowledged hurting my feelings in the past. He got out of bed and left the room. I held my breath, not sure if he were coming back. When he returned, I let out the air that I'd been holding. He slid back between the sheets and pulled me to his chest. I sighed as I relaxed into his arms. Moments like this that made all the pain worth it. This was the gentler side of Ronald—more like the man who I had fallen in love with.

He kissed my neck and shoulders. His hot breath sent shivers down my spine. My body arched toward his waiting mouth. He turned my face toward his and kissed me deeply. His arms snaked behind my back as he held me close.

"I love you, Gina," he whispered as he pushed me back onto the bed.

His fingers traced tiny circles around my nipples. A low moan escaped my lips. I loved it when he took his time to bring me pleasure. I trembled in anticipation. He lowered his mouth to my waiting nipple and gently suckled it. Briefly, an image of feeding his child flitted through my mind, but I pushed that thought away.

"You taste so good to me. I missed the way your tit fills my mouth."

I squirmed beneath his touch. He was exciting me with his words and his fingers. He pushed my breasts together and pleasured them both as moisture leaked from my vagina. We had only been at it for a few moments and already I was coming.

"Do you like that, Gina?" His lips brushed against my skin sending pulsating tremors throughout my body.

"Yes, baby, I like it." I wanted him to go lower. I needed him to go lower. I yearned for him to taste me.

As if he were reading my mind, his lips traced a delicate path. He blew against my stomach and my body jerked upward. The puppet master was pulling my strings again. He sat up in bed and positioned himself between my thighs. Instead of dipping his head down into the valley, he inserted his finger inside me and twirled it around.

He said, "It's tight."

His breathing was ragged. I opened my eyes and saw his dick pointing straight out. He was as aroused as I was. I wanted him to stick it in and forego the oral pleasure. Ronald had other ideas. He pulled his finger out and a cold chill settled inside my pussy. I wanted to demand he put it back. He stuck his finger into my mouth and I sucked it like I was sucking his dick.

"Damn, girl, you still hungry?" He chuckled. Ronald was the master of seduction, and I had fallen under his spell. "Are you gonna suck my dick like that when I give it to you?"

"Try me and see." I attempted to sit up but Ronald gently pushed me back down on the bed.

"Relax, baby, let me do what I do." He eased himself down on the bed with his mouth poised above my steamy center. Before he dipped his head down he looked at me one more time, a small smile lingered on his lips.

My juices creamed the lower half of his face as I cried out in ecstasy. Ronald entered me at the peak of my climax. As much as I wanted to feel his hot dick inside of me, he was hurting me. I cried out, but Ronald must have misunderstood my pain for pleasure. He was pounding inside of me like he was trying to punish me.

"Take it easy, Ronald. It's been a long time." I clawed at the sheets trying to pull away.

Instead of slowing down, he intensified his stroke. His mouth covered mine so I could not scream. Not that screaming would do any good, no one else was there. Hot tears seeped out my eyes as our beautiful lovemaking turned to straight fucking. Ronald held me by my hair, pinning my head to the pillow. My eyes searched his but he had them closed. I lay still waiting for his assault to be over. Finally, he collapsed on top of me. I pushed at his chest until he rolled over like a fallen log. Less than one minutes later the sound of his snores filled the room. He came and went at damn near the same time. If I hadn't been so sore, it would have been laughable.

I climbed out of bed, careful not to disturb Ronald. I needed to make sure my baby was intact. His dick felt like it could have penetrated my womb. I stumbled to the bathroom, trying to hold back my sobs. I couldn't understand why our lovemaking became almost vicious.

I used the bathroom and was relieved to find that there was no blood on the toilet paper. As I left the room, I knew one thing for certain: I could not let Ronald do that to me again.

Ronald was sitting up in bed when I came out of the bathroom. He startled me.

"You're pregnant."

It wasn't a question. It was a statement. I panicked because I didn't know what to say.

"Don't bother lying about it. I know pregnant pussy when I feel it."

I turned away so he wouldn't see the panic that I knew was written on my face. My body felt warm. It seemed like I was about to faint. I wanted him to know about the baby, but not like this.

Ronald continued to precisely list the reasons why he thought I was pregnant. "I'm not a novice. I know pussy. Your nipples are hard as pebbles. Your vagina is wet as hell, and it feels different.

A sudden awareness came over me. "Is that why you were so rough with me?" Anger replaced my fear. I never thought in a million years that he would try to deliberately harm me. Obviously, I was wrong.

Ronald grunted. "I don't want any more kids. You've got to take care of this."

I stared at him in disbelief. Surely he wasn't suggesting that I abort our child.

"Ronald, you can't be serious. Do you know how long I've wanted a child?"

"You are already raising children Gina. You're done. You have two boys. It don't get no better than that."

"Need I remind you that those are your children and not mine. I'm raising those twins because of my love for you." I was beyond pissed.

"That is beside the point. Why would you want to mess things up now? Do you realize how traumatized those kids would be if you tried to bring someone else in here? They might think they weren't good enough."

"How am I traumatizing them? When you left them with me, a stranger, that was more traumatic to me."

"They survived didn't they?"

Ronald got out the bed and began putting on his clothes. He didn't even bother to go in the bathroom to wash his nasty ass. He just stuffed his dick in his pants and zipped them up. It was going on one o'clock in the morning and he was leaving.

"They appear to be okay." I wanted to add no thanks to you, but I bit my tongue.

"You're not thinking straight. We can't have a child right now. Merlin and Gavin are just getting in school. Another child will ruin all my plans." He sat down on the bed and put on his socks. What motherfucker puts on his pants before his socks?

"What plans, Ronald? You keep telling me that we are going to be together and live like a family. But, I think you are blowing smoke up my ass. At the end of the day, this is just another visit and you'll be leaving again. That's no kind of life for me."

"And you think things will get better if you bring another child into the equation? I'll have to work even longer to provide for another mouth."

"That's not true and you know it. If you would come back home, we wouldn't be spending the extra money on your apartment in Ohio. Not to mention your apartment here. Maintaining these households is what's killing us. Can't you see that?"

"No, what I can see is a selfish person that is only thinking of herself." Ronald stood up with his chest heaving in and out like he had been running.

I could almost see rockets with red glare bursting before my eyes. That's how angry I was. "Selfish? Are you kidding me?"

If Ronald was looking to cut me deep, he succeeded. I had sacrificed everything for that man and he accused me of being selfish. It was all bullshit and once again I was shown a glimpse of who he really was. "You're a son of a bitch. You call me selfish? I'm not the one that is driving around in a $40,000.00 car and living in a penthouse apartment. I'm not the one—"

"Who fucking what, Gina? I have all those things because I work hard."

He had the nerve to be angry, but so was I. I felt a fire burning in my veins headed straight to my heart. "You have all those things because you're a selfish prick." This was the first time that I had expressed my feelings about his opulence. I spoke the truth. The paltry sum he sent to me to help with the kids wasn't a drop in the bucket compared to what he spent on himself.

Ronald started flinging his shit into the duffle bag that he'd brought home with him. Fear oozed through my body. As much as I hated him at the moment, he was still my world. I didn't want him to leave me. I reached for my nightgown and slipped it on. I felt foolish arguing with him while naked.

I had to make him understand my position. "I wanted to work too, damn it, and you ruined that for me. Every dime you send me goes into this house and your children," I said.

He didn't look at me as he continued to shove his shit into his bag. My pride kept me from saying anything else to him as he grabbed his cologne that I had brought him off the dresser.

"And don't forget to mention your freeloading friend. You run this fucking house like it's a fucking shelter and you expect me to foot the bill."

My head was reeling. I could not believe the venom in his voice. It pissed me off that he wanted to talk shit about Tabatha but he didn't have a problem with my asking her to babysit his children. I wanted to hurt him like he was hurting me.

"I let Tabatha stay here for a few months and that was over two years ago. She even paid me rent while she was here so I don't know why you would have a problem with that, other than the fact that you don't like her. Those other people that you are referring to were brought in here by you. They gave me nothing but grief!" I was screaming at him and I didn't even care.

Ronald's hand dipped into his pocket and he peeled some bills from the knot he had in his pocket. He threw the money on the dresser.

"Take care of your problem, Gina, because if you have this kid, you're on your own. You will never see me again." He slung his bag over his shoulder and walked out the door.

I collapsed against the bed. I couldn't move even when I heard the front door slam. He said it was my problem as if I got pregnant all by myself. I couldn't decide if I was more hurt than mad.

Ronald's words played on a continuing loop inside my head. His threat to never see me again didn't clarify what would happen to his children. I had grown to love them and it would break my heart if he decided to take them from me as well. By the same token, the boys were the spitting image of their father and it would always be a constant reminder of our failed relationship. All of these thoughts were going through my head when I finally fell asleep.

10 GINA MILLS

Last night should have been a wakeup call for me. Once again, Ronald showed me who he was but in my head, I continued to make excuses for him. There should have been no way to justify the way he treated me or his children for that matter. Yet I continued to try to think of ways to salvage our relationship. The only reason why I hadn't picked up the phone to call him was because of the crumbled up bills that were still sitting on my dresser. Those bills were a stark reminder of what Ronald expected me to do.

I clutched my stomach each time I walked past them. It seemed so unfair that it all came down to this. If I did what he wanted me to do, it wouldn't be the first time. When I was sixteen, Ronald persuaded me to get an abortion. Back then, I thought it was the only thing to do. I was still young, in school and living at home with my mother. Had I told my mom's she would have forced me to have it. So I didn't. Physically, I survived the abortion but the mental and emotional anguish continued to torment me. There wasn't a day that went by that I didn't think about the child I aborted. I vowed to never put myself in that position again and I failed. While in Ohio, I could have easily stopped Ronald long enough to put on a condom. But I didn't. I knew the possibility of pregnancy existed since I wasn't using birth control. I assumed Ronald had thought about that too and was ready to take that chance. I didn't think he would try to use abortion as a means of birth control again. It was too much and so unfair.

Not knowing where Ronald was, was killing me inside. No matter how angry I was with him, I still didn't want him with anyone else. Sending him out the house mad was the fastest way to another woman's arms. My only consolation in that whole mess was the scent of my pussy on his breath. Ronald was a smooth talker, but there was no way he could convince some other bitch she was smelling Chanel instead of cum. I wouldn't put it past Ronald to try it.

He switched shit up on me so much, he might even have been able to do it. It was times like these that made me realized how he played with my head. I wasn't dumb by anyone's stretch of imagination. It was my heart that was stupid as hell.

Tabatha had dropped the children off at school before she went to her class. She'd left about ten messages on my phone but I wasn't ready to talk to anyone yet. Especially her. She knew I planned on telling Ronald about the baby and I didn't feel like hearing her say I told you so. She earned the right to say it, but it didn't make it any easier to listen to.

My phone began vibrating on the table. I didn't want to answer it but since if could have been Ronald I had to answer it. I cautiously picked up the phone as if the caller could see me on the other end. I didn't recognize the number, but I answered anyway. I was in the mood to cuss someone out so why not curse out a telemarketer. I felt like it was my civic duty to bite their heads off when they called me especially since I was on the national do not call list.

"Hello?"

"Hello, Mrs. Mills?"

"Speaking." I was on immediate high alert because the only people that addressed me as Mrs. Mills worked at the children's school. I sat down on the chair and braced myself for bad news. My imagination ran while as I envisioned a mad shooter in the hallway or something else equally as terrifying.

"Mrs. Mills this is Assistant-Principal Waters down at the school. I'm afraid I have some bad news."

My heart started racing. "Oh, my. Did something happen to my boys?"

"Well, not exactly."

I wanted to yell at the woman and ask her why she was calling my phone. "What is it then?" I politely asked.

"It seems as if Gavin got into an altercation with another student. The aide tried to break up the fight, and Gavin called the aide a cunt. Now Mrs. Mills, we do not tolerate that type of language in our school."

"Are you suggesting that I tolerate it in my house? Because if you are, you are sadly mistaken. I will deal with Gavin when he gets home."

"Uh, Mrs. Mills, I'm afraid you will need to come pick up both of your boys right now or arrange to have them picked up by someone that is on their contact list."

I was stunned. Both boys? While I wasn't surprised at what Gavin did, I was completely knocked off guard by the suggestion that Merlin was involved in anything wrong. "What did Merlin do?" I was already reaching for my shoes.

"I'm afraid, Merlin kicked the aide. I don't believe she will press charges but she does want both boys to spend a few days at home until we can figure out what to do with them."

"Are you freaking kidding me? Merlin is not that kind of boy. He wouldn't hurt a fly."

"We can discuss that when you get here Mrs. Mills."

"Wait—" Damn. I did not want to have to do this. I had half of mind to call Ronald and ask him to go up to the school. The sad part about that was that he didn't even know what school they went to. I went in the bathroom and pulled my hair into a ponytail then washed my face.

This was the part of parenthood that I liked the least. Waking up in the middle of the night to change diapers was the pits. Visiting principals which your child has acted a fool was a close second. Things weren't like what they used to be in the old days when I was coming up. Back then, if you showed your ass in school and your parent had to come, they would whip you right in school and send you back to class. These days it was a big damn production that ended up punishing both the parents and the child.

♥♥♥

"Mrs. Mills, thank you for coming," Mrs. Waters said as she shook my hand and waved me into her office.

The way she said it, it sounded like I had a choice about coming. If I did, I sure wish she would have conveyed it to me before I left the house. Gavin and Merlin were sitting on the bench outside the vice-principal's office. Neither child looked at me.

"Yes, of course."

"I wanted to have a word with you in private before you took the boys home."

Once again she made it sound like I had a choice. Rather than point that out to her, I took a seat in her office.

"Mrs. Mills I am so terribly sorry to be the bearer of such news but I am sure you can understand our position. This is a state funded school and we have so many parents vying for spots.

"Wait, are you saying the children can't come back?"

"Mrs. Mills, this isn't the first time that I have had to call you to come to the school."

"Yeah, but—"

"And, we've tried everything to help them."

"What do you mean you tried everything to help them. Like what?" If this happened they forgot to inform me about it.

"Well, we've tried splitting them up but Merlin doesn't want to be apart from his brother. And the other children don't want to play with Gavin. They say that he's a bully."

"I,—" I couldn't even finish my own sentence on that one because I had seen for myself how Gavin could be viewed as a bully. He could play well as long as he was in charge. His problem came when he wasn't. Or if someone had something he wanted or felt he should have.

"I think it would be best for all parties involved, if you would remove the boys from the school."

"Isn't there something else that I could do, short of that?" My heart was thundering in my chest. This was the only free school in my district that was still accepting students. Since my budget was already stretched to its limits, I didn't know what I was going to do to fix this. I was ready to fall on my knees and beg for another chance.

"I'm afraid not. There is also the matter of the aide. She was very upset with your sons and since I don't want this going further than this room…"

I got the message loud and clear. If I tried to fight their decision, we could be looking at legal problems. I was grateful that they didn't get the police involved but I was still stuck between a rock and a hard place. I heard about cases where children were arrested for kissing their teachers. I could only imagine what they would do to Merlin for kicking one. "I understand." I got up to leave.

"Mrs. Mills, is there something going on at home? Perhaps you can seek some help…"

I drew back in surprise. How dare this heifer try to turn this shit back around and point the finger at me. This woman didn't know how close I was to wringing her scrawny neck.

"Mrs. Waters, I can assure you that nothing is going on in my house and since you are unwilling to work with my children, I don't see where it's any of your damn business. Good day."

I was so damned angry when I walked out of that woman's office, I could barely speak. I was also ashamed and disappointed that they couldn't do something as simple as pre-school. Who the fuck gets kicked out of pre-school?

"Get," I said to the boys. I was digging through my purse trying to find my keys. It was a small distraction that allowed me to gather my thoughts before I got behind the wheel.

Merlin and Gavin leaped up as one and followed me out the door. I didn't know who I was madder with. The boys for getting into trouble at school or that awful lady that seemed to imply that I didn't know what the hell I was doing raising children. As I marched to the car, I asked God to order my words. I didn't want to start raising hell right there in the parking lot. I unlocked the doors and the boys climbed in the back seat and buckled themselves in.

"Don't say a word," I said as I looked at them in the rear view mirror. It wasn't enough that I would have to find someplace else for them to go to school. I had to deal with the humiliation that woman caused me. It was pre-K, how hard could it be? "I'm so disappointed in you Merlin I don't know what to do. And you, Gavin, I could—" I turned around and pointed at both of them.

"Momma, please don't be mad at us. It wasn't our fault." Gavin said.

My hand paused in mid-air. *Momma?* They didn't call me momma.

Merlin looked from his brother than back to me with his mouth hanging open. "Yeah, we're sorry, Momma," Merlin said.

The fire went out from my eyes and nestled down in my heart. "Gavin, we have got to work on that mouth of yours. You can't say words like that, it's not nice. And Merlin your feet belong on the floor." Based upon my conversation with Tabatha, I had no doubt where they learned such words. Once learned it could never be undone but I had to find a way to make them understand the difference between good words and bad.

As much as it delighted me that the twins were finally accepting me as their mother, it came with a large price tag. I was completely invested.

11 TABATHA FLECHER

I was having a Monday on a Tuesday. Nothing was going right for me. I woke up late, tore a hole in my stockings, misplaced my keys and was late for a staff meeting. Since I prided myself on punctuality, I was not in the best mood when I received a text from Gina. My gut instinct was to ignore her much like she had been ignoring me for the last few days but that would have been self-defeating. If it turned out that she really needed me and I had ignored her cries, I would forever beat myself up.

Her text said she was coming by my job during my lunch break. Since she said it was an emergency, I decided to hold my feelings in check until I found out what the problem was. My gut told me it was about Ronald and some of his foolishness. I just prayed for the day that she would finally wake up and see that nigger for who he really was.

When the receptionist buzzed me to let me know Gina was there, I quickly went out to the lobby to meet her. "This had better be good. You know I'm pissed at you, right?" So much for keeping my feelings in check. I had been worried so much about her that I couldn't keep it inside.

"I know you are and I'm sorry. I spent most of yesterday feeling sorry for myself."

"So you ignore me?"

"Please don't take it personal. It honestly gave me time to think about all the things you have been saying to me. So, even though you weren't with me physically, I had you playing in my head. Ronald doesn't want to have anything to do with the baby."

"Really? What a surprise. What I would like to know is why is it that he can have fifty million children with other women but he doesn't want a child by you? What kind of shit is that?" This confirmed everything that I had been thinking about Ronald. However, I couldn't say it to Gina when I could tell she was already hurting.

"I know. Girl, he said he was going to leave me if I have this child. I just don't know what to do."

As much as I wanted to say 'I told you so,' I didn't have the heart to do it. Gina had been through enough and my heart went out to her. As loving as she was, she didn't deserve the treatment she was getting from her asshole of a man. As much as I disliked Ronald, I could not believe he would form his lips to say anything that cold to Gina. I expected him to be upset. I never thought he would suggest she abort his baby again.

"How did all this go down? Were you home when it happened?"

"No. We went to dinner at my favorite restaurant, *Copelands*. It was real dark and sexy. He had a few drinks and appeared to be in a good mood. As soon as I mentioned the children, he cut me off."

"Hold up and wait a damn minute. I thought you hated Copelands."

Gina sucked her teeth. "I do, in the worst way. But Ronald seems to think I still love it. I mean when we first started going there and all, I loved it but after a while, it gets old."

"Gotcha. I'm sorry. I didn't mean to interrupt. I just got confused for a minute. Go ahead."

"He said he didn't want to talk about the children on our night out."

"I guess he didn't."

Gina stopped talking. She looked as if she were about to turn on me. I pulled my lips together tightly.

"Anyway, I backed off about talking about them even though I really wanted him to acknowledge how good of a mother I've been. You know, set the tone before I told him I was pregnant."

"Gina, get to the point. I'm on my lunch hour and I would like to eat something." Gina's look told me she was irritated with me.

"Are you going to let me tell my story or what?"

"You can tell it but I'm going to need the Reader's Digest version if I'm still going to be able to eat lunch."

"So, I was about to order dessert and he told the waiter that I didn't need it because I was getting fat."

"Damn, that's cold." I gazed at my friend sympathetically. She had gained a few pounds, but she was still a beautiful woman both inside and out. Had Ronald really loved her he would see that before anything else.

"I know. He hurt me so bad I almost started crying. He didn't even apologize. In the car, I tried to act like it didn't bother me, but I couldn't. We didn't speak the whole way home."

I tried to imagine how that ride must have been because Gina loved to talk. If she was quiet around me, I would assume she was either sick or asleep. A small smile tugged at the corners of my mouth. Thankfully, Gina missed it.

"I would have cussed that nigga out and ordered dessert anyway. But that's just me. Then what happened?"

Gina shot me an annoyed look. "When I got home, I went to take a shower. I just wanted to go to bed and sleep away my pain."

I felt real bad for Gina. I wanted her to have a wakeup call but not this way. "It's a good thing the twins were with me?"

"I know that's right. He was already in bed when I came out of the bathroom. I could tell just by looking at him that he was ready to fuck, but I wasn't feeling him."

"Humph." That was also no surprise to me. Niggas always wanted to fuck especially when they are mad. It didn't matter what else was going on, their dick's weren't affected. They could be damn near dying but could still get a hard-on. I just shook my head instead of saying the words out loud.

"Anyway, to make a long story short, he said he didn't want any more kids."

"At least he did not lie about it."

"You know what? I thought I was ready to discuss this with you, but I'm not. I gotta go." Gina grabbed her coat from the sofa and started for the lobby door.

"Wait, Gina. If Ronald doesn't want this child, then let the motherfucker go and tell him to take all of his other rug rats with him."

"Tabatha, they are my children now. It doesn't matter that I'm not their birth mother. I love them and I won't turn my back on them."

I could tell that I had struck a nerve but I could not let her leave without saying what was on my heart. "The nigga you slept with is willing to turn his back on you. What kind of bullshit is that? You don't deserve this, Gina. You've given this nigga everything. When is it going to be your turn to be on the receiving end?"

"It's complicated, Tabatha, and you wouldn't understand."

"What the fuck is there to understand? He's using you. And now that you are having his baby, he wants to run and fucking hide like he did with his other babies' mommas."

"I'm not giving up on my kids."

I felt like I was talking to a deaf person and I didn't know how to communicate. "You can be a fool if you want to, but you mark my words, you might live to regret it. I'm not saying you should abandon those children but you should be mindful of what is going on around you. Speaking of children where are they? What time do you have to pick them up from school?"

"That's the other thing I wanted to tell you. They got kicked out of school yesterday."

"Oh, Lord, what happened?"

"Gavin called the aide a cunt and Merlin kicked her. The principal even had the nerve to ask me what was going on at home as if I condoned their behavior."

I laughed in spite of myself. "Girl, that Gavin is something else. So where are they?"

I saw the tears form in Gina's eyes.

"Ronald came by today and took them. He said I needed to think about what I was going to do when they were not with me."

"Get the fuck out of here. You mean he is threatening to take them if you don't give up your baby?"

Gina nodded her head seemingly unable to speak.

"That dirty dog. Now that's low, even for him. You are the best thing that has ever happened for those children. What are you going to do?"

"I honestly don't know. That's why I'm here. I needed someone to hear me out."

"Whichever way you go boo, I'll be there for you."

"Thanks. I needed to hear that. I'll let you get back to your lunch."

I reached over and gave Gina a hug. I wouldn't want to be in her shoes for anything in the world.

"That man is only playing with your head. He is not prepared to take care of those children himself. And if he had someone else to take them to other than you, he would have taken them there to begin with."

"I know. I just miss them is all. Let me go before I start crying right here all out in public."

"Call me if you need me," I said to her fleeing back.

12 TABATHA FLETCHER

"Tabatha?"

"Yeah? Who is this?"

"It's me, Gina. I need to talk to you." It was late I could tell because even the lamps lighting the street appeared to be asleep. Gina never called me after ten so I was on heightened alert. With all the things going on in her life, it could be any manner of things bothering her tonight.

"Why are you whispering?" I said as I whispered back. I turned over and looked at the clock. I confirmed that it was after one o'clock in the morning.

"Because he's in the house."

Alarmed, I sat up in bed. Gina had my full attention as I envisioned an intruder in her home. "Who is in the house? Do I need to call the police?" I felt around for my slippers with my feet as I slid out of bed, ready to make a run if I had to. I wasn't going to let anyone mess with my girl if there was anything that I could do to stop it.

Gina signed heavily. "No. Tabatha. Listen to me. Ronald and I got into this big fight about the baby. He left and I thought he was going back home. He took all of his things with him, even the slippers I brought him that he hates. He just came back in, and I, just can't…"

Even though I didn't like Ronald or the things that he did to my friend, I felt pretty sure that he wouldn't put his hands on her. As Gina's words reverberated in my mind, something stood out. *Fought? What the hell?* I snatched my robe off my bed and walked over to my dresser.

"What did you just say? Did you say fought? Did that motherfucker put his hands on you? Because if he did, I swear before God, that I will kill that bastard. Gina, please tell me that nigger didn't hit you, because I'm on my way." I picked up my panties from the floor and turned them inside out before putting them on.

"No, he didn't hit me. But I can't stand the sight of him right now. Can I come over and stay at your house for a minute."

"Of course, girl. Get your shit and come on. You are always welcome at my house."

"Thanks, Tabatha. I'm on my way and I'll be alone."

"Good, I will be waiting up for you." I hung up the phone and continued to get dressed. I had to search for something suitable to answer the door. I slept in the nude so it was a terrible scramble for me to get my clothes in order in the dark.

"What's the matter?" my bedmate asked as he rolled over.

"Uh, listen, I have an emergency and I'm sorry but you need to leave."

"Are you fucking serious?" Homeboy wasn't very happy about being put out in the middle of the night. If the shoe were on the other foot, I would be pissed too.

"Sorry, boo? It really can't be helped."

"This is some fucking bullshit right here." He got up and started looking around for his clothes as I turned on the light. We had really gotten wild and our clothing was scattered all over the apartment.

"I'm sorry, something has come up and I have to deal with it." I felt a twinge of regret for turning down a perfectly good dick without riding him at least one more time. Unfortunately, there would be no way I would be able to enjoy him once Gina got there.

"Please don't go away mad. This situation is beyond my control and I really had a nice time with you."

"Fuck you and your situation," he said as he stuffed his feet into his loafers.

I could understand his being a little upset but dude was pissed. "Can I get a rain check?" I asked hopefully.

"Bitch, please, your shit wasn't that good in the first place." He slammed the bedroom door on his way out.

Damn, what a waste. He didn't have to insult me. There was no call for that. I went into the bathroom to wash up. I didn't want to smell like sex when Gina got there. When I finished dressing, I went into the kitchen and put on a pot of coffee. It was going to be a long night and I needed something to get us through it.

As the coffee pot began to whistle, I changed my mind and decided that I'd rather have a strong drink instead. I turned the kettle on low, just in case Gina wanted some, and poured myself an apple martini. I had made up a batch for me and William but we never got around to drinking it. I was on my second drink when I heard Gina's car turn into the parking lot. I peeked out the window and saw Gina struggling with two suitcases. I quickly went down the stairs to help her.

"Damn, did you have to bring everything? You do know that's your house you just ran away from. If anyone should have been leaving it, you weren't the one? Are you all right?"

I asked while struggling to carry her heavy-ass bags up the stairs.

"I know, but asking him to leave would have brought about more drama and I just couldn't take it. I just need some time to rest and think.."

"It's not a problem. You know I'm here for you." I dropped her bags in the living room. Even though I was thoroughly against Gina having this baby, I understood how much it meant to her.

"He should have just stayed away. I don't know why he came back to torment me."

"Girl, why, what happened?" I made sure my door was locked before I moved away from it.

"After I left you, I went home expecting Ronald and the boys to be gone. They weren't. He started asking me a thousand questions about where I had been. I told him I was with you but he didn't believe me. He started going in on me and he said it probably wasn't even his baby."

"No he didn't! That bastard. He's the cheater in this relationship and he damn well knows it."

"I know. That's what makes me so mad. We've been together for so long without any children. I was sure I could convince him to accept it so we could finally be parents. Stupid me figured that if I was able to give him children, he would stop cheating on me."

I had to bite my tongue. I knew her ability to have children had little to do with Ronald's infidelity and she had to know this too. He was a lowdown, dirty motherfucker who liked variety in his life. The best thing for Gina to do right now would be to walk away from him. She was still in her thirties and would get over his cheating ass in no time if she just gave herself half a chance.

I said, "So my question to you is, what are you going to do?"

Gina slumped down on my sofa and started crying. Up until then, she had been holding it together. I walked over and wrapped my arms around her. She lifted her head from her chest and placed it on my shoulder. I actually felt her pain.

"I wanted to be a real mother so badly, I just didn't want to be a single parent."

I found myself getting angry and I spoke without regard to how it would make Gina feel. "You have been a single parent for years. The only difference is that the children you raised weren't yours."

Gina tensed up in my arms, pulling away from me, but I didn't let her go. She may not like what I said, but it was the truth. We rocked together for three or four minutes before she pushed away from me.

"It's okay, boo. Everything is going to be okay. We'll figure this thing out together. Hell, I could move in with you and we can raise that baby together." Gina acted like she didn't even hear me as she continued talking it out.

"He was so angry with me. I just had to get out of there."

I tried to change the subject to something lighter. "Damn, girl, what did you put in those bags, cement blocks? They were heavy as hell."

Sniffling, she replied, "I just grabbed everything I thought I was going to need."

"I still don't see what the big deal is. He just needs to man up and do the right thing."

"Tabatha, he was so pissed. I thought he was going to hit me, and for what? Because I wanted to keep my baby."

"I will say it again. Why are you the bad person for doing the same thing that his other babies' mommas have done?"

Gina pushed at me so hard, I almost fell off the sofa. "I'm not like those other bitches. I love that man and I care for his children."

Gina was right. She wasn't like those other women. She was there, day in and day out, fighting for two of the kids Ronald had delivered into the world. "Gina, I'm sorry. You are different from them. You have been there and I can't deny it. I was wrong for even implying such a thing because I know better. I can't help it if I get mad every time I think about how he treats you. I want to whip his ass one good time." Ronald was like dirty laundry to me. If you didn't wash it, it began to stink.

"Nobody wants to whip his ass more than I do, but I can't."

"From now on, I'm going to stop this negative thinking. The bottom line is you are my friend and that is your man for better or worse." Even as I said those words, I wasn't feeling them. I was sure Gina would see right through me but to my surprise, she appeared to believe me.

"It's too late for all of that," Gina said.

"Too late? What do you mean too late?" I was not understanding her. For years she wanted me to accept her relationship and now that I was telling her that I was willing to do it she said no.

Gina looked at me and shook her head back and forth. Tears dripped from her eyes.

My forehead wrinkled. "Oh, God, Gina what did you do?" She didn't have to answer, I already knew. I started shivering as a cold chill went up my spine.

"I couldn't have my baby, Tabatha. I know you don't understand this, but I had to do it. He said he was going to take Merlin and Gavin away. I couldn't let that happen. I couldn't lose them too. It was the only way."

"Lord, have mercy."

Gina put her head down in my lap and cried. I was numb. I had promised myself I wouldn't get emotionally attached to her child but I had. Now that the child was no more, I didn't know how to feel about it. The only problem was that her tears wouldn't bring back the life she had destroyed. How could Gina recover from this? It wasn't even my child and I felt an emptiness inside.

Ronald broke her down to the lowest level so he could control her. He knew she would do anything for his children and he used them like pawns. To me, he was the lowest form of scum on the planet. A leech sucking the life from my friend. I didn't know how she was going to recover from this latest tragedy but I promised myself I would stand by her even if I didn't agree with her reasoning.

13 TABATHA FLETCHER

I was in the mood to celebrate and as usual, Gina was not responding to my calls. I understood that she had been under a lot of stress but she had to know I wasn't the one who put it on her. When I caught up with her ass I was going to tell her about it too.

I had just finished my last class and I wanted to get out of my house and party before I bunkered down to take my licensing test. I hadn't seen much of Gina since she came over to my house in the middle of the night. She stayed with me for two days but when phoned she damn near broke her neck trying to get to him. The bags she could hardly lift when she came over were hefted out like they were empty. The only thing I could do was shake my head.

While I knew she wouldn't be able to go out anywhere because of the kids, I was prepared to bring the party to her. If she just answered the phone.

Since Gina didn't answer the phone, she left me no choice but to go over to her house. I didn't really like to stop by unannounced, but she didn't leave me much of a choice. Celebrating alone wasn't an option. Although I still held some resentment toward Gina for giving up her child for the sake of her worthless man, she was still my girl. It was rough on me, so I knew it was harder for her.

I rang the bell repeatedly at Gina's house and no one answered. I couldn't understand why she had me outside her place looking foolish. I started knocking on the door because I knew she was in there. Her car was parked out front and I could hear the television blaring. After a few minutes of knocking and ringing the bell, I started to get scared. My imagination got the best of me as I envisioned the worst. I pictured them all inside dead or dying.

"I swear Gina, if you don't want the police knocking down this door, you better open it up right now!" I had my phone in hand ready to dial when Merlin opened the door.

"Sweetie, is everything okay? How come you didn't answer the door? Auntie was so worried about you all." I bent down and gave Merlin a long hug. I was so relieved to see his cute little face.

"Momma told us not to open her door."

"I'm sure your momma wouldn't mind your opening the door for me. Where is Gavin and your mother?" It was still strange for me to refer to Gina as their mother.

"Momma is still sleeping and Gavin is watching TV."

I wasn't at all surprised to know that Gavin was engaged with the television. What did surprise me was the fact that Gina had slept through all the ruckus that I had made. Even with the buzzing of the door, she still hadn't come to see what was going on.

I walked into the living room and I felt as if I had walked into somebody else's house. The place was a wreck. Gina had neatness down to a science. Everything had a place and she had even trained the boys to pick up after themselves. Something was very wrong with the picture I was seeing. All her knick knacks and such were scattered on the floor. The throw pillows were all tossed about on the floor and the cocktail table was littered with empty soda cans and dirty dishes. There was also evidence that the boys had abandoned setting their meals in the kitchen.

"What in the heck happened in here?" I caught myself just before saying a bad word.

Merlin hung his head but didn't answer. I walked over to the television and turned it off. Somebody was going to explain what was going on.

"Hey, what did you do that for?" Gavin asked as he finally looked up at me.

"Hi to you to little man. Didn't you hear me knocking on the door?"

"Mamma says—"

"Stop. I already heard it. Who made this mess in here?"

"I didn't do it."

"Well, who did it then?"

Merlin continued to look away but Gavin wanted to get back to the television. "Mamma. She made a big mess, didn't she? Can I finish watching television now?"

I didn't believe for one minute that Gina had messed up the room but I couldn't be worried about that now. I needed to find out why Gina was still sleep at three in the afternoon.

"Yeah, sure. Is your mom in her room?" I tried my best not to let my fear show on my face.

"Yes, she's always in her room."

I turned the television back on. Merlin grabbed my leg and pulled on my pants. "Is momma in trouble?"

"Trouble? No honey, it's okay." I said in my best reassuring voice.

"She won't stop crying."

"Oh, honey. I am sorry. Why didn't you call me?"

"I don't know your number."

"Silly me. I'm going to have to show you how to get in touch with me if you ever need me. Okay?"

Merlin nodded his head. "She's in her bedroom. She doesn't come out much." He was whispering like he was afraid of something.

"Merlin, have you two been eating?" This was starting to sound much worse than I thought. If Gina spent most of her time crying and sleeping in her room, who was caring for them?

I walked in the kitchen which was equally as messy. Merlin was right behind me.

"We have been eating grilled cheese."

"Oh, I can see that now. Well, I'm here now. Baby you go on back in the living room while I go check on your mother."

"Okay."

I smelled Gina as soon as I entered the room. The stench of unwashed arms, ass, pussy and booze, slapped me in the face immediately. Gina was stretched out face down on the bed. An empty bottle of Skyy vodka was lying on the floor.

"Gina Meadows, why the hell does it smell like something has died up in here?" I shouted loud enough to wake a dead person but Gina did not move. I walked over and gently shook her. She stirred a little but her eyes remained closed. Next, I punched her on her shoulder.

"Leave me alone," she mumbled as she swatted at my fist that was steadily giving her jabs.

"Get your ass up out that bed. You stink!" The smell was pungent and if I didn't care for her I would have just let her be. This wasn't no forty-eight hour stench. She was homeless funky.

"I said leave me alone, damn it."

"I'm not like those kids. You can't just tell me to get out and expect me to go. You will have to get up and make me. I just want you to know if you don't get your ass up, I'm going to throw cold water on you."

"What do you want Tabatha? I don't feel like fooling with you today."

I ignored her little funky attitude. "When was the last time you got out of bed?"

"How did you get in my house?"

"Merlin let me in. Now get up and get in that shower before you make me sick."

"I'm going to beat his narrow ass. I told him about going to my door. And, if you don't like the way I smell, you can get the fuck out too." Gina pulled a pillow over her head as if that would be enough to make me leave.

"I'm going to pretend like I didn't hear that last part. You had better be glad that he did open the door for me because I was about to call the cops. If they had busted down your door, not only would you have had to pay for a new door, they would have probably taken those children away from you. What the hell were you doing in the living room?

It looked like I finally had Gina's attention when she pulled herself up on her arms. "Why would they take my children away from me? Why is everyone trying to take away my babies?" Gina wailed.

"I can't talk to you until you take a shower. Seriously, boo, you stink."

"Fine."

I didn't want to touch her but she looked like she needed some help. "You had better be glad that I like you. Or, I wouldn't even be in this room with you."

I walked Gina as far as the bathroom door and then I went back into the kitchen to start cleaning up the mess. Gina came out of her room just as the boys and I had finished straightening up the living room.

"I need a drink," Gina said a little too loudly.

"Are you sure about that? Judging from the empty bottles in your room, I'd say you had enough."

Gina gave me the finger. "Don't judge me until you have walked in my shoes."

I wasn't about to get in that debate with her. "Come into the kitchen and let's talk. I could actually use a drink myself."

Gina shuffled into the kitchen and sat down at the table with her head in her hands. "Did you clean up in here?" '

"Naw, some magic fairy swooped in and cleared it out."

"Well, tell that bitch to hit my bedroom too before they leave."

"I love you but I'm not touching that bedroom. You need to get them sheets off that bed and get some air circulating in that room."

"What for? I am starting to like it."

"Come on Gina, I'm trying to help you."

She laid her face on the table with her eyes closed. "Can't nobody help me. Everything is all fucked."

I didn't like to hear Gina talking this way. "You need to get off your pity pot. The only thing it is doing is making you miserable. If you can't do it for yourself, then you need to do it for your children."

Gina raised her eyebrow at me as she accepted the glass I handed her. "Those are not my children. After you have said this to me about a thousand times, I finally get it."

"Biologically, they aren't, but you made them your own. I recognize that and so do they. Hell, they are calling you mom now."

"Humph. They started calling me that because they knew I was mad at them. They think I'm stupid just like their damn daddy."

"That's not true and you know it. What's gotten into you? You were not talking like this when you left my house."

"It didn't really hit me until I got back here. And of course, Ronald didn't help either."

"Why, what did he do?" I did not want to talk about Ronald. I could give two shits about him. My concern was Gina.

Gina looked away as her eyes filled with tears. I didn't press her. I felt like she needed to tell me in her own way. She played with her glass for several seconds before she emptied it. I had already made up my mind that I was going to be spending the night, so I didn't care if we both got drunk. I refilled our glasses.

"Ronald told them I wasn't their mother. He said they shouldn't call me that."

"Well, they aren't listening. When I asked about you, they both called you momma."

"They did?"

"Yeah, girl they love you. Ronald probably said that because he was mad that you ran out on him."

Gina exhaled loudly. "Ronald called the other day and he was pissed."

"What else is new?"

Gina shot me a warning look. "I'm sorry."

"You know I filed my tax return and claimed the children right?"

I had this sinking feeling in my stomach. I knew what I was about to hear was going to piss me off. I had warned her that fucking with Uncle Sam would not end well. "Yeah, I remember."

"I was counting on that refund to handle some things around the house and get some things for the kids. I need some major work done on my car, you know how it is."

"I feel you. It's always something."

"He wants me to give him the money and he reminded me that they weren't my children."

"He's a prick."

"He doesn't need the money. Girl, you should see his apartment in Ohio. It has everything and then some. And don't get me started on his car! His ass is just being greedy."

"From what you are telling me, he ain't showing you anything new. He's been like this the entire time that I've known you."

"I guess it didn't matter as much to me then. But now that I have to take care of the boys, every dime helps."

"I feel you. But I still don't understand why Ronald's being such an ass. I mean you did exactly what he asked you to do."

"Wait, it gets worse. Since I filled for assistance, I'm not getting the refund either. Seems I have to pay that money back and Ronald is not happy."

"Screw him. Did he think that money would be free? The government would go bankrupt if they did that. Ronald is a prick."

"So, that was one part of the argument we've been having and we're hardly speaking about that but then, the other night, I called him and told him how badly I felt and he—"

Gina waved her fingers in front of her eyes rapidly fanning them. I understood what she was trying to do unfortunately, she was fighting a losing battle.

"He said I should feel bad since I murdered his child!"

My mouth dropped open in surprise. I never had a high opinion of Ronald to begin with, but he had sunk to a new low with this one. "Are you kidding me? Who does that? Where did you meet this motherfucker at anyway? At the zoo?"

Gina could not even speak she was crying so loudly. I scooted my chair over and took her in my arms. I didn't know what to say to comfort her. Ronald was an ass and I would love to meet him in a dark alley with a baseball bat. I would whoop the shit out of his ass.

Merlin walked into the kitchen and said, "Don't cry momma. It's going to be alright." He patted Gina on the leg as he tried to wiggle into them. I could tell he wanted to be comforted too.

If that wasn't proof that they loved her, it didn't exist.

"Fuck off," Gina mumbled against my shirt. I pulled away from her horrified.

"Merlin, go back in and watch television. When I finish in here, I'm going to take you boys to get something to eat." Merlin didn't seem surprised by Gina's reaction and it truly hurt my heart.

"Can we have a happy meal?"

"Sure baby, just go back in the living room until it's time to go."

After Merlin left I grabbed Gina by her arms and shook her as hard as I could. "What the hell is the matter with you? That boy came in here because he heard you crying and to show you that he loved you. It's a good damn thing that I don't think he heard you or I would have slapped you silly."

"Go ahead. Slap me then. Do you think it will hurt me more than I hurt myself?"

"If you want to be mad at someone then take that shit out on Ronald! He's the fucker who deserves your anger. Not those kids and not me. We are the ones that care for you."

"Can I please have five minutes to myself? Can you do that for me?" Gina couldn't see outside the hole she had put herself in and there was nothing I could do about that.

"I can do you one better. I'm going to take the boys with me to my house for the night. You can come get them when you get your mind right."

"Are you serious? You would do that for me?"

"If you have to ask me then you really are messed up in the head."

14 GINA MEADOWS

After Tabatha left with the boys, I finished off the rest of the booze I had in the house and the bottle that she had apparently brought with her. No matter how much I drank, I couldn't get rid of the pain I felt inside my heart. This pain was unlike anything that I had ever experienced in my life. Even when I had my first abortion, I couldn't remember feeling this bad.

I dragged myself to the bathroom and stuck my finger down my throat. It didn't provide much relief to my heart but my stomach wasn't as queasy. As I washed my face, I avoided my reflection in the mirror.

I was more than a little ashamed of myself for the way I acted in front of Tabatha. I couldn't decide which hurt more, my head or my heart. After Tabatha and the boys left, I called Ronald repeatedly but he didn't answer. This was Ronald's way of punishing me. I knew this but it didn't make me feel any better about it. I would have preferred total closure instead of the flux in between.

Realistically, I should have never called his ass again. But I was as dumb as a box of rocks because he was the first call that I made after I fixed my morning cup of coffee.

Unlike the other times I had phoned him, I left a message:

I feel like a sharecropper picking cotton. No matter how much cotton I pick, there is one more piece to get. Just one more piece. Until you realize that no matter how many pieces you pick there will always be more. And you know what happens when you come to that realization, Ronald? You get tired. Sick and fucking tired. Well, I'm tired. I'm tired of you and I ain't picking your motherfucking cotton again. I'm done.

I felt a little better after I left the message. I was empowered for a change. I had never spoken to him like this before. I had also never felt like this before. It was like I was finally seeing things clearly. I wasn't even mad at Ronald for treating me like shit for years. He didn't do anything to me that I didn't allow him to. This realization was the hardest for me to accept because it meant I couldn't be mad at anyone else but myself. I finished drinking my coffee and went to shower. I was going to have to eat a huge slice of humble pie when I went to pick up the kids.

Before I could go to my room, my phone rang. It was Ronald's ringtone. Instinctively, I reached for it but drew my hand back like it burned. I shook my head and smiled. "Not this time boo-boo. Not this time."

I was waving a white tee shirt over my head when I rang Tabatha's doorbell. I was expected her to have a major attitude toward me and I deserved every bit of it. It was one thing to feel sorry for myself but that didn't mean that I had to make everyone around me miserable.

"I know you want to just punch me in the face. I am so sorry for the way I acted last night. Thank you so much for everything you did. Do I need to get down on my knees in order for you to forgive me?"

"Humm, I would almost like to see that. Let me think about it for a moment." Tabatha stood there holding the door as if she was actually thinking about it.

Even though I knew she was joking, if she said that was what she wanted me to do, I would do it. I owed her so much. She was always there when I needed her the most.

"Well?"

"Girl, get in here and give me a hug. You look a lot better than you did last night. And you certainly smell a hell of a lot better. Child, you were humming to the high heavens."

"Don't remind me. Where are the boys?"

"You trying to be funny?"

"I know right."

"Then you know where they are. I swear, last night I hid the remote thinking they would go to sleep. Boy was I wrong. I'm telling you they spend entirely too much time watching that thing."

"I know girl. They just don't want to do anything else."

"You have to stop giving them a choice. Make them pick up a book. Take them to the library. Hell, make them go outside. When did children stop doing that?"

"Beats me. When we were young, we couldn't wait to get outside. Cold, rain, snow, it didn't matter."

The boys said hello when I walked into the room but it was half-hearted at best. It might have been better if I had timed my entrance during a commercial.

"Let's go into my bedroom where we can talk. These boys may act like they aren't paying attention but I know better."

I sprawled across Tabatha's bed while she folded clothes.

"You know you really had me scared last night. You can't keep doing that to me. Even if you don't want to talk, you should still either answer the phone or send me a text letting me know you are okay."

"You're right. That wasn't fair of me. I would be pissed if you had done the same thing to me. I just couldn't see past my own pain."

"I know it's human nature to have tunnel vision when you're dealing with painful issues but as a matter of safety, you have to learn how to push pass the pain."

"Okay, I promise it won't happen again."

"I actually came over last night to share some good news with you."

"Really? What?" I felt a pang of jealousy that she had something to be happy about.

"I passed my realtor exam. You are now looking at a licensed agent with Coldwater Realty."

"Girl, I am so proud of you! It seems like it all happened so fast. Congratulations." Even though I was tickled pink for Tabatha, I couldn't help but to be a little envious of her. This was a dream we had both shared.

"I know girl. I can't believe it myself. I was so nervous I would fail that I didn't tell anyone I was taking it."

"Was it hard?"

"Oh yeah, make no mistake about it, it was. When you get ready to take it, I will help you."

"Yeah, right. When do I have time for school?" I couldn't help but feel sorry for myself in the face of her success.

"You are going to have to make time for it Gina. You can't keep depending on Ronald to help you through. We both know what happens when you do that."

"You ain't lying. I just don't know where to start."

"You start by getting those boys in school. They can't sit home with you all day watching television. Then we find you a job so you can have some money in your pocket."

"Doing what? I haven't worked in a minute."

"When did you become so critical about yourself? You might not have worked in a very long time but you are employable. Have you thought about going back to the job you had before Tiera had her baby? If I remember correctly, you used to like it there."

"Wow, that seems like it was a life time ago. I don't even know if any of the people I worked with are still there."

"There's only one way to find out. You should call. You might be surprised. You could also check down at the unemployment office. I'm sure they have job listings there."

"This is actually a good idea but I think I'm going to try my old job first. That is, after I get the kids enrolled in school."

"Right. Even if you can't get them into a pre-K program, you could at least get them into daycare where they teach them something."

"If anything, they need to learn how to play with others. That's what got them kicked out of school in the first place."

"I can see that. Merlin is very protective of his brother and Gavin can be a bit of a bully."

"Right. I like that they are close but sometimes it worries me. They are very bright boys and I haven't been completely negligent with them. I have started working on their ABC's and I read to them."

"Stop being so sensitive. I wasn't trying to say that they aren't learning with you. But you all need to get out more."

"Thanks. I really needed to hear that this morning. I get so much negativity from Ronald."

"That's because he's an ass. One of these days you will wake up and see that."

"I think I have. I called him this morning and told him I'm done."

Tabatha fell down on the floor in true Fred Sanford style. "Thank you Jesus!"

She was so theatrical at times. I loved that about her. "Get up, girl. I know you have been waiting a long time to hear that."

"I sure have. I swear I never understood the hold he had on you."

"You would, if you ever met him. He could talk the drawers off a nun."

"That's not a good thing. Maybe if he kept his dick in his pants, where it's supposed to be, I would have had more respect for him."

"It's so weird the way you feel about each other. He has no love for you and vice versa."

"He don't have to have any love for me. I love my own self and when that's not enough there is always my portable dick. It never judges me and its sole purpose is to make me happy."

"Girl you are too much. I've got to get me a portable dick too."

"I'm surprised you don't have one. I would be climbing the walls without mine."

"I had the real thing and baby it was enough to satisfy."

Tabatha threw her hands up in the air in apparent frustration. "Honey, you don't need a dick. You need an exorcism."

We both laughed. "I need something."

I woke up to the door bell ringing first thing in the morning. It wasn't quite eight o'clock in the morning so I was good and pissed by the time I got to the door. I yanked open the door only to be greeted by a large bouquet of red roses.

"Delivery for Mrs. Mills," the driver said as he handed me the flowers.

I was outdone. Never before had I received flowers for any reason. Even at the height of my dating Ronald, he never gave me flowers. He once told me he wasn't going to spend his hard earned money on some flowers that were already dead once the stems were cut.

"These are for me?"

"If you are Mrs. Mills it is," the driver waved as he trotted off to his truck.

I was speechless as I counted the roses. There were fourteen of them. I assumed there was one for every year that we had been together. I carried the roses into the kitchen and looked to find something to put them in. I didn't have a vase so I rinsed out a pitcher and filled it with water. The perfume of the flowers filled my small kitchen.

I carefully took the card from the flowers and read it:

I guess I needed to hear you say I'm done before I realized what I was throwing away. You mean the world to me and I don't want to lose you. Could you find just a little love in your heart for me? I really do love you.

I felt the ice that had been surrounding my heart melt. These were words I was dying for Ronald to say. And since he had broken his own rule, I couldn't help but feel hopeful about our future together.

15 GAVIN MILLS

Eight years later

I was responsible for practically every ass whipping Merlin ever had. I did it because I could. He was an easy mark. Most days it didn't bother me in the least knowing that I had caused him pain. But tonight, I might have gone too far. And though I regretted most of my actions, it was too late to undo what I had already set in motion.

I heard mom's key in the door. Now that she was here, things would move pretty quickly. I flipped over on my stomach and feigned sleep. Merlin had dozed off early, falling asleep while reading in bed. He was such a dweeb.

Merlin was the good kid but he was more of a follower. He did well in school, minded his manners, did his homework without being prompted, and kept his side of the room spotless. I, on the other hand, was the complete opposite. The only way I knew how to level the playing field with him, was to create situations that would bring Merlin down a notch or three. It wasn't personal, it was survival. I was sick and tired of all the praise mom lavished on Merlin. Tonight was my night.

Anxiously, I listened to my mom's progress through the house with a sensitive ear. I needed to know where she was so I could plan my reactions. I envisioned her in the kitchen pouring herself a glass of wine and maybe pausing at the table to go thru the mail. My mom believed in schedules. Since it was Wednesday, she would check the calendar to see which chores had been assigned and then she would inspect our work. My heart was racing as I began counting down the amount of time it would take for her to discover what I had done. On cue, my mother yelled from downstairs. I clutched my sheet in my hands as I pretended to lay still. The shit just got real.

"Merlin! Get your ass down here!"

Merlin sat up like a robotic toy. He looked around like he was confused. I knew the expression on his face would be comical. I just wished I could have turned on the light to see it. I laughed quietly anyway at the visual I imagined in my head.

"Huh?" he yelled back as he fought against his covers to get out of bed.

I snuggled down deeper in my covers and pretended not to hear the ruckus he was making. For good measure, I faked a loud snore.

"You heard me boy. Get your skinny ass down here."

"Shit," he mumbled under his breath loud enough for me to hear him. If he suspected my involvement, he didn't let on.

For a fraction of a second, I felt sorry for my brother because he was about to walk into the bowels of hell and had no idea he was headed there. A slow smile came across my face. I loved it when a plan came together.

Merlin pulled on his pajama bottoms and threw on his robe. He was dragging his feet, which only added to the trouble he was about to experience. If he knew, like I knew, he would have hustled his ass downstairs because Mother hated to be kept waiting. Mentally, I went through the list of chores that I had been given and subsequently reassigned to Merlin. I knew he finished his chores, but mine were seriously lacking. Served her right for giving us busy work.

Ever since momma took that part time job, she was trying to make house husbands out of us. I would have preferred that she stayed home if that meant we were expected to clean up her room.

"Don't make me come up there and get you."

Merlin was still pretty much asleep when he walked out the room. He didn't deserve what was about to go down. Nobody did. I was supposed to clean the bathroom, but instead, I made it my business to piss on everything. I let go of about one gallon of water in there. I even peed in the trash can.

I decided it wasn't enough for me to hear the fireworks, I wanted to see them too. I snuck out of my bed to follow him. Momma had her back turned from the stairs.

"What's wrong, Mom?"

She whirled around to look at Merlin. Her face distorted with anger. "Don't be sneaking up on me, boy." She had her hands on her hips blocking the rest of the bathroom from our view.

"I wasn't sneaking," Merlin sputtered as he tied his robe tighter.

"Shut up."

He stood before her shifting from foot to foot. Suddenly, I had to go to the bathroom in the worse way, but I didn't want to do anything that would draw attention to me.

"What day is it?" she demanded.

Clearly Merlin had no idea where this conversation was leading him. I had switched days with him on the calendar our mother kept on the refrigerator.

He said, "Wednesday."

"And what happens on Wednesday?"

This was not a trick question, and I was sure she knew the answer to it. On Wednesday night, my brother and I cleaned. We each had a long list of chores that should keep us busy until it was time to go to bed. It was Gina's way to keep us occupied so we didn't get into trouble.

"Cleaning day." Merlin was smooth. He didn't flinch when he answered our mother because he was confident he had finished his chores.

Usually, Merlin was responsible for cleaning the first floor. I was given the job of doing the upstairs, which included straightening up my mother's bedroom. I hated that detail because she was always throwing her bras and panties around the room. No child should have to pick up their mother's dirty underclothing. I could not understand how she went from such a neat freak to a total slob.

"Exactly. So telling me you forgot won't cut it. You know the rules, right?" Mother began to undo her belt from around the waist of her denim jeans.

"Wait, what? Why are you taking your belt off? I did my chores." I could see the fear written on his face and I almost felt sorry for him.

She whirled around and looked at the room again. I knew for a fact the bathroom was wacked. I made it that way, right after I switched Merlin's name with mine on the calendar.

"You call this clean?" She stepped to the side with a sweeping motion of her hand. "Is this the thanks I get for giving up my own child to raise you and your brother?"

I almost blew my cover when she said this. I was so sick and tired of her talking about the baby that she had given up. That was a choice that she made for herself and we didn't have anything to do with it.

"Mother, this bathroom wasn't on my list. Check the calendar," Merlin insisted as his eyes followed her belt.

I could see the fright in his eyes. The last thing you wanted to do in life was piss off my mother. Merlin was pleading with her, but she wasn't hearing him. I was elated. It was a mean thing for me to do, but I had to do something to bring Merlin down to my level.

"So what are you saying? Are you trying to say that I'm senile or something. I checked the calendar before I woke you up."

If my brother had an opinion about whether or not mom was crazy he wasn't stupid enough to say it out loud. Mom hit him across the lips with her belt. Immediately his upper lip split and began to swell. In spite of myself, I gasped. I wanted her to punish him, but not this way. I was thinking more on the lines of no television or not being able to go to the movies.

Mom turned on me like a viper. "What are you doing down here? Did I call you?" my mother demanded as her beady eyes locked with mine. "I guess I really pissed God off when I killed my own child because he is sure punishing me with you two. My life would have been so much better were it not for you."

I was about to walk into the trap I had created just for opening up my darn mouth. I wanted to back pedal up the stairs but it was too late. I was caught.

"Look at what your brother did." She splayed her arms wide, spilling some of her wine from the glass she was holding but she didn't even appear to notice. The red stain on the carpet resembled the blood on Merlin's face.

In the bathroom comet was spread all over the sink, walls, and floor. Gina marched over to the stairs and grabbed my arm. She dragged me down the rest of the steps into the bathroom so I could get a closer look. Wet wads of toilet paper littered the walls. A note was written on the mirror in toothpaste: *Merln hates chors.*

Mom dropped my arm and slapped Merlin in the back of his head.

"I didn't do this," Merlin said between sniffles. I thought he was still dazed from the pop to his mouth.

"What? Do you think I'm stupid? Your dumb-ass brother did this. You know he can't spell worth a damn. Look at the way he wrote your name and the word chores."

"If you know I didn't do it then why are you hitting me?"

"I hit you because you consistently let your brother set you up and you do nothing about it. This is a mean world you're stepping into and you are gonna have to learn how to handle it."

"How could I have known he did this crap? When I came home from school, I did my homework, ate, finished my chores and I went to bed."

"Your smarter than your stupid brother, figure it out. Everything in life isn't going to be handed to you. I refuse to raise another sucker like me. Your dumb-ass brother knows this, and he sets you up every time and you allow it. You need to check his ass! I can't do it for you." She popped Merlin on his head again.

It hurt my feelings that she called me a dumb ass, but when I realized what I wrote on the mirror, I couldn't argue with her. In my haste, I spelled his name wrong. But she still didn't have to call me stupid. All of a sudden, my childish little prank didn't seem like such a good idea at all. I thought it would make her see that we didn't need busy work.

"If there is one thing that you will learn from living with me, it will be to stand up for yourself." She dragged Merlin closer to the toilet.

I actually felt my heart seize in my chest as mom really got a good look into the toilet. Floating amongst the Comet and the piss I had left in the toilet, was my mother's toothbrush.

"Oh God!" Merlin must have realized it as the same time as my mother did. Merlin shook his head as if he couldn't believe it.

My mother appeared to turn another shade of black. She looked almost blue, and her eyes looked like they were about to pop out of her head. I inched my way out of the bathroom. My brother was on his own.

"Is that my toothbrush?" my mother demanded as her hand balled up into a fist.

I was so sure that she already knew it was hers before she even asked him, but he appeared to be at a loss.

"Oh God!" he said again.

I was afraid—really afraid.

"Don't you dare take the Lord's name in vain." She wacked him upside the head with her fist.

"Momma, you know I didn't do this," Merlin shouted, but it was too little too late. He bent down under the sink to get something to fish her toothbrush from the toilet with, but instead of finding a rag, her wet silk head wrap fell out along with the empty can of Comet. Merlin's honey-bronze face turned bright red. Even with it being wet, I was certain he knew what he was holding.

"I work too damn hard to have to come home and see this bullshit." Mother shouted.

"Momma, I'm sorry. I'll clean it." Merlin was shaking so hard, I could see him trembling.

"You know what a devious and conniving brother you have. You should have double-checked behind him." She slapped him upside the head again. If I was Merlin, I would have moved.

He continued to deny any involvement but she could care less. She was on a roll and there was nothing he could do about it but take his licks.

"I know you didn't do it, but you're too stupid to say who did."

Damn, why should he have to tell her? We were the only ones who lived in the house. She knew it was me so what was the point? I slipped up the stairs because I wasn't in the mood to get beat upside the head.

"You're going to learn how to be a man," she shouted.

I was so confused. *Was she saying real men rat on each other?* Those words reverberated in my head as I sought my bed.

I heard Merlin say, "But, Momma—"

"Momma my ass. Now clean this shit up, and you will be paying for my toothbrush and my head wrap from your lunch money."

"I'll bet you are feeling pretty good about yourself now. Aren't you?"

A feeling of dread came over me. My mother had snuck into our room.

"Huh?" I rolled over and tried to grab my covers, pretending I'd fallen back to sleep.

"Huh my ass. I know it was you that fucked up the…"

I waited for her to finish her sentence, but she left it hanging in the room like a stale fart. I hoped she wasn't waiting for a confession, because it would be a cold day in hell before I'd confess to throwing her toothbrush in the toilet. I looked down and saw what held her attention. My dick was poking up against the sheet.

"Ah, Ma, you messed up a perfectly good wet dream." My intent was to shock her enough to make her leave my room. Although it wasn't my intent to piss her off, it did exactly that. I was batting one thousand.

"You nasty little pervert. How dare you say some shit like that to me!" She started beating me over the head with my own hands.

"I'm sorry. I was sleeping, Momma, I didn't mean any disrespect. I said the first thing that came to mind."

"What do you take me for?" She stopped beating me about the head as if she seriously expected me to answer her question, but I was not falling into that setup.

My whole plan backfired on me when I misspelled those two words. Once she realized I had sabotaged Merlin, she shouldn't have punished him. Clearly she could see I'd targeted her when I destroyed the bathroom, because all of the items I used belonged to her. I couldn't understand why she didn't see that I was calling out for attention.

"Get up. I want you downstairs to mop the kitchen floor and vacuum the living room."

"Mom, I have to go to school in the morning. Don't you know how important it is to get a good night sleep before school?" I was laying it on thick, but I could tell she wasn't buying it.

"Ha. You would have to go to school before that argument would work with me. Don't think I don't know you're spending all your time on the corners instead of in the classroom."

Damn, I was busted! I thought I was being slick and shit and she saw right through my game.

"I hate school. It is a waste of time." I raised up on my arms and looked into her face which was contorted in rage.

"You are fifteen years old! What do you think you're going to do if you don't go to school? You won't be able to get a job. Who do you think will hire your retarded ass? You need an education so you can better yourself. You won't be living off my ass for the rest of your life."

Her comments stung, and even though I knew it was her anger talking, it still hurt. Although she thought I was dumb, I was smart enough to know this whole evening wasn't about me or Merlin. It was about my dad, just like all of our other arguments. Every time she looked at us, she was reminded of him.

"Wipe that damn smirk off your face and go mop the floor, and while you're down there, wax it too!"

I rolled out the bed under her watchful glare. Even though I wound up with additional chores, I still made out better than my brother because he had to clean the bathroom with a toothbrush.

"And you are going to school in the morning, mister and you will stay there. If you miss one more day, I'll kill you." She walked off in a huff toward her bedroom.

Something inside me snapped. "If you hate me so much, how come you don't send me to live with my father?"

Mom threw back her head and laughed. "He don't want your ass either. Why else would you be here with me? I can't believe I gave up my own child for this."

My chest got tight. I was sick of all the constant reminders about the child Gina never had. I gave her the finger behind her back.

"I saw that you rotten bastard."

16 GAVIN MILLS

Mom's wasn't kidding about my staying in school. She took off from her day job and personally escorted me. The whole way there, she talked about how she should have never given up her baby for me and my sorry-ass dad.

"You didn't have to come with me." I was dragging my feet because I didn't want anyone to know we were together.

"Like hell I didn't. You're going to get an education even if I have to sit up in the class with you every damn day."

I paused mid-step. Surely she had to be kidding. I would look like the biggest loser in the world if that were to happen.

"Come on, boy. You don't want us to be late."

I felt like screaming when she yanked open the front door to the school I'd vowed to never step foot in again.

"Show me the way to the office." My mother reached back and yanked me to her side. Her voice was so loud it practically bounced off the walls.

I was so embarrassed, I refused to look up. "Down this hallway and on the right." I started walking fast in hopes that she wouldn't be able to keep up with me.

The sound of her heels clicked harshly against the ceramic tiled floors. Fortunately, the first bell had already rung, so the hallways were clear of other students. The morning announcements were being read as I held open the door for my mother. She marched past me and made her way to the secretary's desk.

"May I help you?" the secretary asked.

"Yes, my name is Gina Meadows and I would like to see about getting my son back in school."

She looked past my mother's shoulder at me and her eyes narrowed in recognition. "Isn't he already a student at the school?"

"I don't know. You tell me. When was the last time that you saw him?"

I prayed the floor would open up and swallow my body.

"Well, uh…now that I think about it…it's been a minute."

"That's my point." My mother looked back at me with a smug expression on her face.

If it were her intent to embarrass the hell out of me, she succeeded.

"Have a seat and someone will be with you."

My mother grabbed me by the arm and pulled me over to a bench in the corner of the office. Part of me wanted to snatch my arm away and find my own chair, but I was no fool. If I had done that, she would not have hesitated to go upside my head or try to dislocate my shoulder.

"Don't you buck up at me, boy, or I will wear your ass out right here in this office."

"I didn't do nothing." I shoved my hands in my pocket to keep from giving her the finger. There was something going on with her that had nothing to do with our little bathroom incident. She hadn't been caring about my going to school so I wondered what triggered her sudden interest.

We were kept waiting for at least a half an hour before the principal finally came to meet with us.

Principal Gaynor said, "Ms. Meadows?"

My mother stood up and pulled me to my feet with her. "Yes, that's me."

"Come with me." Principal Gaynor turned and started walking to her office, which I was very familiar with. She held the door open for us, then we took a seat in front of her desk. She closed the door behind us.

I slumped over in my seat.

"Sit up straight," my mother prodded.

I sat up.

"How may I help you this morning?" Principal Gaynor asked.

"It has come to my attention that my son has not been attending classes like he should be. I want to see what I need to do to get him back in school and on track to graduate with his class."

"Ms. Meadows, the school year is almost over. Most of the students his age will be moving on to their senior year at the end of the term. Gavin has missed a lot of time and I'm not sure he can make up what he has missed and have enough credits to graduate next year."

I hated they were discussing me as if I wasn't in the room with them.

"I know, but he has got to get an education and he will graduate with his class. Failure is not an option. I don't care if he has to go to summer school to do it either."

"I agree, but we can't make him come to school." Principal Gaynor left the comment hanging in the room, but what she didn't say was clear.

"Oh, I'll make him come to school." My mother threatened.

The tension in the room became uncomfortable, and I started to squirm in my chair.

Principal Gaynor cleared her throat. "Ms. Meadows– "

"It's Mrs."

I turned to Gina surprised she had said that as if my dad would actually marry her. Why she still wanted him was a mystery to me. He didn't fuck with me and my brother. He only came around her when he wanted a piece of ass or needed a free place to stay the night while he was in town. My dad obviously knew how to handle the ladies. In that respect, I wanted to be just like him when I grew up.

"I'm sorry, Mrs. Meadows. I didn't mean any disrespect."

"None taken. A lot of people make that mistake. I'm married, but I kept my maiden name."

Mrs. Gaynor cleared her throat. She looked like she wasn't buying that lie either. "As I was saying, the school year is almost over and your son did not do well in the few months that he did attend school this year."

"I understand, but can he get on track?"

"That's up to him. It will take a lot of hard work."

I could feel my mother staring at me, but I refused to look in her direction.

"Excuse me, Mrs. Gaynor, but this is not up for debate. This boy is going to go to school and he's going to graduate with the rest of his class. Right, Gavin?" She said this as if I had a choice.

"Yes," I said between clinched teeth. When all I wanted to do was tell her to go fuck herself. It would be one thing if she really gave a damn but I felt like she was just doing this because I threw her toothbrush in the toilet.

"Yes, what?" my mother demanded.

"Yes, ma'am." I mumbled.

"Fine, but it's not going to be easy. He may need a tutor," Mrs. Gaynor said.

"Don't worry about that. His brother is an excellent student. I'll get him to help Gavin."

"Oh, yes, Merlin is one of our finest and an absolute treasure to have around. Our school is lucky to have him on our basketball team."

I felt like puking. I was sick and tired of living in Merlin's shadow. I just got no respect. "I don't need no damn tutor and I don't need his help either."

My mother wacked me in the mouth with the back of her hand so fast, I didn't have time to duck. Ali wouldn't have anything on her. She could float you one just like a butterfly.

Apparently outraged, principal Gaynor jumped up from her desk. "Mrs. Meadows, we don't condone that type of behavior in this school."

My mother's face was contorted in rage. " Maybe you should. That's what's wrong with these children today. They don't have any manners. I'm sorry Principal Gaynor if that offends you, but sometimes this boy just pushes all my buttons at the same damn time. He reminds me so much of his father, it's criminal."

Mrs. Gaynor continued to stand as I rubbed my face trying to take away the sting. Tears pricked at the back of my eyes, but I refused to cry.

"Well, I..." The principal seemed to be at a loss for words. She was probably trying to think of a way to get us both out of her office.

That was the second time my mother brought up the man who didn't give a fuck about either of us. I wanted to ask her if her dead baby, empty bed and ring less finger weren't proof enough that he was using her, but I didn't have a death wish. My mother would have had no qualms about beating my ass right there in the principal's office.

Instead, I said, "I don't need a tutor. The work was too easy, so I stopped going to class." I slouched down in my seat as all eyes turned on me.

"Is that so? Perhaps we should test your son's abilities Mrs. Meadows." Principal Gaynor sat back down at her desk and opened the folder that she had been carrying in her hands when she greeted us.

"So what are you saying? You think you're some type of genius?" My mother's voice was dripping with sarcasm. Her eyes told me that she didn't believe a word coming out of my mouth.

"I ain't saying all that. I just said that I could do that stuff they were teaching me in them classes in my sleep."

Ma said, "How would you know what they are teaching if you haven't been there?" She had me there, but I wasn't about to admit it.

"I've seen Merlin's homework." A smile inched up from the corners of my mouth, but I wasn't in the clear yet.

My mother turned to Principal Gaynor. "Fine, test his dumb ass since he thinks he's so smart." She stood up to leave and I got to my feet as well.

"Where do you think you're going?"

I was confused. "I thought the meeting was over." I looked down at my feet because I couldn't take the intensity of her stare.

"It is, but this is a school day and you, bright one, have got a test to take. I'll see you at the house. And you better not think about leaving out this building until the dismissal bell rings. Are we clear?" It was a rhetorical question. She shook the principal's hand and walked out of the office with her head held high.

I nodded as I sat back down.

"Gavin, it's going to take me a minute to get a proctor to handle the test. Have a seat out in the waiting area and I'll have someone come and get you when we're ready for you."

I thought about giving the principal my ass to kiss but I wasn't ready to be homeless. I walked out into the waiting area and took a seat.

17 MERLIN MILLS

I was leaving my second period class when I heard the bad news.

"Hey, man, I guess they finally caught up with your brother. I just saw him down in the principal's office," Braxton Harris, my best friend, said as he patted me on the back.

"What?" I froze in my tracks. I knew I should not have been surprised, but I was. When I left Gavin at home sleeping, I assumed last night's theatrics was all wine talking. Mom hadn't taken an interest in Gavin's schooling before, so I didn't know why she wanted to start now. Especially when things were going so good for me at school. Having Gavin around was a distraction that I didn't need. This was the worse news ever for me. Without Gavin's presence, I was finally making friends.

Braxton pointed. "They got your brother sitting down in the office."

"Shit," I mumbled to myself. Instead of going straight to my next period, I detoured to the office and took a seat next to my brother. "I guess mom wasn't playing with you."

"She practically dragged me in here."

Gavin was pissed, but so was I. My life flowed better when my brother wasn't in it. He was the source of most of my pain and it took my being away from him to realize it.

"Why though? It ain't like you are going to do anything while you are here except get in trouble." I was not happy about this latest development. Gavin thrived on chaos and discomfort. When he was around, people tended to lump us both into the same category. I hated that shit. I was nothing like my brother.

"She said I had to finish school and graduate with my class."

"So what you going to do?" I secretly hoped he would say fuck it and walk away although realistically I knew that wasn't going to happen.

"I don't see I have much of a choice but to finish. She said she would kick me out the house if I didn't stay in school."

I didn't understand. Gavin hadn't been in school in months and it never seemed to bother my mother before. "So when did she became such a concerned parent?"

He grinned, "Maybe when I threw her toothbrush in the toilet and wiped my ass with her head scarf."

Damn, with one stunt, Gavin managed to fuck me twice.

"That was some foul shit you did. I can see why you could be mad at her, but why you always got to be fucking with me?"

"Man, I don't feel like hearing your whining right now. I've got bigger fish to fry. You are going to have to help me pass this year."

I wanted to ask him how I was supposed to do that, but now was not the time. I needed to get to class before I found my own self in trouble.

"So what are you waiting in here for?"

"They supposed to give me some type of test to find out where I should be placed."

I almost told him exactly what I thought, but decided to keep my big mouth shut. The last thing I needed right about now was to get into a fight with my brother and risk being cut from the basketball team. I saw basketball as my ticket out of my mother's house and to a higher education. High school was the stepping stone to my future. Since I already knew my mother couldn't afford to send me to college getting a scholarship was my only option. If that didn't work, I would enlist in the military. Unlike my brother, I had plans. It wasn't that I didn't appreciate Gina for all that she'd done for us, but the woman she was today versus the one we met when we were younger, was like night and day. I didn't like this new Gina very much. I believed she only kept us around to remain relevant in our dad's life.

Gavin slumped back on the bench as I left him. He didn't look too happy. But then again, neither was I. I went to class with a heavy heart. Fortunately for me, I made it before the bell. One of the hardest things about being on the basketball team was that the teachers used that shit against you to keep your ass out of trouble. If I missed doing my homework, I sat out a game. If I was late to class, I sat out a game. Because I planned on using basketball as my ticket out, I couldn't afford to miss shit.

"Did you see him?" Braxton asked when I slid into my seat next to him.

"Yeah, I saw him." I didn't want to talk about Gavin but Braxton knew my pain when it came to my brother.

"So, what's he doing here. He told us he was never coming back." Braxton whispered.

"He's a dumb ass. He had to know that our mother wasn't going to let that happen."

"She ain't been concerned, why now?"

Braxton voiced the million dollar question that we were asking ourselves. "We were just saying the same thing ourselves." Normally, I would have gotten upset if someone had something negative to say about my mother. I was very protective of her even if she was callous at times with me. I couldn't forget the sacrifices she made for us even if she did remind us about them damn near every day. Braxton got a pass from everyone else. He wasn't saying something negative to be mean and hurtful. He was speaking the truth. He knew how raggedy my family relationships were. He had been to our house and witnessed it for himself. He also understood that no matter how wrong Gina might be she was still the only mother I knew.

"So, do you think he will stay in school?"

"He might not have a choice. She was pretty mad at both of us last night."

"Is that where you got that shiner?" Braxton asked as he pointed to my eye.

"Yeah, she was hot."

"What set her off this time?"

"My brother, as usual. He didn't do his chores and tried to blame me for it."

"So why didn't she take that shit out on him? He didn't look like he had a black eye."

"I know, right. I was so sleepy I didn't know what was going on until I got popped."

"Aww, man. What did she do, wake you up and yell at you?"

"She sure did. I was sleeping good too."

"I just wish you would tag your brother one good time for me. It's not like he doesn't deserve it."

"I wanted too. I know he thinks I'm scared of him but that ain't even the case. If I would have knocked his ass out, mom would have come down on me like a mountain. She's big on loyalty and shit. Man I can't win sometimes."

"Dag bro. I hate to hear that. I was going to ask you if your mom would let you come over for the weekend. That girl Kim is having a party. I hear her parents are going out of town."

"No thanks. Those girls are wild as hell. You know if I get in any trouble, I'm off the team."

"Damn man. This is the weekend we are talking about. It has nothing to do with school."

"Those girls go to this school. Therefore, that counts me out. I might have gone if it was someone else that I didn't know."

"Shit. I was hoping you would run point for me. These girls all seem to love you. If they knew I was your boy, they might even look at me a little differently."

I started laughing. Even in the midst of all my pain Braxton found a way to make me laugh. "Man you need to quit. You look like someone's lost puppy. You don't need me to run point for you. If you just show them who you are, you will have them eating out of your hand."

"Man, I don't want them eating out my hand. My lap maybe, but not my hand."

I doubled over laughing. He could be downright crude sometimes. I wasn't as pressed as he was when it came to girls. I liked them and all, but I was a little intimidated by them. Gavin, on the other hand, was like a male whore. According to him, he could talk the drawers off a saint. I knew I wanted to be a different man than my father when it came to women. I didn't like what he did to them and the way it changed them. Even without a role model for the proper way to treat a woman, I knew I was going to be different.

"Braxton, why don't you ask Gavin to go to the party? I'm sure he would love to go."

"First of all, you know I don't roll with your brother like that. Secondly, I doubt he would help me get a girl. He would try to fuck them all. You and I both know your brother doesn't like to share.

"You got that right. Now that I think about it, he wouldn't have your best interest at heart. Hey, I thought you had to work on Saturday."

"I do but I'm going to call out."

"Don't call out man, I will work your shift. I need a few more shifts so I can finish paying off this car."

"Okay man, that's cool. You can work it. I have to be there at noon. I really can't believe you have saved enough money for a car and you can't even drive it yet."

"I will be taking the test next month and this car might not be available. It would have been dumb to wait until after I passed the test to start saving."

"I hear you. I wish I would have started saving when you did. Then I would be getting my car about the same time."

"It's all good. You can ride with me until you do. You know I've got your back."

"Your brother is going to hate you."

"I know. But it's not my fault he never wanted to work. He could have gotten a job just like us."

"I know. I can't wait to see his face. Have you told him about it yet?"

"I can wait. It will just be something else for him to worry the shit out of me about. But I'll tell you what, he won't be driving my car. That's for sure. He doesn't know how to appreciate anything. I'm not about to let him fuck up my shit."

"You say that now Merlin, but I know how you are. You have too kind of a heart."

Braxton's words disturbed me. I hadn't really given much thought to Gavin's reaction to my getting a car. He knew I was saving my money but I never discussed with him what I was going to do with it.

"Who knows, he might not even trip. We'll just have to wait and see. Even as I said it, I knew he was gonna trip. I started working when I was twelve at the neighborhood car wash drying off cars for tips. Gavin thought I was stupid for working for change. That change added up when I could keep it hidden from Gavin and Gina. She didn't hit me up as much as he did but it still happened. It would be a relief to spend the money so they would stop asking for it.

18 GAVIN MILLS

I was playing nice just like my mother wanted me too. I was going to school every day and applying myself. With Merlin's unknowing assistance, I was also passing my classes. Every day when I got home school, I would copy Merlin's homework. I didn't copy it verbatim, I changed a few things so it wouldn't noticeably be the same.

It wasn't that the work was hard, it was just boring. I could care less about history or social studies. The only thing that I applied myself to was math. This was something I thought I could actually use outside of school. I knew I had to be able to calculate my money.

I put away my books and looked around the room I shared with my brother and I tried not to get pissed off. Merlin's side of the room was always so damn neat. It drove me nuts. I stifled the urge to throw his shit up in the air and stomp on it. It wouldn't make me feel any better because Merlin would pick it up and put them away as if nothing had happened. It was getting so it wasn't even fun anymore to fuck with him. I was about to go downstairs to fix myself a sandwich when I noticed that Merlin had left his precious laptop on.

"What do we have here?" I said out loud when I sat down on his bed. He was on Facebook and must have forgotten to log out of his account. I rubbed my hands together devilishly.

"I wonder what I can do to mess up his life?" I thought about taking a picture of my dick and posting it on his page, but quickly decided against it. It would be just my luck that he would land a girlfriend out of it. Much to my surprise, Merlin had quite a few friends.

I got up off the bed and closed our bedroom door. I wasn't expecting my mother home for a few hours, but there was always that chance that she would chose this day to get off early. I sat back down on the bed again and started clicking on his photos and friends.

"Damn, this nigger got game. Who would have thought it?" I clicked through his friends list until I found the cutest girl I had seen in a long time. Without even thinking about it twice, I sent her a message. I wasn't sure which one surprised me more, the fact that I sent this beautiful girl named Cheryl a message or the fact that she responded back.

Merlin: What are you doing beautiful?
Cheryl: Oh, now you want to talk? We've been Facebook friends on Facebook for almost six month."
Merlin: I know, I'm sorry. I don't do this much?"
Cheryl: Do what?

I felt a tingling in my dick that I normally only experience with my hand. It was so cool, I wanted more. The only problem was that she thought I was Merlin. If I walked away from the computer and he never allowed me access to it again, my connection with Cheryl would be lost. I had to find out more about her.

Merlin: I don't mess around on Facebook much. I just use the computer to do my homework and stuff.
Cheryl: Oh. I thought you were being stuck up.

Merlin: If I was on here often, I would certainly talk to you. I prefer to have my conversations in person.
Cheryl: Wow, that's nice. I don't talk much on here either.
Merlin: Can I, uh, call you on the phone instead of talking on this thing?

I almost had a orgasm when she typed her number. I copied down her number, erased our conversation and told her I would call her in a few minutes.

I was elated. I went downstairs and fixed myself a quick snack and called Cheryl. She answered the phone on the first ring.

"Hello?"

"Hey Cheryl, it's Merlin." I knew I sounded lame but then again, I was pretending to be my brother. His personality was a lot different than mine.

"I'm really happy that you called me."

"Oh, yeah? Why so?"

"Because, silly. I've been trying to get you to notice me for months."

"When? You mean I saw you somewhere and I didn't speak to you?"

"You wave at me but I didn't even think you knew my name. I see you all the time when you play against my school."

"Ah, you're a sports fan. I get it." I was a little bit disappointed with this news. I wasn't the least bit interested in basketball and I didn't want to pretend that I was.

"I'm a cheerleader. I thought you knew that. Why else would you have accepted my friend request on Facebook?"

"I'm sorry. I told you I'm not on Facebook like that. I don't really know any of those people that are on my page."

I wasn't lying about that because I didn't know most of Merlin's friends. We didn't travel in the same circles at all.

The only one that I knew about was his friend Braxton and that was because he was always hanging around him.

"Oh, I thought you weren't interested in being friends with me."

I chuckled. She was fishing for another compliment. "Well, I am a little shy. I'm trying to get better though. What school do you go too? I swear I've never seen you walking our halls."

"I go to Southwest DeKalb."

"Tell me a little about you. I know that you are a cheerleader, what else do you like to do?" If I could keep our conversation away from sports, I was sure we would find something else to talk about.

Cheryl giggled. "You want to know what I like to do?" She giggled again.

"Yeah, like do you like to bowl? Go to movies? What do you like to eat?" I was asking her all those questions when I knew good and well that I didn't have the funds to do any of them. The only thing my dad taught me about bitches was that if I wanted to get in their panties, I had to get in their mind first. He said the best way to do that was to get them to talk about themselves.

"Yes, I like all of that."

This conversation was a lot harder than it needed to be. It was like I was pulling teeth.

"A pretty girl like you, I'm sure you have a boyfriend. Where is he at?"

More giggles followed by boisterous laughter. And just as suddenly as that tingle appeared, it died. Cheryl wasn't my type of girl. I could see this already. At the rate this was going it would take a year just to get a touch of her breasts. I had no desire to go through all that just for a little pussy.

"No, I don't. My mother says I'm too young for a boyfriend. Uh, do you have a girl friend?" Her voice sounded deeper, a little sexy too.

"I have friends. Just waiting for that special girl if you know what I mean."

"Yeah, I know what you mean."

There were a few seconds of awkward silence. I had run out of small talk and I didn't think she had any in her to begin with.

"Well, it was nice talking to you." I said as I prepared to hang up.

"Wait, will you call me again?"

I felt myself getting angry. Why should I call her again? I wasn't trying to catch a case of blue balls dealing with her.

"Uh, I don't really see the point. I mean, it's not like you can go out on a date with me or anything like that."

"I didn't say all of that. I said my mother didn't want me to have a boyfriend. But you know what they say, what she doesn't know won't hurt her."

I was beginning to feel more confident about my chances of getting the panties. "I think you have an unfair advantage over me."

"How's that?"

"Well, the only picture I've seen of you is all small but you have seen me in person."

"Well, I could send you some pictures of myself. If you want me to."

"You would do that for me?" I was smiling from ear to ear. This was a lot easier that I thought it would be.

"Sure, give me your cell number."

"Are you going to take some special pictures for me?"

"Um, yeah. I can do that."

"404-589-1234"

"Okay, give me an hour or so okay?"

"Sure, I'm not going anywhere. Just trying to get my homework done. I'll talk to you later."

I was feeling a little hopeful when I hung up the phone. Perhaps things were going to turn out better than I thought they were. I went into the living room and turned on the television.

19 MERLIN MILLS

I waited until Saturday morning while Gavin was still sleep to approach momma with my news. She was sitting at the kitchen table sipping on coffee when I walked into the kitchen.

"What are you doing up so early?"

"I wanted to catch you before you got busy with your day."

"Is this going to piss me off? Because if this is going to make me mad, you can march your narrow ass right back up those stairs and save it for later."

"I hope it doesn't piss you off. I mean, it shouldn't." I was a little skittish because these days everything pissed her off. If I could have figured out a way to do what I wanted to do without her knowing about it, I would have.

"Fine. Long as you remember I can still bash you over the head about it."

I swallowed a rather large knot in my throat. "Well, you know I have been saving my money from my jobs ever since I started working right?"

"Yeah, and." Momma was tapping her finger nails on the table making me even more nervous.

"You know my birthday is next month and I found a car that I want to buy and I need you to—" I tried to get it all out before she interrupted me but it didn't work.

"I am not co-signing for shit. Your daddy done already messed up my credit fooling around with him. So you are shit out of luck with that one."

"I wasn't asking you to co-sign."

"Well, what do you want then? I ain't got no money either. It takes all the money I make to take care of this house and make sure we have food on the table."

I was trying very hard not to show any emotion on my face. I knew my mother was struggling. She wouldn't let any of us forget it either. But I resented it when she made it seem like all we did was take from her. Unlike my brother, I had been working, one way or another, since the age of nine. If I wasn't cutting grass, washing cars or walking dogs, I was in my room studying. She could not have gotten a better son than me even if she had me herself. And I was always giving her money to make things better so I couldn't help but to feel a little resentful about her remarks.

"I bought the car already. I just need you to drive it home since I don't have my license yet."

My mother's mouth dropped open. Clearly she wasn't expecting me to say that. "What do you mean you bought a car? Who would sell you a car at your age?" She sounded pissed.

"My boss sold it to me. It's a nice car Mom. There is nothing wrong with it. It belonged to his son and he stopped paying on it."

"What about insurance. You know you have to have insurance in order to have a car. Have you thought about that mister smarty-pants? They are going to want an arm and a leg for it at your age. And, you're a boy, so that's going to make the rates even more high."

For the life of me I couldn't figure out why she was so negative all the time. It wasn't like I was asking her for anything. She should have been happy. "Yes, I know about the insurance. I already called and got several quotes. I already have enough saved for the first years premium." I was feeling a little proud of myself and she was really sucking the wind out of my sails.

"Humph. And are you prepared for all the maintenance a car requires? What about your tags and title? Do you know anything about all that boy?"

I cringed. It was almost like she were trying to devalue me and it hurt immensely. I loved her, but I also hated her at the same time.

"I believe I have thought about everything. If I haven't mom, I will save for it just like I have been until I have everything that I need."

"What about driving? Who is going to teach you how to drive it? I don't have the time nor the patience for all of that."

I repressed the urge to scream at her. I couldn't remember if she acted this way around my dad or not but if she did, I could understand why he didn't spend any time with her. She was acting like a real bitch.

"I know how to drive. I will just need you to go with me to take the test."

Mom didn't say anything for a few minutes as she sipped her coffee. I couldn't think of anything else that would sway her to say yes so I stood there silently praying that she wouldn't fuck up all of my plans.

"What about your brother?"

I stood there stunned and at a complete loss for words for several seconds. "What about him?"

"Have you thought about how he will react?"

"No disrespect intended mother, but Gavin is not my child. I have looked out for him all my life. He had the same opportunity to do something for himself as I did. If he doesn't like my car, that's his problem."

"It's about time you stood up for yourself! When do you want to go get this car?"

A slow smile slid across my face. After years of trying to get her approval, I had finally done something that she could be proud of. "We can go get it whenever you're ready? I have the keys to it and I know where it is parked."

"Let me finish my coffee and get dressed. I want to see what you spent all your money on."

"Thanks, Mom."

I wanted to go up to her and give her a big hug and kiss but I was afraid to ruin her good mood. She was just that volatile, so I decided to wait and let her make that move herself.

20 GAVIN MILLS

After months of silly conversations, I finally made a date with Cheryl. I was excited because the daily pictures we exchanged were getting more and more risqué. I was ready to taste those breasts that she so willingly shared with me.

This date meant a lot to me. It represented more than me just getting my fingers wet. It was also a big fuck you to my brother who had been acting like his shit didn't stink after he got his car and his license. Even though I hated to admit it, I kind of admired the way he went about it. In hindsight, I wished I had done the same thing. But it was too late for me to cry about that.

Not only was I about to steal his car for my date, I was also about to steal a girl who continued to believe she was talking to my brother. It would be like a double victory for me. One that I intended to dip his nose in once I got back with her panties.

I snuck into the kitchen and raided my mother's wallet. Unfortunately for me, she didn't have much money in it. I already knew what would happen if I took her last twenty dollars. She would have my shit sitting out on the porch by the time I got back to the house. I went back into our room and started going through Merlin's drawers. I had hit Merlin up so many times in the past, he opened up a savings account to protect his money. But I was not discouraged, I knew he had a secret stash of mad money and I wasn't going to give up until I found it.

"Bingo," I said as I held up the two twenty dollar bills and kissed them. I wasn't worried about Merlin saying anything about the money. Car or no car, he was still a pussy as far as I was concerned.

The other thing that bothered me about my brother's bold move, was the way our mother treated him. She was finally giving him the respect I thought we both deserved from day one. She didn't yell at him like she continued to yell at me. I tiptoed past my mother's room and snuck down the stairs. This little stunt was a fuck you to her too for treating us differently.

I took Merlin's keys from the rack in the kitchen. It served him right for leaving them in plain sight. I snuck out of the house and locked the door. I didn't really relax until after I had started up the car and drove it down the street. Cheryl didn't live that far from our Covington home, so I wasn't worried about not having a license. I figured as long as I stayed off the main streets and obeyed the traffic laws, I should be straight. If everything went as I planned it, I would be back home before Merlin came home from work.

Merlin's car was nice and for a second, I felt proud of my brother. That feeling only lasted for a few seconds. I kept looking in my rear view mirror paranoid that someone was following me. After several blocks, I started to relax.

Cheryl was looking hot when I picked her up. She came out to the car after I tooted the horn, and stood by the door with her arms crossed across her breasts. I could not remove my eyes from their swell. Seeing her in person was so much different from looking at her on my phone. I envisioned myself tasting her breast so much, it was the only thing I saw when she came out.

She cleared her throat. "Aren't you going to open the door?"

This bitch was tripping. I fought back the urge to ask her if her fingers were broken. I wasn't used to playing the role of gentleman. For some pussy, though, I was willing to play along. I got out of the car, and sauntered around the back, and stood facing her. I wanted a kiss but knew it was too soon to be taking it, especially while standing in front of her parents home. I reached past her and opened the door. "You look nice," I said as I closed the door behind her.

She seemed to unthaw with those few words. Cheryl was a attention whore. As long as I plied her with compliments she was cool. It was mentally draining trying to come up with fresh new things to say to her.

"Thanks, Merlin, you look cute too." I was wearing black jeans, a black Frankie Beverly and Maze tee shirt, and a black hat. I walked back around the car with a little pep in my step. I was feeling cocky and sure of myself as I got back into the driver's seat. Although, I never heard a single song that Frankie Beverly sang, he just seemed like the type of artist that Cheryl would appreciate, so I borrowed the shirt from my brother. I didn't actually borrow the shirt, 'cause that would require my asking his permission, so I guess you could say I stole it too.

"Nice car. Is it yours?"

"Yup, I just got it a few months ago."

"Where are we going?" Cheryl was looking in the mirror putting on lipstick. She wore a tight pair of blue jeans and a yellow tank top.

My eyes kept going back and forth from the road to her breasts. I couldn't help it. I was smitten with them.

"Merlin?"

I heard her talking, but I forgot I was pretending to be my brother until she nudged me.

"Huh?"

"I asked you where we're going." Her voice was beginning to get on my nerves.

In our conversations over the phone, I never noticed the whiney quality to her voice. It was like nails on a chalkboard in the tight confines of the car. It took everything in me not to tell her to shut the fuck up. It was only the possibility of getting the panties that kept me silent.

"Relax, baby, I got this."

Cheryl sat back in the seat with her hands folded in her lap. I was taking the shortcut though the Indian Reserve when the car sputtered and jerked.

"What the fuck?" I muttered as the car quit moving altogether.

"Why are we stopping? Did you just run out of gas?"

In my haste to get the car out of the driveway before my mother stopped me, it didn't even occur to me to check to see if there was any gas in the car. "Shit." I hit my hand on the dashboard in frustration. All week long Merlin had been catching a ride to school and work with his buddy Braxton, but he never said why and now I knew.

"Please tell me you didn't run out of gas." There was attitude in Cheryl's voice.

This was not good. We were on a deserted part of the reservation at the bottom of the hill, which was a disaster waiting to happen.

Rather than sit there and bitch and moan about the situation, I decided to take charge. I could get mad at Merlin later when I got his car back to the house. "You are going to have to steer the car while I push it off the road." I opened the door and went around to the back of the car with my hands resting on the trunk.

"Are you for real? I don't know how to drive." Cheryl protested.

I wanted to tell her neither did I, but we didn't have time to argue the point. "Just turn the wheel to the right and keep your feet off the brake. Put the car in Neutral."

She slid over the seat. Any hope of getting some pussy tonight went right out the window. I'd be lucky if I got a kiss on the cheek.

She put the car in gear and I started to push. Getting the car to move was harder than I thought it would be. I had to dig real deep before it began to move.

"Now straighten up the wheel," I yelled grunting with exertion.

"How do I do that?" She yelled back.

Ooh wee, I was sick of her. "Turn it a little to the left."

She stomped on the brake, stopping the car.

"Get your fucking foot off the brake!"

"Who the hell are you cussing at?"

That had to be the dumbest question ever. We were the only people out there.

I counted to five before I answered. "Cheryl, please. We have to get the car off the road before someone comes and hits us." I pushed again and the car glided to the right. "Okay, that's good. Put the brake on and put it in Park." I leaned against the bumper as I tried to catch my breath.

Cheryl got out the car and stomped around to the back. Her high heels made a clicking sound on the pavement. "What now?" She had her hands on her hips and was working her neck like she was some ghetto chick. It was not a good look for her.

Wiping the sweat from my forehead, I said, "I guess we walk."

"Walk? Are you out your mind? Do you see these shoes I'm wearing?" She lifted her foot for my inspection.

"Do you have another suggestion?" I could care less what she had on her feet. She was quickly getting on my nerves.

"Merlin, there is no way that I can walk with these shoes on." She was whining again.

"Fine, stay here. When I get some gas, I'll be back."

Cheryl sputtered as if she couldn't believe what I was saying. "You expect me to wait out here all by myself?"

Her question didn't even warrant a response. I just wanted to get as far away from Merlin's car as my feet would carry me. I was going to use the money I had stolen to get some gas, drop this bitch off at her house, and park Merlin's car back like nothing ever happened.

I said, "If we stay here, we're liable to get hit so the choice is yours." I opened the trunk. I prayed that Merlin had a gas can in there, but luck was not on my side. "Shit." I slammed the trunk down and started going toward Salem Road.

"Why are we going this way? My house is back there." She was pointing her finger back in the direction from where we came.

My blood was starting to bubble. "Look, I'm not trying to be a dick but you really are being stupid. I have to get gas, and the last time I checked it wasn't in that direction."

"But if we walk that way, we will have to walk back."

"Duh!" I was done being nice to her. If she thought I was going to walk her home first then go get gas, she was dumber than I originally thought.

"You don't have to be an ass, Merlin. It's not my fault you ran out of gas."

So now the bitch wanted to play the blame game. I started walking again at a rapid pace. The way I figured it, the quicker I got the gas, the quicker I could get rid of this pesky clickety-clacking chatterbox next to me.

Cheryl huffed loudly. "Must you walk so fast?"

"This date is fucked anyway and I ain't trying to be out here all night. I told you, you're welcome to wait in the car." I could tell that she was thinking about it, but while she was thinking, I was walking. The road going through the Indian reserve was dark and without a sidewalk, so we had no choice but to walk on the road.

"Did you see a flashlight in the trunk?"

Dumb bitch. "If I saw a flashlight, don't you think I would have brought it along?"

"You don't have to be so nasty, I was just asking a question."

Once again, her comment did not deserve an answer. The walk was beginning to take its toll on me. We had just started up the hill when we heard an approaching car. Without thinking, I grabbed Cheryl's hand and quickly crossed to the other side of the road. The car rushed past us.

"What are you doing, idiot? That car could have given us a ride."

"They could have run us over too. Didn't your mother ever teach you to walk against the flow of traffic?"

"You leave my mother's name out your mouth." Cheryl shouted.

The second she said it I realized my mistake. Cheryl's mother had passed away a few months before. Even I wasn't insensitive enough to joke about someone's mother.

"I'm sorry, Cheryl, I didn't mean it the way it sounded. I wasn't talking bad about your momma." I felt like kicking myself. Although she was getting on my nerves, I didn't mean to hurt her like that.

She stopped walking. "We could have hitched a ride." She was sulking.

"You would have gotten into a car with a stranger?" I was surprised.

She said, "It's not like I would have been alone, you would have been with me."

"What good will that do if they have a gun?" I started walking again. We were wasting valuable time standing around talking.

"You wouldn't throw yourself in front of a bullet for me?"

I couldn't tell if she was being serious or not so I didn't respond. I kept walking and she started following me again. I was glad because I really would have hated to leave her on the side of the road.

"My feet hurt," she whined.

I ignored her and kept on walking.

"How far is it to Salem Road?" she asked.

"After we get off this reserve, probably about two to three miles."

"Miles? Have you bumped your head? I'm not walking no three miles." Once again she stopped walking.

"Suit yourself." I kept going.

"You're going to leave me out here by myself?" She sounded genuinely surprised.

"If you don't come on, yeah, I will. We've got to get to the gas station before it closes and pray that they have a gas can for sale. If it makes you feel any better, we can try to get a cab from the station."

She appeared to think about it for a minute before I heard the distinct sound of her heels clacking against the road.

"Some date this turned out to be." She ran to catch up with me.

I overlooked her chatter. I understood why she was pissed. I was too.

"I can't wait to get back to school and tell everyone on my cheerleading squad what an ass you are."

For a second, I almost stopped, until it dawned on me that she wouldn't be smearing my name, she would be attacking

Merlin. A chuckle slipped from my mouth. Hell, she didn't even go to my school which made it even better.

"Oh, you think that's funny?"

I wanted to tell her so badly, that it was, but I wasn't ready to disclose my true identity. Cheryl would have never gone out with me in the first place if she knew who I was. According to her Facebook page, she was on the A-list at school, a good student, and the vice president of the junior class. A bad word from her would be the kiss of death to someone who gave a damn. I, on the other hand, was a second-class citizen. I had a bad reputation of being a shit starter and a womanizer. I was in numerous fights, struggled through my classes and was a social reject when it came to my peers. So yeah, it was funny to me. I had nothing to lose.

"I wish your feet would move as fast as your mouth."

She punched me in the shoulder. Part of me wanted to slug her back but I held my composure. It wasn't her fault that we had to walk, but it wasn't mine either. If Merlin had put gas in his car, we wouldn't be in the situation we were in.

She nudged me. "So what are you trying to say? Are you saying I talk a lot?"

"You tell me. I think a hit dog hollers loudest."

"What's that supposed to mean?" She started walking so fast that she breezed right past me. I didn't complain because it gave me the opportunity to watch her ass jiggle in her jeans.

"I know you're watching my ass. Take a good look 'cause this is the closest you will get to it."

This time I didn't bother to stifle my laughter. She was so full of herself, I just couldn't control it. "Girl, your ass is okay, but I've seen better. Leave the jiggling to Jell-O and firm that shit up."

She fell back in step with me and raised her hand to strike me as a car came barreling down the hill. I don't know what came over me but something told me to push the big-mouth bitch, so I did. Her excruciatingly loud scream permeated the night. The awful sound of crunching bones met my ears. The car rolled right over her stomach cutting off her screams.

"No!" I yelled as I stared at my hands in horror. I could not believe I acted on my own impulse.

The driver of the vehicle swung wildly in the road before they seemed to regain control of the car. I rushed to Cheryl in disbelief. Blood was pouring out her mouth. Her eyes were wide open with a shocked look on her face.

"Cheryl, I'm so sorry," I said as tears streamed down my face.

She looked as if she wanted to say something, but her mouth was not cooperating. All she managed to do was blow bubbles with her blood.

"I didn't mean it. I swear I didn't mean it."

The car finally managed to stop in the middle of the road several hundred feet from where we were. The passenger door opened and I saw two figures running towards me.

"I don't have a phone. Could you please call for help?" I pleaded.

"Gavin?" One of the men inquired.

I looked up confused. The voice sounded so much like my brother's but I knew that was impossible. My brother should have been at work.

"Call for an ambulance please," I begged.

"Oh, God, Gavin, what have you done?" Merlin ran toward me and dropped to his knees.

"It was an accident. I swear it was an accident." I felt like I was losing control. Images that shouldn't be there were popping in my head like in a virtual movie, making me nervous. I saw my mother's face. She had a perpetual frown. My father's face had a look of disgust, but the facial expression that hurt me the most was the one on my brother's face. His look of revulsion and fear was real.

"Is that Cheryl? Oh my God!" Braxton shouted as he came up to us.

'Oh, shit, Gavin," Merlin cried as tears rolled down his face. He kept bringing his hands to Cheryl's head and pulling them back without touching her.

I tried to shake Merlin's voice from my head, but as much as I tried, his face remained. He was crying and yelling at me at the same time.

"What have you done?" Merlin leaned over and started beating me about the head.

Braxton tried to pull Merlin away, but he kept trying to hit me. "We've got to go get help."

Since I thought this was all a dream, I tried to protect Cheryl as best I could, but her eyes were no longer open. I prayed that she had only passed out and was not dead.

I pushed Merlin off of me and crawled over to the side of the road. My stomach heaved as I let go of everything that remained in my gut. This whole ordeal was turning into a pure nightmare. Not only did I have to contend with the body in the road, I had to deal with my brother's ranting.

"What are you doing here?" I demanded once I got myself together. Braxton and Merlin had their arms around each other's shoulders. I recoiled from the sight. Merlin should have been holding me up instead of his stupid friend.

"Did you just push that girl in the street?" Braxton demanded.

"What? I, uh…" I could feel the sweat trickling down from under my arms. I could not believe Braxton saw me shove Cheryl.

"Oh, God, Gavin," Merlin was openly moaning as he held his hand over his mouth.

"Wait, no. I didn't push her. She was trying to flag down a ride and I was trying to grab her out of the way."

"It didn't look that way to me," Braxton insisted a little loudly.

"Merlin, tell this fool that I wouldn't do anything like that," I pleaded.

"What are you doing out here?" Merlin asked as he seemed to get control of his emotions.

"See, what happened was…" I couldn't even finish my lie.

"You tried to take my fucking car didn't you?" Merlin rushed toward me with his arms outstretched. Braxton rushed behind Merlin and grabbed him by the waist, holding him back.

"I'm going to kill you," Merlin shouted as he struggled to get free.

"I didn't crash your precious car! The fucker ran out of gas."

"You didn't have any business being in it in the first place!"

"Merlin stop, we have to call the police."

I started to panic. "What are you going to tell them?"

They didn't have time to answer as the ambulance came to a screeching halt on the road followed by two patrol cars. I watched in terror as the officers rushed from the car over to us.

"What happened here?" One of them demanded.

I couldn't even look at my brother. He held my fate in his hands. I just prayed he would do the right thing.

21 GINA MEADOWS

"Oh God, Gina. I just heard about Gavin on the news. Please tell me that it isn't true," Tabatha said.

"Girl, I wish I could. I was at the police station half the night trying to figure out what the hell happened my own self. They had both my boys down at that jail."

"Both? What do you mean both?"

"That poor girl's family told the police that she went out with Merlin. He was down there trying to clear his name."

"What kind of foolishness is this? You can't mean that Gavin actually pushed this girl like they said on the news. What is he saying?"

"He swears he didn't, but he also told the police that Merlin let him take his car. It's just a big old mess."

"Sweet Jesus. Do you want me to come over there? What does Merlin have to say about this?"

"You don't have to come over. I'm going to get some sleep in a minute. They had me miss work for this shit. I swear these are some ungrateful children."

"Come on, Gina. I'm sure they didn't intentionally make this happen just so you would miss work."

I was slightly taken aback by the anger I heard in Tabatha's voice. I expected her to be on my side with this one since she knew how much I struggled to keep those kids out of trouble. It hurt me that she was defending them over me.

"It doesn't matter whether it was intentional or not. I am the one that has to worry about getting a lawyer and shit. Do you think I can count on Ronald to get his son a lawyer?"

"Don't you think that is something you should be working out with Ronald?"

Her voice was dripping with sarcasm and I hated it. Tabatha knew that Ronald wasn't taking my phone calls these days. I had drunk dialed her way too many times to try to deny the fact that Ronald and I were on the outs.

"Well, that nigger is on his own with this one. Gavin is just going to have to take his chances with the public defender."

"Damn, Gina. Remind me not to piss your ass off."

"What? You don't think I have a right to be mad about this shit?"

"I'm not saying that at all. But that nigger you are referring to is your son. Ain't that what you told me?"

"He's still a nigger. Just like his damn daddy. Ain't neither one of them niggers' any good."

"You can be mad at Ronald's sorry ass all day long, Gina. Those boys didn't ask to be born. Don't take your frustration for their dad out on them."

"I don't have time for this shit either. I'll talk to you later Tabatha." I hung up the phone. I was not in the mood for a lecture. I was tired and irritable and more than a little frustrated. No matter what I did, I had to realize that Gavin wasn't going to do right.

"Merlin, get down here." I yelled up the stairs. I followed his heavy foot fall with my eyes as he walked across the floor. His eyes were red and his shoulders were slumped.

"Yes?"

"Sit down. I want to talk to you."

He sighed loudly. I could tell he was tired too. He was still wearing his uniform from the night before.

"I'm going to ask you this one time. Are you sure you saw Gavin push that girl?"

Merlin shook his head no. "I'm not sure what I saw. He might have been trying to grab her like he said he was."

"Boy, don't lie to me. We both know your brother ain't shit."

Merlin appeared to cringe.

"I'm not lying mother. It was dark out there and he was wearing all black. He could have been helping her for all I know."

"But your friend said he saw him push the girl."

"That's what he told the police but I can't tell you what he saw. He wouldn't lie on Gavin, if that is what you mean."

"Sounds like you are protecting your friend over your brother."

"I'm not protecting anybody. If Braxton said he saw something, then I believe him. He was paying attention more than I was since he was driving."

I couldn't argue with that logic. I was torn. "And you're sure you didn't tell your brother it was okay to drive your car?"

"Seriously? Do you remember how hard I had to work to get that car? You think I would jeopardize all of that for this shit?"

"Boy, you had better watch your mouth."

Merlin's eyes were lit like small candles. "Then maybe you should think before you say some dumb stuff like that!" He shouted.

I raised my hand to slap him but Merlin caught it. His fingers locked on my wrist and pressed it back down on the table.

"Have you lost your mind?"

"You can't hit me for this one. Don't you see how this is tearing me apart? That's my brother they are talking about on the news."

"Well, that same brother tried to drag your ass into this mess so don't get it twisted."

"Don't you think I know this already? Why do you have to keep on hammering at me like I'm too stupid to understand it. I get it! You have been trying to tell me my brother ain't shit for years. I heard you the first time. But just because he doesn't have a moral compass that doesn't mean that I don't have to have one."

All the fight went out of me. Gavin had hurt us both for the last time. "They are going to lock that boy up. I just hope they don't throw away the key."

"Can I go now?" Merlin wouldn't even look at me.

"Yeah, go ahead. Ain't nothing that we can do about this now." As he walked away, I could hear his sniffles. He was hurting but he was also learning. It was the hardest lesson I could teach him.

I called Ronald because I thought it was the right thing to do. He deserved to know his son was about to go to jail even though I didn't know how I was going to form my lips to say it. Ronald would assume that I failed again, even though I gave his kids my all. He wouldn't accept any of the responsibility. I knew this, but I still made the call. As usual, he did not answer the phone so I felt no remorse when I sent him a short text saying *Gavin is in jail, deal with it.*

♥♥♥

The whole time I was getting dressed for Gavin's arraignment I kept waiting for Ronald to call. I kept thinking he would walk through the door and make everything alright. It was silly of me to think that he would, given the fact that he had never done so in the past.

"You ready to go?" I asked Merlin as I stopped by his room. He was sitting on his bed with his head down looking at the floor. He wore the only good suit he had left, a dark blue one.

"Yes," he mumbled. There was another suit laid out on Gavin's bed.

"Are you taking that suit for your brother to wear?"

"Do you think they will let him have it?"

"I doubt it, but you can bring it with us just in case." It felt like I had a lump in my chest instead of a heart. If I had a heart, it would have been bleeding.

"I don't see why I have to go down there anyway. I don't have anything to say." I understood where Merlin was coming from. I didn't feel like going down to the courthouse either.

"Let's go, we don't want to be late."

Merlin got up off the bed and grabbed the suit following me to the car. He got in and buckled up.

"Does my dad know what's going on?"

"I tried to call him but he must have been working so I left him a text."

"Figures."

I couldn't even get mad at Merlin for saying it. It was one thing to turn his back on me, it was something else to turn on his babies.

"He wouldn't be able to do anything now anyway. It's too late."

"What do you think they are going to do to Gavin?"

There was no mistaking the quiver in his voice. "You really love your brother, don't you?"

"Yes, even though he doesn't deserve it."

"I know what you mean, I feel the same way about your father."

22 MERLIN MILLS

When we got to the court house the room was packed. I searched the room for Gavin but I didn't immediately see him. My heart skipped a beat.

"Are you sure we are in the right room?" I asked Gina.

"Yeah, I think so."

"I don't see Gavin. Do you?" I couldn't imagine what things were like for him. This was the first time that I could remember ever being apart from him for any considerable length of time. Even though he sometimes worked my nerve, he was still my blood and I loved him.

"No, I don't see him. They might not be ready for him yet."

Although Gina remained calm on the outside, I could tell she was just as nervous as I was.

"All rise," the bailiff said.

We all stood as the judge walked into the courtroom. She was a small white woman with black horn-rimmed glasses and white hair. The chair she sat in was almost bigger than she. She banged her gavel and everyone in the room sat back down. The whole atmosphere in the room was intimidating to me and I wanted Gina to put her arms around me and tell me it was going to be okay.

The side door opened and another officer led in six black boys, all in orange jumpsuits and strung together with handcuffs like cattle. Gavin was in the middle of the pack. He held his head down so I couldn't see his face. My heart went out to him. He had fucked up good this time.

The officer led them over to a bench off to the side of the room and undid each of their handcuffs and secured them to their chairs. I thought it was unnecessary because all of the boys looked broken. Armed guards were all over the room, so I seriously doubted any of them were bold enough to make a run for it.

I looked around the room again and noticed Braxton sitting on the back row. He waved at me with a small smile on his face. I could tell he didn't want to be there any more than I did. I nodded my head back to him. I wanted to tell him to come sit with us but I was afraid to draw attention to Gina and me.

I leaned over and whispered in Gina's ear. "Can I go and sit with Braxton? He is in the back."

"No, it's too late to be moving around the room. It won't look good."

I didn't like it, but I understood what she meant. The room was very quiet. The only sound I heard was the ticking from the clock mounted on the wall.

The judge banged her gavel once again. She read off the names of the six boys that were brought into the room. Each boy raised their hand when their names were called.

"Before we get officially started, I am giving each of you an opportunity that will only come once in your life time. I sincerely hope you will think about my offer before you make a decision because you will never get this chance again. Most of you are charged with crimes that could easily result in long prison sentences if your cases were to proceed to trial. Ultimately this could cost the state a lot of money. Since you are all juvenile offenders, I will offer you the chance to take sentence before judgment. What that means is, that before the court reads into record the individual charges each of you have, I will render a sentence. Once that sentence is completed, your convictions will be removed from your permanent record unless the same or worst crimes are committed. Do you each understand what I have explained to you?"

Each boy nodded their heads in agreement.

"Good, this court will be in recess for ten minutes to give you all a chance to think about what you want to do."

We were ordered to stand again as the judge exited the room.

"Should Gavin take this deal?" I whispered to Gina.

"Yes, I think he should."

"But we don't know what the punishment is. That sounds crazy to me."

"I know. But Gavin could be charged with some serious offenses. I don't know what the minimum sentence is for each crime, but he could be sent away for ten or fifteen years."

"For what? Borrowing my car? I won't tell the judge that he stole it. I just can't do that to him."

"This is out of your hands Merlin. That little girl died and the judge could charge him with murder or manslaughter. And even if you didn't tell the judge that he stole your car, he still was driving without a license and proof of insurance. They will throw the book at him."

"But what if they sentence him to ten or fifteen years anyway?"

"I think that's a chance he should take because at least when he gets out, there won't be any record of his conviction."

I slumped down in my seat. Either way this thing went, it was going to suck for my brother. I looked up and Gavin was staring straight at me. I clutched his suit in my hands wrinkling the fabric.

"Take it," I mouthed. He nodded his head and looked away.

The judge came back in the room. "Have each of you reached a decision?"

Of the six boys, five of them decided to take the deal. They were all sentenced to a youth correctional facility until they turned twenty-one. The other boy was given a court date and they were all escorted out of the court room. We didn't even get a chance to say good-bye.

When I walked from the courtroom, I was numb. It was like I had left a part of myself in the room. I might have walked into that courthouse a boy but I came out as a man. Gina tried to console me during the drive home but I didn't want to hear it. Nothing she could say could take away the emptiness I felt inside.

"This is going to be good for the boy. Make a man out of him and teach his ass a lesson or two."

"Really? Is that what you think?"

"Look, I don't like this any more than you do. But Gavin brought this on his self. There was nothing that I could have done for him."

In my head, I knew she was right but my heart wasn't listening. We drove the rest of the way home in silence. When the car pulled up in front of the house I quickly got out of it and ran up the porch stairs. I unlocked the door and stopped abruptly in my tracks, causing Gina to bump into me.

"What the hell are you doing? Go in the house."

I could not move. The man standing there looked exactly like me, only older. We were almost the same height and build. The major difference between us was that his head was shaved whereas I wore my hair cut low.

"Ronald," Gina gushed like she was sucking on a delicate pastry.

I actually saw red spots dancing before my eyes. "What are you doing here?" I demanded.

"I came as soon as I heard," my father said.

"Bullshit. Gina said she called you the day he was arrested. That was over a week ago."

"Boy, don't you take that tone with me! I got here as soon as I could."

"Well, you're about ten years too late. We don't need you now." I waited for Gina to back me up but she just stood there with this glazed look in her eyes.

"Seriously, Gina? You gonna let this negro walk back into your life just like that after the way he's dogged you for all these years?"

"Merlin, I, uh…"

"You can't get over him as long as he is on top of you. Even I know that." I pushed past Gina and went back out the same door I had just entered.

"Merlin, get back here," Gina shouted.

"Let him go. Niggah thinks he's a man all of a sudden. He'll be back." I heard Ronald say before the door slammed shut.

23 GINA MEADOWS

I reached up and patted my hair suddenly feeling self-conscious. I had dreamed about seeing Ronald again, but none of my dreams happened like this.

"You could have at least phoned and told me you were coming." I was trying to get a hold on my raging emotions. Ronald was looking panty dropping hot.

"I was driving Gina. Aren't you happy to see me?" Ronald took a step closer to me sending my senses on overload. The scent of his cologne tickled my nose. He was wearing the scent I had purchased for him. However, the stench of pot spoiled it for me and made me step back. I hadn't been around it in years so it stung my nose. "I would have been happier if I had known you were coming."

"I'm here now baby. Don't that count for something?"

I had longed to hear those words for so long, it actually made me smile. But even as the smile threatened to take over my lips, a frown surfaced. "How long are you here for this time?"

Ronald fell back and walked into the living room. His bags were sitting next to the sofa. "If you didn't want to see me Gina, why didn't you change the locks?" He took a seat.

"For what? You were never around. I didn't need to waste the money."

"Shade don't look good on you Gina but that dress does. Got my dick thumping in my pants."

"Ain't nobody throwing shade. I'm just speaking the truth. You never answer my phone calls and you don't come thru that often."

"I see you every chance I get girl. You don't complain when I have your heels pointed at the ceiling so why are you complaining now?"

"Maybe I don't. But when I put those bitches on the ground again, I realize it is only temporary and by then, you are gone."

"I didn't come here to get into an argument with you Gina."

"Then what did you come for? Did you come to check on your son? Because I don't recall you even asking about him."

"See, this is why I don't come and see you more often. You got too much lip. Can't appreciate a brother for his efforts."

"Efforts! You want to talk to me about efforts? What about my efforts?"

"I send you a check every month for those." Ronald picked up the remote and turned on the television. If I hadn't purchased the television, I would have put my foot through it. How dare he try to equate everything I done to a check.

"That little chump change you send me ain't shit."

"I don't remember you ever sending it back."

"I wouldn't waste my money on the stamp to send it back."

"Are we going to fight the entire time I am here or are you going to come over here and put your fine ass on my dick?"

Ronald unzipped his pants and pulled out his penis. The sight of it made my knees feel weak. My pussy juice drenched my panties. This was how he got me each and every time. I was powerless to saying no to his dick. Even as my clit was twitching, Merlin's words were replaying in my head. It was the only thing keeping my feet on the floor instead of bouncing in the air.

My feet were hurting so I took off my shoes and kicked them in the corner and sat down on the couch. "I don't want to do this with you Ronald."

"Are you sure about that? Your nipples say otherwise."

"I can't control how my body reacts. It's been a long time."

"You keeping that pussy tight for me?" Ronald stroked his dick faster and I had to tear my eyes away from it as my mouth watered.

"Please don't jack off on my couch. We have to sit there."

"I wouldn't be jacking off if you came over here and sat on it." Ronald closed his eyes like I wasn't even in the room with him.

"And maybe I would be sitting on it if I didn't have to wonder who else was sitting on it last. See unlike you, when you're not around I'm not fucking with the next dude."

"So you are keeping my pussy tight."

"It's my pussy Ronald. You lost the right to call it yours. I use to loan it to you when you came to town."

"I don't like it when you talk like this Gina. Makes me think you don't love me."

I sighed. "I will always love you Ronald. My problem is, I don't like you."

"In the dark, they both look the same. Let's pretend it's midnight up in this bitch."

"Let's be honest, it's not." By denying him, I was hurting myself. It truly was the first time I said no to him and meant it.

Ronald zipped up his pants. "Fine. If you don't want me anymore I'm cool with that. It's a good thing you are telling me now, before I made that move."

My head jerked up. "What move?" My heart started beating double time.

"I was coming back home, but I see now that I don't have a home to come back too." Ronald stood up and grabbed his bag off the floor.

My heart nearly skipped a beat as I stood up as well. "What do you mean? Home?" It wasn't like he actually lived with me when he was here. But the thought of being able to see him more than once a month excited me.

"I put in my transfer papers. I'm just waiting for them to be approved."

We were at a standstill. He was saying what I had been dying to hear for years. My mind said it was too late but my silly heart could not have been happier.

"Why didn't you say that?" I was already contemplating taking off my stocking and doing him right there in the living room.

"Did you even give me a chance? You didn't even say hello to me."

"I'm sorry Ronald. Things have been a little rough around here lately. What with Gavin being in jail and all."

"So what did the boy do?"

"He stole Merlin's car and he may have caused this girl to get killed."

"Merlin has a car? Where did he get a car from?" Ronald seemed more interested in the car than whether or not a person was killed.

"He actually brought it with his own money he saved from working." I could not help but to feel a little proud of Merlin's accomplishments.

"Where was Gavin's car?"

"He doesn't have one. He didn't have the same drive and determination Merlin does. That boy is going to be somebody someday."

"Are you saying that Gavin is not?" I heard the ire in Ronald's voice. He had some fucking nerve.

I left my pride on the couch as I sank to my knees before Ronald. I was practically slobbering as I tried to unzip his pants.

"What are you doing Gina?"

"Welcoming you home."

Ronald pushed me away as if I was some worrisome bug. I felt like a fumbled football that was bouncing out of control down the field waiting for someone to grab it.

"I thought this was what you wanted."

"I wanted it when I first asked for it. Now, I've changed my mind. I think I'm going to go out for a minute and clear my head."

"But you're coming back right?" I could not keep the pleading out of my voice. He had filled me with dreams for tomorrow and I couldn't get them out of my head.

"I might." Ronald strode to the door leaving me on my knees. He didn't even look back when he shut the door behind him. My only consolation was that his bags were still in the living room. As long as they were there, there was still a chance for me to make things right.

I was still in the living room when Merlin came back home. At first it looked as if he was going to walk pass me without speaking but he stopped with his foot on the step.

"Is he gone?" His right eye appeared to be twitching. His fingers wrapped tightly around the banister as if he needed it to stand up.

"For now, he left his bags here so he will be back."

"How could you just let him walk in here as if everything was alright?"

"Merlin, you are too young to understand."

"I understand enough." He started walking up the steps.

I didn't like his attitude. He was talking to me like he was the adult and I was the child. "Merlin, you may be angry with your father. You have every right to be. But at the end of the day, he is still your father and you will respect him."

"He can't buy my respect, he has to earn it."

"So what are you saying? You think your father bought me? Are you insinuating that I'm a prostitute?" I was beyond mad. I was pissed.

"I may not like everything that you do, but you have earned my respect. You stayed with us when he didn't. Even after he made you make the ultimate sacrifice, you still loved him. But you know what? It changed you. I didn't understand it then, but I do now. You hated us because we reminded you of him."

"Merlin, that's not true. I never hated you two."

"Oh, I think it is true. I could see it in the way that you looked at us. And when I saw him today, I could understand when you looked at us, you saw him. We look just like him."

Merlin was striking all kind of nerves because most of the things that he said were ringing true.

"You can't help who you love." I said it as if it were an excuse.

"If this is what you call love, I don't want any parts of it. Love shouldn't be painful." Merlin continued walking up the stairs.

He made some valid points about love. For someone so young, he was so wise. I agreed with everything he said, yet I felt like I was powerless to change anything as it related to me.

24 MERLIN MILLS

I rushed downstairs to speak with Gina before I went to school. I found her in her regular place, at the kitchen table sipping coffee. It was hard to believe but ever since Gavin went away, Gina and I were actually getting along better. I could not help but to think my talk with her had something to do with it too. In any event, I wasn't as afraid of her anymore.

"Can I speak with you for a moment?"

Gina looked up with red rimmed eyes and nodded. I wanted to ask her if she had been crying but I really didn't want to know the answer to that. "I know you don't like me getting in your business and I'm not trying too. I just want to know if it would be okay if I stayed over to Braxton's house until my dad leaves. I have already spoken with his mother and she said it would be okay."

"Merlin since your father is here, don't you think this would be a good time for you to get to know him?"

"When? He doesn't come home until one or two in the morning and he's sleep when I leave for school. How's that going to work?"

"I know but, if you were to make an effort—"

"I don't mean no harm, but it's not up to me to get to know him. He should want to get to know me! I am not about to beg that man for his attention." I left unsaid how I felt about her begging. She already knew where I stood about that.

"It won't be begging. You could ask him to go to one of your games."

"Basketball season is over Gina."

She fidgeted with her cup. "Oh. Well you could ask him to check out your car or something like that. It could bring you two together."

I thought it was interesting that she would suggest that I invite him to my games when she had never showed up at any of my games either. For all she knew, I sat on the bench each and every time. "It's okay. I'm over it."

"Then why do you want to leave? I don't think he will be here all that much longer."

"Honestly?"

Gina emptied her cup before she answered. "Yeah. Honestly."

"I can't take waking up to the sound of the headboard banging every night. There are some things that I don't need to know about." I was exaggerating a little bit. The headboard didn't bang every night. On the other nights I had to listen to Gina crying. I didn't know which one was worse.

Gina blushed and hide her face behind her hands. "Oh, my goodness. I didn't realize you could hear us."

"It's an old house. Sounds echo," I said shrugging my shoulders. I couldn't help it if she got embarrassed. She should be.

"I don't even know Braxton and his family."

"He's been my friend since elementary school."

"Really? You never talk about your friends."

Now was not the time to beat her over the head with the facts. She never took an interest in me or my brother. "Can I go?"

"Honey, I don't know."

"Don't know what?" Ronald asked as he walked into the kitchen. He wasn't wearing his shirt. Disgusted, I turned my head. The least he could have done was throw on a shirt. His state of undress left too much to my imagination about what he and Gina were doing behind closed doors.

"I asked Gina if I could go stay with my friend for a few days. It's no big deal." I hated talking to him as if he meant something to me.

"Then why are we talking about it then?"

Gina interjection, "It's all settled, Ronald. I was about to tell him yes."

I grew angry. He hadn't said five words to me since he came back into the house and now he was butting his nose in our business. I couldn't take it. I needed to get out of that house before I did something I would later regret.

"That nigga want to go, let him. Then maybe you could make me some breakfast because I'm starving."

I pushed my chair away from the table and went upstairs and grabbed the bag I had already packed. I rushed down the stairs and out the door without another word.

♥♥♥

I called Braxton from the car and he met me at the door so I wouldn't have to ring the doorbell. It was too early in the morning to be ringing the bell. I wasn't trying to piss off Braxton's mom.

"You ready to go?"

"Yeah, I just need to leave my bag here. If that's okay."

"Sure, it's cool. I'll run it up to my room and be right back."

I went back in the car and waited for Braxton. I was hoping he didn't ask me a lot of questions because I really didn't have much to tell him.

Braxton got back in the car and handed me the key. "Let's go man. We don't want to be late."

I let out a sigh of relief. That was one good thing about our friendship. It was like Braxton could sense when I needed my space and didn't press me.

"I can't wait for this school year to be over. Seems like it just flew by didn't it."

"I know right. Next year we will be the big men on campus. That is going to be the shit."

"Next year hell. We're going to big men on campus in a few weeks. Once these seniors walk across the stage, we're officially it!"

"You know something, you're right. Now that you're staying with us for a minute, I don't want to hear any excuses about going to this party with me tonight."

"Come on, man. I wouldn't even know how to act."

"Don't you worry about a thing. All you have to do is follow my lead."

"I don't know. I'm not trying to go somewhere and make an ass out of myself."

"What are you afraid of? Girls?"

"No. I mean yeah. I don't have a lot of experience in that area."

"Just be yourself man. You don't have to impress anyone. Hell, half the girls in school are already in love with you and you don't even know it."

"You are just saying that to get me to go to the party."

"That's not true and you know it. I've been telling you this shit for years. You just don't listen."

"Okay, I'll go to the party but I'm driving my own car in case I want to leave before you do."

197

"That's cool. I am so sure you're going to have a great time, you are going to wish you had someone else take the wheel. I just hope you don't make me regret inviting you by stealing all the girls from me."

♥♥♥

I was more than a little nervous as I followed Braxton to the party. Despite his assurances about my popularity with the ladies, I still had my doubts. I wasn't trying to get my feelings hurt my first time out. So my strategy was to play it safe, hug the wall and hope for the best.

"You good?" Braxton asked before he rang the bell.

My heart was beating fast in my chest. Every bone in my body wanted to bolt for the car and not look back. Had I been alone, I probably would have. I didn't have the same type of personality as Braxton did. He could have a conversation with a rock. "Yeah, I'm good."

The party was all the way live when the door opened. A lot of familiar faces were dancing in the middle of the room and more familiar faces stood around in small clusters talking.

"See, it's not too bad, right?" Braxton asked as he nudged me with his elbow.

I had to admit it wasn't. It would have been different if I didn't know anyone in the room. However, after several sweeping glances around, I realized that I knew everyone. Well, almost everyone. I pulled Braxton's arm and leaned over and whispered in his ear.

"Who's that girl standing by the fireplace?" She was absolutely beautiful to me. Her long legs, shapely hips and tantalizing smile mesmerized me.

"Damn, bro. You scoped out the pick of the litter. That's Cojo. She's new and I don't know too much about her other than her name."

"She goes to our school? Where the hell have I been hiding?"

"Do you really want me to answer that?" Braxton said laughing.

"Man, she's a twenty." My eyes connected with Cojo and she smiled at me. I felt like Charlie Brown when the red-headed girl smiled at him. I could count on one hand, the number of girls in my school that made my heart rate increase. Those girls weren't my type. They were beautiful and they knew it.

"You feeling lucky?"

I felt like Braxton was enjoying himself at my expense. "No, I'm feeling thirsty. Let's go see what they got to drink." I stole one final look at Cojo as we went in search of some libations.

When I got my beer, I fell into a conversation with some of the guys from the basketball team. They kept my mind off of my fear about approaching the honey in the next room. It wasn't easy but I stuck around until the last person wandered away. I walked back into the living room and searched the wall for Cojo. Much to my dismay, she was gone. I looked around the room and noticed her on the dance floor and I felt sick. She was dancing with Braxton.

I had never felt so betrayed in all of my life. This was the type of thing that Gavin would have done. I would have never expected it from Braxton. I slammed my glass on the table. It was all I could do not to rush over to him and punch him right in the face. He knew I had eyes for her, she should have been off limits to him.

My eyes grew wider when I saw him whisper in her ear. As far as I was concerned, our friendship was over. I was going to go back to his house, grab my bag and be out of there before he got back. I started working my way to the door when Braxton caught up with me.

"Hey, man, where are you going?"

I didn't feel like I owed him any explanation. "Move out my way."

"What's wrong with you?"

"You know good and damn well what's wrong. Now get the fuck out of my way."

"Man, chill. I want to introduce you to Cojo. I told her you were shy and wouldn't come to her."

I looked up stunned. Cojo was standing next to Braxton with the brightest smile I've ever seen. I was humiliated.

"Uh, hi," I stuck my hands in my pocket because I suddenly didn't know what they were there for.

"Hi, Merlin. It's nice to meet you."

I was speechless. Braxton leaned over and whispered in my ear again. "Be yourself man. You got this. She likes you." He patted me on the back and went deeper into the living room disappearing in the throng.

"My man told me you went to our school, but I swear I don't remember ever seeing you."

"That's because you walk through the halls like you have tunnel vision."

I was thrown off for a minute. "You mean you have seen me before?"

"Of course. You've made quite an impression on all the girls so they were quick to point you out to me."

I started laughing. "It wasn't me. None of those girls know me like that. The most I've said to any of them is hi."

"That's what makes you so popular. The ladies like a good foot race."

"Darn, you make it sound like I'm the prize or something like that."

"Aren't you?" Cojo asked suggestively.

All of a sudden I was feeling a lot better about myself. "I guess I am although I never really thought about it that way.

"You said you don't fool with the girls in school. Who do you fool with?"

Cojo was taking me on a ride and I liked it. She was making me feel things I had never felt before. I was both in awe and intrigued. "Are you always this direct?"

"What's the point of beating around the bush?"

"I guess you have a point. I honestly didn't realize I was a social retard until now. I've been so focused on school and work that I never paid attention to it."

"I like a man who is focused." *Was she coming on to me?* I was so inexperienced and it was beginning to show.

"Since you've heard about me, what about you? What's your story?"

"I just recently moved to town. I'm an army brat. My dad is stationed in Saudi. He's been there for over two years and my mom got lonely. So we moved here from North Carolina to be closer to my aunt and her family until my dad comes back state side."

"That must have been hard on you leaving in the middle of the school year. What about your friends?"

"It's not that bad. I'm close enough that I can go back for a visit if I want to. The main thing is my mother is smiling again. She was very unhappy."

"How many broken hearts did you leave in the Carolina's?" I was feeling more and more confident the longer we spoke.

Cojo laughed out loud causing several people to look our way. "None that I know of. I am rarely anywhere long enough to make those kind of friends."

"It doesn't take that long," I said suggestively trying to use the same tactic she had used on me but I think I fell flat. I was barely comfortable in my own skin. I couldn't try to pretend to be something I wasn't.

"Were you getting ready to leave? You looked like you were pissed off about something."

I was busted. I couldn't decide whether to fess up about what had pissed me off or lie like a dog. In the end, I decided to be truthful. I wasn't very good at lying anyway. "You got me. I was feeling a little salty when I saw you talking to Braxton."

"Why?" Cojo stepped closer to me. Her breast brushed my arm sending tingles down my spine.

"Uh," I felt like I was turning three different shades of red and I was thankful for the semi-darkened room.

"What?"

"I told him I was feeling you and I thought he was making moves on you."

"Wow. Don't trust your friends much, do you?"

"I, uh." I shook my head feeling self-conscious. I didn't know much about girls but what I did know was that they liked a confident man and I had just showed her I didn't have that trait.

"It's okay, I don't trust many people my damn self."

"That didn't come out right at all. Braxton has never given me a reason to distrust him. I've just never been interested in someone before and I let it cloud my judgment."

"Are you saying you're interested in me?" Cojo said smiling.

I swallowed a little knot in my throat. "I guess I am."

"Do you want to go somewhere a little less noisy?"

"Sure. Let me say bye to Braxton."

"Cool, I'll meet you outside."

25 COJO WINFREY

I still couldn't believe my luck with hooking up with the most elusive man in the senior class of Milford Mills High. Rumors had it that girls had been throwing panties his way since grade school and he had been walking right over them. The other rumors were that he was gay. Catching his eye was a major feather in my cap and I instantly went from the new girl to the IT girl. Merlin had elevated my status.

It was almost like it was too good to be true and most days it left me feeling anxious. I wasn't used to this type of attention. At my old school, people didn't pay me much attention and I just blended in. It seemed like there was something in the Georgia water that made my booty pop and my tits swell. The biggest problem with having the most sought after man in school was keeping him. I knew first hand how treacherous females could be.

When I got to school, the entire building seemed a buzz. People that had simply ignored me were going out of their way to speak to me. At first, I didn't put two and two together but as the girls became more brazen with their questions about my weekend, I figured it out.

"I saw you at the party the other night. Did you have fun?" This was coming from a girl in my second period class who went out of her way to snub me my first week at school.

"Sure, it was good."

"Really? You left kind of early. What else did you do?"

"Nothing really. Me and a friend went to get something to eat."

"A friend? Oh, it's like that?"

"What?" I feigned ignorance. I wasn't about to let this girl get all up in my business.

"I saw who you left the party with. You do know he might be gay, right?"

"Oh, really? He didn't act gay to me. He might have mentioned something about some girls being desperate at school, but I don't think he likes skanks."

The girls eyebrows shot up in surprise. It looked like she was trying to decide whether or not she should be offended. While she was making up her mind, I side stepped her.

"Talk to you later," I said loud enough for her to hear. I didn't start laughing until I was out of her eyesight. I wasn't trying to get into a physical altercation with anyone. That just wasn't my style but I felt like I needed to shut her down before she tried me.

"What are you smiling about?" Merlin asked as he fell into step with me.

"This girl who tried to get all up in my business. Heifer doesn't even know me like that, and she wanted to question me."

"Did you check her?"

"I sure did."

"What was she asking about?"

"You already know. She called herself telling me about you."

"For real? Why?"

"Merlin, I'm not about to blow your head up."

"Wait, I wasn't asking you too. It just seems so bizarre to me. None of these girls paid me any attention before so why are they acting like they care now?"

"They were paying you some attention, you just didn't notice. Hell, I noticed it on my very first day here."

"Well, it's news to me. But anyway, I wanted to ask you if you wanted to go get something to eat later? I don't have to work tonight so I was hoping you would be free."

I was secretly thrilled that Merlin wanted to spend more time with me but I didn't let my eagerness show on my face. I let the invitation linger in the air for about five seconds as if I needed to think about it before I accepted. "Sure, but I have to ask my mom first. Where and when?"

"I'm flexible. Let me know what she says and I'll plan it."

"Oh, really?"

Merlin looked confused. In so many ways he was still like a boy and I liked that about him. He reminded me of myself in a lot of ways. I thought that I was more advanced than most of my peers but I was still naïve in other ways.

"What's wrong?" His concern was clearly visible on his face.

"Nothing. I just liked the way you said you would plan our date. I like a man who takes control." I winked my eye as I said it. I didn't know what it was about Merlin that made me tingle inside. Whatever it was, I wanted more of it.

"Cool. I've got to get to class now, but holler at me later."

"Okay, I'll phone my mom at lunch and let you know what she says after that."

"All right then." Merlin trotted off down the hall leaving me left staring at his ass.

"Close your mouth," Braxton teased as he walked by.

I was immediately embarrassed to have been caught. "And don't you dare tell him either," I said laughing.

Braxton placed his fingers on his lips and pinched them shut. He seemed to be a good friend to Merlin and I was glad that he had him. Being an army brat, I never got the chance to form meaningful friendships. That is why I never allowed myself to completely let go with anyone. Somehow, I thought things were going to be different with Merlin and me. It was like we were made for each other.

♥♥♥

Merlin took me to Red Lobster for dinner and I was pleasantly surprised when he handed me a rose. "Gee, do you treat all your girls like this?"

"Oh, now you want me to blow your head up?" He said laughing.

He had me. I wanted some type of confirmation that he was feeling me like I was feeling him. "Okay, you can't blame a girl for trying. You're not exactly vocal with your thoughts."

"The fact that I'm here with you at all should tell you something. I believe you already know that I see something special in you."

"A girl needs to hear it too, Merlin."

"Humm, I thought actions spoke louder than words."

"You have a point. I stand corrected. I'd much rather someone showed me how they felt instead of told me."

"Don't get me wrong, I love the way you look. But that is not what attracted me to you in the first place."

"It isn't?" Now he truly had me baffled. If it wasn't the booty and the butt what was it that drew him to me from across the room? I couldn't imagine what made me stand out in the crowd to him.

"It was your confidence. Those other girls just seemed thirsty to me. You owned the room and I liked that."

"Wow, really? And I thought it was my MAC smokey eye shadow."

"Hey, it was dark, what can I say?"

"Don't worry about it, I'm not mad. It just goes to show you that all that other stuff isn't necessary to get somebody's attention."

"Oh, so you were trying to get somebody's attention?" Merlin playfully asked.

"Hey, who goes to a party to be by themselves?"

"It's all good. I am just glad it worked out the way that it did."

"If your boy hadn't come up to me, would you have made the move yourself?"

"Honestly?"

"Yeah, I would always prefer honesty when you are dealing with me. I don't need anyone blowing smoke at me."

"I don't know. I'd like to think that I would have, but I really don't know. I hate making a fool out of myself if you know what I mean."

"I get that and I can respect it too."

"Would you have approached me?"

"Me? Naw, I don't think so. I'm too confident to sweat a nigga."

Merlin looked at me a little strangely.

"I'm just kidding. You said you liked my confidence. So I'm playing the part."

"What about honesty? Is that just a one-way street?"

"Of course not. I can give it as well as I can take it. I didn't realize that was such a serious question. I probably wouldn't have approached you either. I have never approached a guy before and I don't think I would have handled rejection well. If a dude ever said no, I might have had to call him a few choice words."

Merlin laughed. "I can actually see you doing that. I'm glad that wasn't necessary for either us. Remind me to thank

Braxton the next time we see him. He saved us both a lot of pain."

I wasn't sure where this conversation was going. One minute we were laughing about silly stuff and the next minute it got all serious. Hoping to totally change the mood at the table, I leaned over and gave Merlin a big kiss.

"What was that for?" He asked as he touched his lips.

"I'm trying to save us from that uncomfortable moment, when the date is over, and you try to figure out whether or not it's safe to kiss me. Now you know."

"Thanks. I really do appreciate that." He leaned over and kissed me back.

"What was that for?" I asked.

"Just in case you felt weird about kissing me first. I wanted to let you know I was down with it too."

I didn't know where this relationship was heading but I was anxious to get there and enjoy the ride.

26 COJO WINFREY

Merlin and I had been dating for several months and while everything was going well, I still felt like there was something missing in our relationship. He had already won the approval of my mother but I had yet to meet the woman who molded him into the man he had become. For some reason, this bothered me. If we were going to have a chance of taking our relationship any further, I felt like we needed to get over that hurdle as well but when Merlin suggested a meeting, I grew nervous.

I changed my clothes about fifteen times before I finally settled on a nice pair of gray slacks and a cute pink blouse. For the occasion, I had also pulled my hair up in a bun hoping for a more sophisticated look.

"How do I look?" I twirled around so Merlin could see me at all angles. Even though I had kept him waiting, he didn't seem to mind.

"You look great. Then again, you always look nice."

"You sure she won't mind my wearing pants? I could go put on a dress if you think she'll like it better." I chewed on my fingernail. This was a sure sign that I was stressed about our meeting.

"Relax. You're fine. Just don't let her intimidate you and it will be okay."

"Do you think she will try to run me away from you?"

"Honestly, I don't know what to expect. I've never brought home anyone to meet her before."

"No one? Not even Braxton?"

"Nope. You're the first."

"Why?"

"It's complicated."

Merlin's kiss stopped me from asking any more questions. As he pulled away, he asked, "Are you ready?"

"I guess. I sure hope that she likes me."

"Me too," Merlin mumbled as he got to his feet.

"What did you say? I didn't hear you."

"I said we'd better be going." Merlin went out the door leaving me no choice but to follow him.

"That's not what you said and you know it."

Merlin didn't answer me until we were seated in the car. "If you know what I said, why did you ask me to repeat it?"

"Babe, I don't want to fight with you. I'm just nervous I guess."

"I'm nervous too."

"Why should you be nervous?"

"Because with my mother I never know who I'm going to get. Sometimes she can be a bit much. If she gets to be too much, I'll cut our visit short. I promise you."

"But what if she doesn't like me? Then what?" I was on the verge of crying. I had been thinking about that possibility all day and it frightened me.

"No matter what she thinks, that won't change the way I feel about you. So if that is what you are thinking, don't worry about it."

"How do you feel about me?" It was as if all the air in the car got sucked out the window.

"Aww, come on, you know how I feel." Merlin started the car.

"No, I don't. Not really."

Merlin turned off the car as his eyes sought mine. "If I didn't love you, I wouldn't be taking you to meet Gina."

His words were like music to my ears even if I felt like I had to twist his arm to get him to say it. "Okay, I'm ready," I said quietly. Merlin leaned over and kissed me.

"It's going to be fine, don't worry."

"I'll try not to."

Merlin and I didn't talk during the short drive to his mother's house. Despite his assurances, I could tell he was nervous too. His fingers gripped the steering wheel tightly and he kept his eyes focused on the road. Normally, Merlin held my hand whenever we drove somewhere. I reached over and turned on the radio just so we weren't riding in complete silence.

Merlin came around and opened the door for me. "Thanks, babe." My heart started fluttering as we walked up the stairs to this rather old and imposing house.

"I didn't realize you lived so close to my house."

"I guess that's because I'm hardly here anymore. Most of the time we meet up we're at Braxton's or your house."

Merlin used his key and opened the door and stepped back so I could enter the house which was eerily quiet.

"Is anybody home?" I was used to hearing some household noise. Even though it was just my mother and me in our apartment, there was always something on, even when we were not home. She left the radio playing for her plants.

"She should be, her car is out front." Merlin stepped in behind me and shut the door. I was so jumpy, I could barely stand still.

"Have a seat in the living room while I go see where Gina is." I followed Merlin up the stairs with my eyes.

Merlin's use of his mother's given name confused me. If I called my mother by her first name, she would have knocked me into next week. I surmised this was something he did when she wasn't around. That wouldn't work for me because I knew I would slip up.

I walked into the living room and was surprised to see a rather attractive woman sitting in an easy chair glaring at me. I jumped as my heart raced. She had to be his mother yet she didn't say anything when we came into the house.

"Oh, wow. You scared me." I took a seat on the sofa too frightened to move.

The woman didn't say anything. She just continued to stare at me with this dark look on her face.

A few minutes after Merlin went up the stairs he walked into the room. "That's weird, she's not...oh, there you are mother. I thought you were upstairs." Merlin came over and sat on the sofa next to me.

"Mom, I'd like you to meet my girlfriend, Cojo." She was not what I had in mind at all. I expected a much older woman. I stood up, dropping my purse to the floor.

"Hello, it's so nice to finally meet you," my voice sounded foreign to my own ears. I cleared my throat.

"Hi," Gina said as she continued to stare at me. She reached over and lifted a glass to her lips and took a large swallow.

I looked at Merlin with a confused expression on my face. He shrugged his shoulders and grabbed my hand and held it in his lap.

"Is she angry?" I whispered barely moving my lips.

"Refresh my drink." Gina commanded.

"Wait here," he whispered back. Merlin got up and took the glass from his mother and started to leave the room.

Gina followed him with her eyes. The feeling in the room was so uncomfortable, I wanted to leave. I regretted not driving my own car. Merlin came out of the kitchen a few minutes later carrying two glasses one of which he handed to me.

"What is this?"

"Iced Tea." His lips were pressed together in a firm line as he walked Gina her drink.

I wasn't thirsty but I didn't want to appear rude. I took a small sip under Gina's watchful eyes.

"How long have you two been going out?"

I didn't know whether her question was directed at me or Merlin, so I kept quiet. There was something about her tone of voice that I didn't like.

"A little over six months," Merlin replied.

"And your just now bringing her over to meet me?"

Her tone was accusatory. I felt like I didn't need to be there for their conversation. Gina didn't even look at me.

"It's been kind of crazy mom."

"Crazy how?" Gina held a glass up to her lips and took a long swig. Her glass didn't look anything like mine.

"You know, with dad being around and all. We haven't seen much of each other."

Gina's eyes squinted together. I wanted to grab Merlin by the arm and drag him out the door.

"What's that got to do with anything? Have you met her mother yet?"

Merlin chuckled a little bit. "Uh, yeah. Her mom wouldn't let me take her out until I did."

"Ain't that special."

"Um, if this is a bad time, I'm sure we can come back another time," I said. I had had enough. I was ready to leave.

Gina scoffed at me. "You got a problem with me asking my boy some questions?"

Her boy? Could she not see that Merlin was a man? Or was she trying to downgrade him for her own reasons. "I wasn't trying to be disrespectful. I just thought you two would like to discuss this when I wasn't around."

"Don't it involve you?"

"Well, yeah."

"Then you should be present. I don't believe in sugar coating shit. If something stinks, I'm not afraid to say it."

Merlin grabbed my hand and squeezed it.

"I can appreciate that. I'm the same way." I wasn't going to let this woman brow beat me. Merlin kept me away from her for a reason and now I understood why.

"Are you? Humph."

The smell of alcohol permeated throughout the room making it clear why my glass was different from Gina's. Suddenly it was all making sense.

Merlin said, "We didn't plan on staying long. I just thought it was time for you two ladies to meet."

"Where's the lady at?" Gina sneered.

Merlin stood up. "I think you've had too much to drink."

"Boy, who you think you are talking to?"

Gina attempted to get up from the chair but she slipped back down into it.

"Mother, I don't mean any disrespect but I don't see why you have to be so rude to my guest."

"I wasn't being rude. I was just asking a question."

I didn't know what to do. Never in my life had I witnessed something like this. To think that she would embarrass Merlin in this manner was inexcusable to me. Not to mention the fact that she appeared to take an immediate dislike to me without even saying ten words to me. I stood up beside Merlin.

"It was nice meeting you." I tugged on Merlin's shirt signaling my desire to leave.

"I'll be back later, mother."

"Oh, no, you won't. Your black ass is going to be right here with me." Gina stood up and my mouth practically dropped to the floor. Her pants fell down around her ankles and she was naked from the waist down. The rubber dildo that she had obviously been playing with rolled to the floor as well.

"What the fuck are you doing?" Merlin shouted as he rushed over to Gina and pushed her back in the chair.

I thought it was pretty clear. It was like a scene from a very bad movie. I could not tear my eyes away as I watched Merlin try to pull up Gina's pants.

"Get away from me boy. I can do it." She was squirming around in the chair trying to dress herself.

There were no signs of remorse or regret on her face as she pushed back in her chair and extended her feet. Gina appeared to be enjoying our discomfort.

"Shit. I'm going to take Cojo home and I'll be back."

"Don't you swear around me! Is that what she's been teaching you?"

It was all I could do not to cuss his mother out but my mother taught me better manners than that. I didn't know what was wrong with that woman but I refused to stoop to her level.

"It's okay Merlin. You don't have to drive me, I can walk home." I wanted to get out of that house so bad, I would crawl if I had to.

"That won't be happening. I brought you here, and I will be taking you home."

Gina managed to get out of the chair and started walking up the stairs. "Run the tramp on home and bring your ass right back here. I got some things I want to say to you."

"Come on, babe. Let's get out of here." Merlin grabbed my hand and we practically ran out the door. He was walking so fast, I could barely keep up with him. He let go of my hand to open the door. I noticed his hand was trembling and it made me feel so bad for him. To be honest, I wasn't even concerned about his mother's reaction to me. I was confident that I would be able to win her over given time.

"Breathe baby, it's not that serious."

Merlin swiveled around and yelled at me. "How can you say that. She was downright rude and drunk as hell! She disrespected you and she fucking disrespected me."

"It's not that big a deal, Merlin. I'm good."

I had never seen Merlin so upset. He had never cursed or raise his voice before at me. Not to mention the distinct tremble in his hands. I got in the car and he barely missed my foot before shutting the door. He got in slamming the door and rested his head on the steering wheel. I didn't know how to react to this situation.

"Babe, I said it was no big deal and I meant that. In a fucked up kind of way I almost understand what just happened." *I understood the animosity but that dildo, she could have that one.*

"How can you understand that crazy shit when I can't and I know her?"

"Because I'm looking at it from another angle. If I was a mom, and my son, who never brought anyone home before, came home with a girl, I might feel some kind of way. I would automatically assume that the chick was special and that I might be losing my child to someone else."

"What are you talking about. Of course you are special why the fuck else would I bring you over there?"

"Okay, I know you are turnt up but I'm going to need for you to turn it down for a minute. I understand you are upset too, but this car is too small for all that yelling."

"I'm sorry. I wasn't directing it at you."

"I know that. Like I was saying. Mothers expect their little girls to grow up and grow away but their boys are something different. It's almost like they are being replaced by another woman."

Merlin's mouth dropped open as his eyes got wider. "Are you serious? Is that what this is about? My replacing her?"

"I believe so. It just makes sense to me. Why else would she start throwing shade at me and she doesn't even know me?"

"Damn, you might be right. But how do I fix this? I won't have her disrespecting you and I'm not going to stop seeing you just because she is bugging."

"I'm happy to hear that last part. Now as far as how to fix this, I'm not sure. Maybe you can start with a honest dialogue with her. Let her know that she will always be your mother and a major factor in your life. Make her see she is not losing a son but gaining—" I sucked in my lips. I got caught up in the moment and almost said too much.

"Gaining a what?"

"Um, I just got caught up in the hypothetical."

"Oh, okay."

Merlin didn't sound convinced but I was thankful he didn't pursue it further. I didn't want to lie to him, but I wasn't ready to confess my desire for a happily ever after with him.

"I swear, that shit was whack. I did not see that coming. I am so sorry."

"Don't worry about me. Why don't you drop me off so you can get back and talk to her. Although you might have to wait for tomorrow to talk because she looked like she was ready to put it down."

"Thanks, babe. I really appreciate your understanding in this. She's not such a bad woman when you get a chance to know her."

Merlin leaned over and kissed me. I could see the torment in his eyes.

"Like I said before, if you need to talk, I'll always be there for you."

"You know this is starting to make sense to me now too. Because of my mom's fucked up relationship with my dad, she might feel like I'm walking out on her too."

"Right. You've got your work cut out for you. Call me later if you can."

27 MERLIN MILLS

After I dropped Cojo off at her house, I drove around in circles because I didn't want to go home. I wasn't sure how I was going to be able to face Gina after the way she embarrassed me. Part of me wanted to go over to Braxton's house and try to forget it ever happened. But the other more protective side of me wanted to go home to check on Gina and make sure she was okay.

Gina was an impulsive drunk. If I didn't go home, I could see her going out to find me, which would only make this situation ten times worse than it already was. If she got picked up for drunk driving, I wouldn't be able to forgive myself.

I was almost at the house when I decided to call my mom's friend for some advice.

"Hey auntie Tabatha, it's Merlin."

"Well, this is a surprise. How are you doing sweetie?"

"I'm okay. I just got some things on my mind and I needed to talk to someone."

"What kind of things? Are you sure you are all right?" I could sense her uneasiness over the phone. She hadn't been around much and I wondered if she had had another falling out with Gina.

"Actually, I wanted to talk to you about Gina."

"Oh."

Her response said it all. "Are you two fighting again?"

"You could say we are not seeing eye to eye, but I wouldn't necessarily call it fighting. We've just agreed to disagree."

"I'm sorry I bothered you then." I was a little disappointed. I felt like I needed some advice from someone who knew Gina better than I did.

"Honey, no. Even when I'm mad at your mother, I wouldn't turn my back on her. What seems to be the problem?"

"Do you think you can over to the house? I really could use some advice."

"Merlin, you are scaring me."

"Don't be scared. You probably won't even see Gina. She will probably be passed out by the time you get here."

"Oh, Lawd. She's drinking again?"

"Yeah."

"I'm on my way. Give me about ten minutes."

I timed my arrival to coincide with Tabatha's. When her car pulled up behind mine, I got out to meet her.

"This must be serious if you are waiting outside for me instead of going in the house."

"I just don't know what to do auntie. I met this girl, and I really like her. I mean really, really like her."

"Wow. Can we go inside? If we're going to have a deep discussion I'd rather do it sitting down."

"Of course. Let me just check to make sure Gina is not in the living room." I slipped inside the house and after walking around the downstairs and finding it clear, I went back to open the door for Tabatha.

"Boy, why you got me creeping in this house like a stranger?"

"I brought my girlfriend over here earlier and Gina was tore up. She was sitting in the chair, half naked. I was trying to save you from the same embarrassment that I felt if she had come back down stairs."

"What do you mean half-naked?"

I shook my head sadly back and forth. "I guess she was jacking off and we came in and interrupted her. She must have forgotten what she was doing, because when she stood up, the dildo was still, uh…in her."

"Oops." Tabatha fell on the sofa laughing.

I was stunned. "Auntie, it's not funny. When that shit dropped on the floor, she just walked over it like she didn't see it. Her pants were down around her ankles and she was grinning like there was nothing wrong with that picture."

"Oh, Lord. This is too much." Tabatha was rolling around the sofa with tears coming out of her eyes from laughing.

"It's not funny. I had my girl with me!"

Tabatha said gasping, "It might not be funny to you now, but in ten years, this will be hysterical. For me, it's funny right now. Oh, wee, I wish I had seen that shit. I might have taken a picture of all of your faces."

This day kept getting stranger and stranger to me. First Gina and all her craziness and now this. "Auntie, I asked you over here for some advice, not to entertain you."

"I'm sorry, Merlin. I really am. There were a lot of things I was expecting you to say but I can promise you, this wasn't one of them." She sat up straight on the sofa and wiped the tears and the smile off her face. Her actions did nothing to hide the merriment from her eyes.

"Are you better now?" I asked sarcastically.

"Yeah. What did you do with the dildo?"

"She left that thing shaking on the floor. I put it in the kitchen."

"Did you turn it off? You don't want to run down the battery, do you?"

"I could give two fucks about the battery." I was really getting mad now.

"Hey, watch your mouth. My joke might have been in bad taste but I'm still your elder."

"I'm sorry. I wasn't trying to disrespect you."

"Since when did you start calling your mother Gina?"

"To be honest, ever since Gavin went away."

"Went away? Where is Gavin?"

"You didn't know?" I was really confused. I thought Tabatha would be the first person to know given her close ties to the family.

"Know what?"

"Gavin was arrested and sent to a detention center. It all happened so quickly. They even tried to drag me in that shit."

Tabatha raised an eyebrow but otherwise didn't say anything about my cursing. "Oh, Lord. I can't believe Gina didn't tell me about all of this."

"If you don't mind me asking, why are you two at odds this time?"

"We had a disagreement about your father. I don't think he's good for her."

"Tell me about it. He treats her like crap. I hate him for that."

"Me too."

"He started coming by again after Gavin was taken away. It made me sick to hear them going at it. So I started staying with my friend from school just to avoid him."

"Is that where you met this girl?"

"I didn't meet her at his house but he did have something to do with us talking. She goes to my school."

"Are you serious about her?"

"Yeah, I am. I brought her by the house to meet Gina and she was absolutely horrible to her. She called her a tramp."

"Oh, shit."

"She didn't even take the time to get to know her. She just started in on her for no reason."

"Is that before or after she dropped the dildo on the floor?"

I looked at Tabatha sharply. If she wasn't going to take me seriously, I didn't want to waste any more time talking to her. "Are you going to let that go?"

"I'm sorry. I had this visual and it keeps tickling me. So what did your girl say about all of this?"

"She was actually pretty understanding. She said that Gina might think that she is trying to take me away from her."

"I actually agree with her to a certain extent."

"You do?"

"Absolutely. See, the tricky part to this whole situation is the uncanny resemblance between you and your father. Gina is never going to forget him as long as she has to keep looking at you and your brother. It's like a constant reminder to her. It sounds sick, but I believe it's true. I swear, I don't understand how he got to her like this. He's a real ass if you ask me."

"I agree with you. But the funny thing in all of this is how well Gina and I had been getting along when he's not around. When he was here it all went up like a puff of smoke. Now that he's coming around less and less, we're getting along again. It's like the man is poison to her."

"In some ways, I think he is too. He's her kryptonite. As long as he's around he drains her power."

"That's a great analogy. Now how do we fix it. I can't have her messing up my thing with Cojo."

"Cojo? Is that your girlfriend's name?"

"Yeah," I said smiling.

"That's a really interesting name."

"She's a really interesting person. I can't wait for you to meet her."

"I would be honored to meet her. I've never known you to be so excited about someone before. I'm happy for you."

"Thanks. I thought Gina would be happy too…"

"Give her time. She'll come around."

"I sure hope so. I really do love her."

"Oh, wow. It's that serious?"

"Yes. I can see actually see her in my future."

"Now I know how Gina feels. I'm feeling a little jealous my own self."

"Stop playing auntie."

"So what do you want me to do? Do you want me to go upstairs and speak to Gina?"

"I don't know whether it will do any good right now. She was pretty wasted when I left out a while ago."

"Then she is probably sleeping it off. I'll stay here until she wakes up. If she remembers what happened, she might need someone to talk to."

"That would be great auntie. I'm not sure I could look at her right now without getting angry."

"If you don't want to be here when she wakes up, I'll stay with her."

"You would do that for me?"

"Of course."

"Thanks, Auntie." I ran upstairs and packed a bag to spend the night with Braxton.

"Be safe." Tabatha said.

"I will. I'm going to my friend's house. Call me if you need me."

"I will."

28 GINA MEADOWS

My head was fucking pounding when I woke up. I stumbled into the bathroom for something to drink. I cupped my head over my hands and drank water directly from the tap.

"Ahh," the water was soothing to my parched throat but it wasn't enough. I looked down and realized that I was naked from the waist down.

"Where the hell are my pants?"

"That's a good question," Tabatha was standing in the doorway to my room shaking her head. I reached for a towel to cover myself.

"What are you doing here?"

"Checking up on you."

"The least you could have done was knock. How did you get in here?"

"Merlin let me in."

"Oh, God. Where is he?" I felt a rush of panic as flickering images flashed before my eyes.

"He stayed the night at a friend's. You know you probably scarred that boy for life don't you?"

"Oh, Lord. I hope I didn't do what I think I did."

"The Lord don't have nothing to do with this one. The devil, maybe, but definitely not the Lord."

"Ah, shit. I cannot believe I allowed that shit to happen. I wanna just go through the floor right about now."

"I told Merlin that he would laugh about this in about ten years. I don't think he believed me though."

"You are getting a big kick out of this aren't you?" I was getting mad.

"Humm. Let me think about that. Uh, yeah. I think it's funny as hell."

I felt sick to my stomach and it had little to do with my drinking. I hated that Merlin saw me at my worse and then spoke to Tabatha about it.

"That's fucked up and you know it. I was having a moment which should have remained private."

"Did you or did you not know they were coming?"

"Well, yeah, I knew they were coming."

"Then it was no longer private. What were you thinking, jacking off in the living room? Why not do that shit in the privacy of your room?" Tabatha doubled over laughing.

"Don't you have something better to do?" I could not get the image of Merlin's face out of my mind.

"Oh, absolutely. But I'm glad Merlin called me. When were you going to tell me what happened to Gavin. I swear you test the boundaries of our friendship daily. It's a good thing I love you and those boys, or I swear I wouldn't have shit to do with you."

"Damn he told you that too?" I was more than pissed.

"Why wouldn't he tell me. I'm not the average Joe blow off the street. I have invested my time into both of those young men. I should not have had to hear this from your son, you should have told me the moment it happened."

"Yeah, right. Do you think I'm proud of what he's done? How was I supposed to tell you that? I'm so ashamed."

"The same way you tell me every other fucked up thing you do. You gave your best to those boys, it's not our fault if one of them chose a different path."

"I keep trying to tell myself the same thing but when I'm here all by myself, I can't help the evil thoughts that plague my head."

"Evil? Girl get a grip. There isn't anything evil about those young men. If anyone is evil in the equation, let's talk about their daddy. That nigga has cast a spell on you."

I felt as if she slapped me as my head rocked back. "I know you didn't just go there. I thought we agree to never talk about him."

"That was your idea, not mine. I didn't give a fuck what you do with your pussy. If you want to filet it for Ronald, then so be it. What I do care about is those two innocent bystanders. I didn't want to care about those kids until you made me do it."

"Whatever. That was then, this is now. You don't know the half of the shit I've been through with them."

"I beg your pardon. If there was something that I needed to know, you should have fucking told me. Just because I can't stand your man, doesn't mean that I don't give a fuck about you. We've been down this yellow brick road before Gina, we don't have to go down it again."

"When Gavin got into trouble, I felt like everything was all on me. Ronald couldn't care less. He didn't even bother to come until after Gavin had been sentenced. I couldn't turn to Merlin because he was also implicated in the bullshit. I never felt so alone in my life."

"That was a bed you made for yourself. If you had called me you wouldn't have been alone. And what do you mean Merlin was implicated? He said that too but he didn't bother to explain it."

"This girl that Gavin was with was supposedly a friend of Merlin's. She told her family she was with Merlin the night of the accident not Gavin. The police confiscated Merlin's computer because that is how they communicated. It seems as if Gavin used Merlin's log on to connect with the girl. He assumed his identity and stole his car."

"Damn."

"Can't you understand how that made me feel? The shame of it all?"

"No. How the fuck would I if I didn't know about it?"

"Tabatha, you made it clear from the beginning how you felt about my taking on those kids."

"And, that was umpteen years ago. How many times have I been there for you and them? I earned my fucking right to know what's going on with them."

I drew back. I had no idea that Tabatha felt so strongly about this. It wasn't something that we had ever discussed before.

"Well, damn, bitch. How was I supposed to know you changed your tune. I've been keeping all this stuff to myself all these years. You could have said something yourself before now."

"I swear, sometimes, I don't know what to do with you. How many times must I tell you that you are my friend and your pain is my pain? What do I have to do to make you understand this? But instead of doing that, you sit at home alone getting drunk, bitch please, you could have called me. We both could have had our panties around our ankles."

I gulped and laughed at the same time. Snot dripped down my nose and I couldn't have been the least bit concerned about it. "Are you serious?"

Tabatha sighed loudly. "This is the last time I'm going to say this. Yes, I'm down. You have to stop forgetting this. It's not fair to me or those kids, who by the way are no longer kids. They are men and you and I have to start treating them that way."

"Who the fuck are you and why are you in my bedroom?" Tabatha was acting like she was truly concerned and shit and I wasn't used to it.

I said, "You've changed. Why?"

"Everybody can't stay the same. You of all people should know that. So what's going on with Ronald? I heard he's been around lately."

"He has, but I know you don't want to talk about him."

"I could care less about him. I am concerned about Merlin running away from his own home because he can't stand to hear the sound of your headboard beating on the wall."

"Shit, he told you all of that. What goes on in this house needs to fucking stay in this house."

"Gina, he didn't use those words, I kind of filled in my own blanks, but he wasn't telling on you. He just doesn't know who his dad is and he cares enough about you to not want to see you hurt any more by him."

"Ronald isn't hurting me!"

"Oh, really? I seemed to remember many nights sitting with you, wiping away your tears. I swear the man must have a golden dick."

"Wouldn't you like to know about it?"

"Negro please, I don't want no dick that makes me crazy thank you very much."

"Oh, now you are calling me crazy?"

"What else would you call it? This man got you so strung out you're willing to wait on him to throw you pebbles. When is the last time you have been on a real date? Tried somebody new?"

"Why should I look for someone new? I have a man."

"Well, his batteries might be dead. Merlin said he threw him in the kitchen."

"Fuck you Tabatha. If the only reason why you are here is to make jokes then you can leave."

"Why are you always trying to put me out of your house? Just because I'm not saying what you want to hear I'm supposed to leave?"

"Don't you think I feel bad enough? Do you really think I want or need you to rub my nose in it?"

"Maybe you do need it, like when you're training a puppy. When they pee on the floor you rub their noses in it so they don't do it again."

"You are disgusting."

"I'm disgusting? Honey I think you should take a look in the mirror. But since you have all the answers, I really am leaving. I strongly suggest that you make this right with your son. He's not your baby anymore and if you don't want to lose him you had better fix this. And, you might want to visit Gavin too. He might be fucked up in the head but you made him that way."

Tabatha slammed the door on her way out. I would have run after her and cussed her out if I had some pants on.

29 COJO WINFREY

I was in my room when my mother got home from work. I had had a few hours to think about the fiasco that occurred with Merlin's mother and I still came to the same conclusion. I was blaming it on the alcohol.

Mom was sitting in the living room going through the mail when I came down the stairs. "How did it go?"

"It was awful mom."

"Awful? Why?" She pushed the bills off to the side and patted the seat next to her.

"His mom was drunk and nasty to both of us. It was terrible."

"You're kidding me. Did she not know you were coming? Does she drink often?"

"I don't know what to think. She knew we were coming but I guess she started to party before we got there. Poor Merlin was so embarrassed."

"That's a shame, he's such a nice kid."

"He is mom. He's everything that I have ever wanted in a guy."

"You are that serious about him?" Mom asked as she turned off the television which had been left on for the plants.

I cringed because I had divulged too much information. I wasn't ready to have a deep conversation about Merlin especially since I didn't know how things were going to turn out.

"Can we not have this conversation now mom?"

"If we don't have it now, when? I've been asking you about this for months and you've never indicated it was serious and you keep pushing me away."

"I'm not pushing you away, it's just that I don't know how to define it. You know I've never been serious about a guy before ,so this is all new. It's new to both of us."

"That's sweet but that doesn't mean I am not concerned for you. You know our move to Atlanta is only a temporary thing. I don't want you getting your feelings hurt when we have to pack up and leave."

I felt like someone had their fingers around my throat and was choking me. "What do you mean leave? Why? Is it dad?"

"No honey. I'm not talking about right now, but it is something that you have to remember for when the time comes."

"Every time we move, I never complain. Even when you yank me out of school in the middle of the year I never say anything. But this is my senior year mom and I will be graduating in a few months. I am finally making friends. Please don't jerk me around this year."

"Are you sure this isn't more about Merlin than your friends or your school?"

"What difference does it make? Don't I deserve some stability too??"

"How dare you say that to me. Haven't I always provided for you? What has gotten into you?"

"Stability means more than having a roof over my head. I want a chance to develop normal relationships with people."

"This is about that boy. Are you two having sex?"

"Oh, God, Mother. Must you go there?"

"Well are you?"

This was a conversation that I had been dreading for months. Every time it came up in the past, I found a way to get out of it, but this time, I couldn't think of a single thing to say to end it.

"Uh." I didn't want to lie but realized this might be my only way out.

"You are aren't you?"

"Mom, I—"

"Shit, I knew we should have had this conversation before. What about protection? Are you using any?"

"I don't want to talk about this right now."

"Oh, we are going to talk about it. Tomorrow I'm taking you to the doctor's and get you on some type of birth control."

"That's not necessary mom. We haven't done anything yet."

"Yet? Then now is the perfect time to do something about it. Obviously y'all are talking about it."

"It's not something that we have even talked about. I'm telling you Merlin is special. We want to wait until we get married."

"I hope you do wait. Giving your virginity to your husband on your wedding night is the most precious gift a woman can give to her man."

"Then you promise me we can stay at least until graduation?"

"I will if you promise me that you will speak to me first before you have sex."

"Okay."

♥♥♥

"Merlin, is everything okay?"

"Yeah, why?"

"I had this terrible dream and I couldn't get you out of my mind."

"I'm fine."

"Oh, okay."

"What about you?"

"Me and my mom got into it a little bit but it's all good now."

"Why? What happened?"

"She started questioning me about our relationship. Wanted to know if we were…you know…having sex."

There was a significant pause on the other end of the phone and I wanted to kick myself for even bringing it up now.

"Did you tell her?"

"Of course not. She already wants to take me to the doctors to get on birth control."

"That might not be such a bad idea after all. We should be careful. The last thing I want to do is bring a child into this world out of wedlock."

"I think we would have a beautiful baby."

"No doubt. Be we have to do it right. My mom never married my dad. I won't do that to another child. I just won't."

I understood where Merlin was coming from. I didn't want that either. "Where are you?"

"I spent the night over at Braxton's."

"Have you even spoken to your mother?"

"Not yet. I had my auntie go over there to check on her. I still can't believe she did that shit."

"I don't think staying away is the answer. You are going to have to face her sooner or later."

"I know. But right now, I can't even look her in the face."

That was perfectly understandable to me. If the shoes were on the other foot, I would have a hard time looking at my mom too.

"My mom is also worried that I will get my heart broken when we have to move again."

"Why is she saying that? Is she thinking about leaving?"

"I don't know. I think because it has never mattered to me before. I made her promise me that we would stay here at least until graduation."

"I don't like the way that sounds."

"I didn't either. I don't want our folks to break us up."

"They won't babe. I won't let that happen."

30 GAVIN MILLS

I wasn't really surprised when I didn't get a visit from Gina. She had pretty much laid her cards on the table when she didn't get me an attorney. She had no idea things would turn out the way that they did and she kind of threw me to the wolves. What did surprise me was the fact that Merlin hadn't come. When all else failed, I should have been able to count on him. I couldn't imagine anything keeping him away if he really wanted to come.

For as long as I could remember, it had only been the two of us. Even though we sometimes didn't get along, we were brothers and that should have counted for something. This of course had only made my resentment for him grow. Every day when visitors were allowed into the center, I seethed about the injustice of it all.

My first day in was a little scary. We were taken as a group by bus. We were led shackled together onto the bus single file. We weren't allowed to talk. I thought it was like a big joke, so I played along. I was pretty certain the guards wouldn't risk their jobs by hitting us. I mean if it was unlawful for our parents to strike us, surely a stranger wouldn't hit us either. Even with my certainty, I was going to let someone else be the test dummy in that theory.

As we reached our seats, we were unshackled from each other and re-shackled to our seats. The bus was painted white with blue letters on the side. The windows were covered in screens which obstructed our view of the outside. It should have been an omen but I ignored it.

The drive was tediously long and quiet. I kept waiting for some of the bad asses on board the bus to start squabbling over something or other but they all kept the peace. The only chatter on board was between the bus driver and the armed guards. That was another thing I was trying to get used to. I wanted to pretend they were props and didn't hold real bullets. It was the only way I made it through the drive without freaking out. I lived with the fantasy until we stopped at the juvenile correction facility in Millersville, Georgia. That's when shit got real to me.

The building was truly intimidating with its high fences, guard booths, vicious looking dogs and more guards with guns. The bus pulled up before the gate and stopped. My heart started beating real fast. I heard the loud groan of the gate opening. To me it sounded more like a scream. But what was more disheartening than the screams of the gates, it was the finality of them closing behind us.

"They have got to be kidding me," I muttered to myself.

One of the boys next to me frowned. "Shut the fuck up," he mouthed.

I wanted to tell him to mind his fucking business but something told me now was not the time to show my ass.

"Stand up and show your hand," the guard ordered. We presented our free hand in front of us as we were reattached to what I considered to be our umbilical cord once more. I was already over this practice and it was the very first day.

My annoyance rose to another level when we were lead into the large room and were strip searched. Twenty-five naked boys all clutching their privates. It was humbling and inhumane for us.

"Arms out to the side," the guard ordered and they removed the handcuffs.

I wanted to scream with every fiber in my being but in the end, I did as I was told, as did the other boys in the room. Our black and white striped uniforms were taken away and we were given orange jumpsuits and orange flip flops. I had never worn a pair of flip flops in my life. The plastic between my toes irritated me.

"I can't wear this shit," I mumbled.

"What did you say boy?" The guard demanded. It seemed like the entire room got quiet as the same precise moment.

I cringed. "Nothing."

"I thought so. You ain't home any more little boy. Welcome to our house."

I resented being called a little boy. I had more hair on my face and probably under my arm than the officer did. This was some bullshit.

The facility was five stories high. The youngest offenders were housed on the first floor. I was moved to the third floor and shown to my room. There were six other boys in my room which contained our beds, a sink and a toilet. I took the only empty bunk in the room. It was right next to the toilet.

I expected an orientation of sorts but at the Millersville Correctional Facility, all I guessed they believed in was baptism by fire. When we made a mistake, we were quick to know about it.

"What's your name son?" Asked the guy closest to my bunk.

"I ain't your son." I was pissed. I didn't care if I was the newest addition in the cell, I wasn't about to sleep with my head next to the damn john.

"Relax youngin', it's just an expression. There are plenty of people in this bitch to be mad at. I'm not one of them. You ought to be trying to make a friend in me."

There was wisdom in his words. I needed someone that I could trust, but I wasn't sure he was it. He was a burly white dude with a shaved head. I didn't like white dudes with shaved heads. They looked crazy to me. "It's Gavin."

"I'm Leo. This here is Ryan, Eric, Sean and Mike."

Leo seemed to be the spokesperson for the motley clan. The other boys nodded their heads.

"We look out for each other in here. It won't be like that out there. You down with that?"

"I guess so." *Did he think I was a fool? Why would I turn protection from anyone?*

"Nigga, either you in or you are out because I am sure I can find a way to have your ass removed from this cell."

Nigga, who did that fool think he was talking too? I had his nigga but I couldn't show it to him right now. "Hey, I ain't trying to start no shit. I just don't like laying my head next to the crapper."

Leo laughed. "Shit. You lucky your head ain't in the crapper. Ain't that right fellas?"

"Yeah. We could initiate you with it. That way the smell won't bother you all that much," Mike said smiling.

Eric laughed. "Yeah, I'll grab his feet."

"And I don't mind dropping a few gifts in there before we do it," Ryan added.

"Okay. None of that will be necessary. I'm down." Some lessons I didn't need to learn firsthand.

Leo clapped his hands. "Good. I'm glad you didn't need any convincing. Those lessons can be a little messy. We like to keep a clean bunk. If you're going fuck some shit up, do it out there." Leo pointed to the hallway.

I sat down on my bunk after I stored the few belongings I had in the drawer under my bed. "What now?"

"You wait. Some of us have television time coming up. It's a privilege, you have to earn it."

"How do you earn it?" Television was my weakness. It always had been since I was a little kid.

"Doing your chores, taking classes, doing work around the center. Shit like that."

"Hey, I didn't do none of that shit when I was on the outside. I damn sure don't want to do it in here."

"Did you ever stop to think that's why your ass is in here in the first place?"

"Can I ask you a question Leo?" I was already sick of his ass.

"It's a free country. You can ask anything you want. Whether I will answer or not is up for debate."

"How old are you?"

"Fourteen, why?"

"Shit, your ass is younger than me. What's up with that?" I smiled. I wasn't taking no damn orders from this teenager.

"How old are you?" Leo had a smirk on his face. Almost like he knew something that I didn't.

"Seventeen," I said proudly.

"Goes to show you older is not necessarily wiser. I started on the bottom and now I'm here."

I thought he was singing a song and didn't immediately get the correlation.

Sean chuckled, "This ain't no rap song nigga. He means he was on the first floor when he got here, dumb ass. We all were."

Awareness came slowly, but I got it. These guys may have been young, but they knew a hell of a lot more than me about life inside.

"I get it. I don't know shit."

Mike said, "Right. So if you decide you want to break the rules and do some shit, don't do it in here. If we get our privileges taken away because of your ass, you won't like it very much. I can promise you that."

I was at least a foot taller than everyone in that room but at that moment I felt like the runt of the bunch. "What are these rules that I need to follow?"

Leo spoke again. "The rules out there are a little different from the rules in here. In here, you keep your damn hands to yourself. You don't touch our shit, we won't touch yours. If you come across some shit, we share it. We don't snitch on each other and if one of us gets in trouble, we help if we can."

"I can live with that but what about the rules out there?" I asked why pointing to the corridor.

Sean said, "There's only one rule out there. Don't get caught."

31 MERLIN MILLS

"Are you sure this is such a good idea? We can always go back to Braxton's house. His mom is cool like that and you know she hardly ever comes in the basement."

Cojo kissed my neck. "It's okay Merlin. My mother is working late tonight. I know Braxton's mom is cool but I get tired of creeping pass her. It makes me feel cheap and slutty."

"There isn't a damn thing slutty about you. Besides, Braxton is my oldest friend and his mom loves me like one of her own. She used to tease me because I didn't have a girlfriend. Now that I do, she couldn't be more happy for me."

"It's one thing for you to have a girlfriend and quite another to bring her over to their house to have sex."

I laughed. "I told you she doesn't think that way about it. All these years she probably thought I was gay."

"Is that supposed to make me feel any better?"

Cojo opened the door to her house and pulled me inside. Even though this was not the first time that I had been in her house, it was the first time I had been there when no one else was at home.

"I was just saying it was cool and all."

"Will you relax. We have the house to ourselves for a few hours. This doesn't happen all that often and I'm going to take full advantage of it. Do you want to take a bubble bath with me?"

"Are you serious? That sounds crazy, sexy cool."

With those two words I was ready to throw all my caution to the wind. I couldn't wait to see all of Cojo's sexiness covered in bubbles.

"Wait right here while I set it up. I'll only be a minute."

"I'll be right here."

I tried not to think about what was about to happen. My time with Cojo came in quick snatches. This would be the first time we could actually explore each other's bodies and I could not deny how excited I was about it. I suggested getting a motel room numerous times but Cojo never wanted to do it. She said she would die a thousand deaths walking into the room. She was so afraid of running into someone we knew.

"I'm ready," Cojo yelled seconds before the sultry sounds of Kem filled the apartment.

"Where am I going?" I yelled back as anticipation crept up my spine.

"Follow my voice lover."

I smiled as I pulled my shirt over my head as I entered the bathroom. Candles were lit around the tub and a naked Cojo was posed in between them.

"Damn, girl. You look good enough to eat."

"Promises, promises. Now can you get out of those clothes before I change my mind." Cojo stepped in the tub and covered herself with bubbles. The flowery smell might have bothered me were she not immersed in them. I quickly stripped off my clothes leaving them in a heap on the floor.

I dipped my toe in the water and almost changed my mind about going in. "Girl, are you trying to boil my nuts? That water is way too hot. My dick is sensitive."

Cojo laughed long and hard. "I'm so sorry. I thought the hot water would help you to relax."

"I don't need any help in that area. I just need a little more cool water in this sauna."

"It's not a sauna silly. But if the water is keeping you out, by all means turn on the cold water."

I turned the faucet and let it run for a few minutes before I stuck my leg in. "I'll heat the water back up. Just give me a minute." I turned off the tap.

I slide in between her thighs as a deep moan escaped my lips.

"What took you so long?"

"I came as soon as you called me."

"Can you wash me?"

"Shall I use my tongue or do you prefer a wash cloth?"

"You are such a bad boy. I think I want a little of both."

I started out slow washing her feet and her legs. My dick was doing double time anxious to get to the prize. It bounced when she tickled my balls with her toes.

"If you want to finish tis bath, I suggest you leave those boys alone."

"What are you going to do if I don't stop?" She teased.

"I'll carry your ass out of this tub and—"

"Actions speak louder than words."

I grabbed one of the towels stacked over the hamper and threw it on the floor. I stepped from the tub and picked Cojo up in my arms.

"You are getting water on the floor." She said giggling.

"You are going to have to make up your mind what you want from me."

I lowered Cojo to the floor and took the time to dry off the water from both of our bodies. Then I carried her into the bedroom.

"Is this your room?" The bed was too big for their tiny apartment.

"Hurry, Merlin. I cannot wait to feel you inside of me."

Her words clouded my thoughts and hastened my actions. With our bodies still damp, I plunged inside of her. My dick sloshing against her pussy walls. "Damn, girl. You're so wet."

"Harder," she demanded. Her eyes were closed as she grunted through her teeth.

I threw back my head and started giving her everything I had. It was the most glorious feeling in the world. Until her mother busted into the room.

"What the hell is going on in here!" She shouted although I was certain it was as clear as day to her.

Cojo scrambled from beneath me as if she weren't clutching me around the waist mere seconds before. "Momma, it's not what you think."

"Are you kidding me?" Her mouth screeched.

I felt my dick shrivel up as I attempted to cover myself.

"I knew something was going on. Something in my spirit told me not to go to work today."

"Momma, I'm so sorry." Cojo was sobbing.

I crawled off the bed in search of the towel I had dropped at the foot of the bed. If her mother was going to start swinging at me, I at least wanted to have something over my dick.

"So much for using protection. Cojo you lied to me. I can't believe you sat right in my face and lied to me." Her mom rushed from the room.

"Does she own a gun?" I whispered as I ran into the bathroom and grabbed my clothes. I had seen some stuff like this on television before where a guy got shot in the ass by this girl's father but I never thought I would be dumb enough to audition for the part. Her mother had every right to be upset with us.

"No," Cojo's face was strained as her eyes kept darting around the room.

"Honey, you should get dressed too before she comes back."

"My clothes are in my room."

"Oh shit. This is bad. This is real bad. She's probably going to call Gina too."

"Is that all you can think about right now? What about the mess I'm in. I have to live with this woman."

For a brief moment I thought about reminding her that this was all her idea but thought better of it. She didn't twist my dick to make me come in this house. I walked in all by myself.

"Then put this towel on. We are going to have to go out there and talk to her. Don't worry. I won't let you go through this by yourself. I am just as much to blame as you are."

I finished putting on my clothes while Cojo tidied up the bathroom and threw on some clothes that she had taken from her mother's closet.

"You ready?"

Cojo nodded. Her eyes wide as tiny plates. Her hand grasped mine as we walked out into the living room. Mrs. Winfrey was seated on the coach nursing a drink. I wanted to ask her to pour us all one but I wasn't trying to get killed.

"Mrs. Winfrey I can't tell you how sorry I am that you had to come home and see that."

"I suggest you get out of my house before I do something that I can't take back."

Cojo looked terrified. Her nails digging into the back of my hand. I knew she was afraid but how much could I do if Mrs. Winfrey threw me out.

"I understand how you might be feeling. But with all due respect, I would rather not leave Cojo to face this music all by herself."

"How I deal with Cojo is none of your concern. Now would you please leave before I call the police and tell them something to make them arrest you."

I did not take kindly to threats even if they were well warranted or deserved.

"Mom, please."

"Mom my ass. Something told me that you two were getting too close and I should have followed my gut and taken your ass away from here. I asked your ass if you needed birth control and you assured me that you were going to wait until y'all got married. Did something happen today that I should be made aware of?"

"Mrs. Winfrey…"

I don't know how I missed the big ass knife lying across her lap but I saw it when she stood up.

"Are you still fucking here?" Mrs. Winfrey had the knife pointed at me.

"Oh, shit." I started to run but Cojo jumped in front of me shielding me from her mother.

"Mother no!"

"I'm done with being nice to his ass and if you don't move…"

"Mrs. Winfrey, I love your daughter and I want to marry her." I surprised myself with my admission. It's not that I was telling a lie but realistically we were too young to think about marriage. However, once the words left my lips I could not take them back. You're damn right you are going to marry her. Just as soon as school's out. I'm going to see to that. You better break the news to your mother because I will be calling on her within the month. Now get your black ass out of my house."

I gently pushed Cojo over to the side.

"Merlin don't make me tell my husband about this. Trust me when I say, you wouldn't like that."

"Don't worry, that won't be necessary."

32 GINA MEADOWS

I had just gotten back from spending the weekend in Ohio with Ronald. I was unpacking my bags when Merlin knocked on my door.

"Gina, can I talk to you for a minute?"

"Uh, sure." I wasn't exactly in a conversational mood. After a disastrous weekend where nothing went as planned, I was looking forward to some peace and quiet. However, I tried to keep my emotions off my face and give Merlin some attention. He was finally speaking to me again after I showed my ass on him and I didn't want to ruin the peace we had obtained.

Merlin sat down on my bed. "I just thought you should know that when school lets out next month, Cojo and I are getting married."

My heart felt like it was going to leap out of my chest.

"I like your nerve coming in here telling me what you are going to do like you're running shit up in here."

"Dag. That didn't come up like I wanted it to. I'm a little nervous."

"What do you mean you're getting married," I yelled. I felt like he was much too young to get married.

"She and I have been talking about it for a minute and we really want to do it." He poked out his narrow chest and stared at me defiantly.

Something about the suddenness of this announcement didn't set well with me. As far as I was concerned, he didn't even know the chick. "Why so quickly? Is Cujo pregnant?"

"Her name is Cojo, not Cujo. And no, she is not pregnant"

I was really trying to wrap my head around what he was saying but I was having a major disconnect. Merlin was the spitting image of his father and I had to keep reminding myself who I was actually talking to.

"Then why the big rush to get married?" I demanded.

"We're not rushing. We just know what we want and there is no point in waiting."

"Yes, there is. You hardly know this heifer." I was really getting mad now. This was Ronald's seed so I expected the same type of procrastination from him as I got from his father.

"If we are going to continue with this conversation, I would appreciate it if you would stop calling my future wife out of her name."

I was stunned. Merlin was standing up to me like a man who knew what he wanted and I didn't like it one bit. I reached back and slapped the shit out of him. He rubbed the side of his face but he didn't back down. I immediately regretted hitting him. "I'm sorry. I didn't mean to do that." He did not respond right away, and I assumed that he was trying to get his emotions under control before this conversation went to a whole different level.

"We're getting married on May twenty-third, one week after we graduate. I'd like for you to be there, but if you don't feel like it, I will try to understand." He turned and walked out the door.

"Wait, I'm sorry. You caught me off guard. I didn't mean to hit you."

"It's not like it's the first time you've done it," he mumbled.

I waved off his words. "Where do you plan on living? You can't bring that girl over here. I don't need another mouth to feed."

"Did we ask you to live here? Do you think I want to start off my marriage with this? With you? Think again."

"You ungrateful son of a bitch. You can't just use me and throw me off to the side like a damn Kleenex. After all I have done for you…"

Merlin's face contorted in apparent rage. "I'm not your man! I'm you son Gina. Don't get it twisted." Merlin stomped out the room and a few seconds later I heard the front door slam.

I opened my mouth to call out to him but my words stuck in my throat. He would not have heard them anyway. I couldn't understand what was wrong with me? I felt like I was really losing my grip on reality and I was helpless to do anything about it. About the only way that I could have a decent conversation with Merlin was if I didn't look at him.

I went into the kitchen and fixed myself something to drink. I had almost promised myself that I wouldn't drink today but with the way I was feeling, I needed something to ease my pain or at least make me forget it.

The hardest part about my accepting that Merlin had become a man, was the fact that he was going to leave. He didn't need me anymore. With Gavin already gone, it was like I was losing my purpose.

When Tabatha first mentioned my visiting Gavin, I hadn't given it any thought. Now with the threat of Merlin leaving, I began to entertain the idea. He wouldn't run out on me. He still needed me. I carried the bottle back to my room. I felt like it was going to be a long night.

I woke up at nine in the morning clutching the phone. "Oh shit. Who did I call?" I felt a feeling of dread spread through my body because I had the feeling that I had done something terrible in my sleep. I bolted to the bathroom, barely making it before I threw up. My head was pounding as I clutched the toilet bowl. I rested my face against the cool porcelain surface. Even the pungent odor of urine wasn't enough to make me move my face. I felt horrible.

After several long minutes on my knees, I finally had enough energy to get up. I leaned over the sink, brushed my teeth and rinsed my mouth out with water. I staggered out of the bathroom and retrieved my phone. I had to know if I was just clutching the phone or if I had actually used it.

My call log confirmed my worst suspicions. I had called both Merlin and Ronald a total of eleven times each throughout a two hour time span. That was a lot of calls but it didn't look like any of them lasted more than a second or two. My very last call was to Tabatha and it appeared as if we spoke for fifteen minutes. Lord only knew what we talked about.

I went back to my bedroom and sat on the bed to think. However, before I could get comfortable the doorbell rang. I really didn't want to see anyone but I was curious as to who would be ringing my doorbell that early in the morning. I eased my way downstairs because my head was still pounding as the bell rang for the third time. I cautiously peeped through the blinds. Tabatha was on my porch. I took a deep breath and opened the door.

"Damn. Why aren't you dressed?"

I couldn't even fake the funk. "For what?"

Tabatha gave me a quizzical look. "Are you shitting me?"

I tried my best to think of where we could possibly be going and I came up with nothing. "If this is about that phone call last night, I changed my mind."

"Changed your mind? How you going to just change your mind and not call me and let me know?"

"Uh…"

"Uh, hell. That's just plain inconsiderate Gina. My time is valuable too."

"I'm sorry." I wasn't about to tell her that I didn't have a clue what she was talking about. It was too humiliating.

"I don't know about you girl. Lately, this hasn't been much of a friendship and this sista is getting tired."

I was stunned. In all the years that we had been friends, I couldn't recall one time when Tabatha questioned the validity of our friendship. "So you're saying I'm not a friend anymore because I canceled on your ass one time?"

"That's the thing, it's not just one time Gina. You drunk dial me at least once a week. Most times I just hang up on your ass. But this time I thought it was going to be different. And it ain't even about that. When's the last time we just hung out and chilled like girlfriend's do? When was the last time that you called me just because you wanted to see how I was doing. Everything can't be about you Gina."

I was highly offended. It was bad enough that I wasn't feeling well, but having to deal with this bullshit was testing my temperance. "How the hell am I supposed to go out with you Tabatha, I've got kids."

Tabatha gave me the side eye. "What have you been drinking? You have been acting dick dumb and liquor stupid."

I couldn't even get mad at her because what she said was so funny to me. I started laughing at what I thought was an original assessment. I was letting a dick drive me crazy and the liquor allowed me to believe it was okay.

"So I'm funny now and this is a big joke?"

I could tell that Tabatha was not amused. "Honey, I'm not laughing at you. Everything you said is the truth, it's just the way that you said that was funny."

"Wait, you're agreeing with me? That's a first. Are you still high?"

"Yes, I am. What did I agree to do yesterday when I called you?"

"You didn't agree to anything. You suggested it so what made you change your mind about visiting Gavin?"

"I can't. I wouldn't know what to say to him."

"I told you I would go with you. It's the right thing to do and you know it."

"Maybe I do but I feel like such a failure."

"Do you hear how you sound right now? When did you become a quitter?"

"I'm not quitting on anything."

"You quit on your son and I never thought I would live to see that." Tabatha slung her purse over her shoulder as if she were about to leave.

Fuck. Tabatha was absolutely correct. I had thrown the towel in on Gavin. "I didn't know what else to do with him. I feel like I gave him everything that I had to give and it wasn't enough. I'm afraid I don't have the energy or the desire to give him any more. What do you do when your best isn't good enough?"

"Was it really your best? And before you answer that, remember I've seen you do more for their no account father."

If Tabatha had a microphone, she should have thrown it on the floor. Instead, she just walked out the door and more than likely out of my life.

I

33 COJO WINFREY

I ran into my mother's room and plopped down on the bed. I was super excited as I watched her put on the finishing touches to her makeup.

"How did the interview go?"

"I got the job," I shouted.

"Honey, that's great. I knew you could do it. But listen baby, I really want to talk to you."

The smile slipped off my face. I did not like it when my mother used the I want to talk to you line because it usually preceded bad news. Her timing couldn't be better because this was supposed to be my day. "About what?" I felt my hair stand up on the back of my neck much like a cat waiting to pounce.

"It's about you and Merlin."

"Mother please."

"No, hear me out. Okay?"

"I'm listening."

"I know I told you I wanted you and Merlin to get married but I'm having second thoughts about it."

"Why? I love him."

"I know you do, but it is all happening too fast. I really think you both need to take your time and make sure it's right.

"Mother, please. You promised me we would go looking for dresses today."

"But sweetheart, don't you hear what I'm saying to you? We don't have to look for dresses now. I am not going to force you to do this."

"You are not forcing us. We want to get married."

"Well, I don't think it's a good idea anymore and besides, it's not necessary. It's been a few months since you had unprotected sex and unless you were blowing smoke up my ass, you're not pregnant. There's no harm, so no foul."

My mother had an almost crazed look in her eyes. It was so creepy it kind of scared me. "What are you talking about. We love each other and we want to be together."

"I just got a bad feeling about this and your father is going to have a heart attack if I have to call him and tell him this news."

I didn't want to upset my father unnecessarily, but I couldn't live my life for my father or my mother. I had to live it for me. "Mother, this is so unfair of you to lay this guilt trip on me. You and daddy are living your lives. How come you don't want me to live mine?"

"Baby, we want you to live your life. But there is no need to sign up for some additional heartache when you don't have to."

"What do you mean heartache? Merlin would never hurt me."

"I guess I'm not doing a very good job of explaining myself. Am I?"

"No, you're not." I folded my arms across my chest. I didn't know where her sudden change of heart was coming from but I didn't like it one bit. I still needed her consent to get married so she was about to ruin everything.

"How is Merlin planning on supporting you? You know you can't live off love."

"Momma, Merlin has a job."

"He works at Chick Fil A. What about basketball? Didn't you tell me he was some hot shot on the team?"

"He's an assistant manager mom, not a fry boy. His boss told him that he would get his own store when he graduates. And now that I'm working too, we should be okay." I wasn't even going to discuss the basketball thing because I was also confused about that. He didn't even try out for the team this year.

"Should be? Do you know how that makes me feel when you are basing your future on a should be? We don't live in that world honey. Our lives are structured and planned. When you talk about marriage and building a future together, you have to start it with a strong foundation."

"I don't know of any foundation stronger than love."

"You can't pay your bills with love either. Where will you live? Have you thought about that?"

"We'll get an apartment. Something small until we can do better."

"Do you have any idea of about how much apartments costs? You have to have money for utilities, groceries, gas for your cars. It's not easy in the real world. You kids have no idea how difficult it can be."

"We're both smart, we can figure this out. Why are you doing this?"

"Because I've had a chance to think about it and it's not the best thing. I think we should go back home for a while and give you two a chance to really think about this. And after say, six months, if you still feel the same way, I'll bring you back and you two can get married."

"Six months! Are you kidding me? What about my job?"

"You can get another job back home."

"And I'm supposed to tell Merlin he's to wait for me. Just like that?"

"If he loves you, he won't mind waiting. He can use the time to get things set up if you do end up getting married."

"I think you are setting us up for failure. Did your mother treat you this way?"

"Things were different back then and has nothing to do with now. I'm just not comfortable with Merlin's situation and he hasn't proven himself to me."

"Why does he have to prove anything to you? He's not marrying you, he's marrying me."

"You know I would have felt better about all of this if I had the chance to meet Merlin's parents. I don't know nothing about them, not even their names."

"Mom, I told you that Merlin's real mother has been MIA his entire life. He was raised by his stepmother, Gina."

"What about his dad?"

"I don't really know him. Merlin never talks about him except to say that he lives in Ohio and that he wasn't around much when he was growing up."

"Honey, if you are going to marry someone, you marry their families too. That's why you should take the time to get to know them as well. I'm telling you, families can make your life a living hell and you don't want that when you are just starting out."

"Is that why I know absolutely nothing about daddy's family?" My mother recoiled and her patient smile turned into a crooked grimace. I could tell I struck a nerve.

"Your father's family, well, that's an entirely different matter."

"Oh, really? How so?" If she was going to grill me about Merlin's family than I could certainly grill her about my dad's. It was a weird argument for her to make since we spent almost no time with our extended family. With the exception of my aunt, we never saw any of them. Most of them I couldn't pick out of a line up.

"Um, you know. It's complicated with your father's job, and the traveling…kind of makes it difficult…you see, your father's family…you know, if we're going to look at those dresses we had better get going."

I jumped off her bed and ran to my room to get my purse before she could change her mind. I knew that she was dodging bullets by agreeing to go shopping, but I didn't care as long as it shut her up about stopping our marriage. Merlin believed that his mother would eventually come around so I had to trust his judgment. For now, keeping our mother's apart was the best tactic because my mom would dog walk his.

I drove over to Merlin's job and met him when he got off work.

"Hey, babe. What are you doing here?"

"I wanted to see you silly." I reached up kissed him briefly on his lips.

"You know I don't like for you to see me like this, I smell like chicken."

"Oh, please. You don't think I've smelled chicken before? Besides, we are going to be married so what will you do then when you come home smelling like your job? Take a shower before you get home? That don't make sense."

"Yeah, I guess it doesn't," Merlin laughed nervously.

"What's the matter with you? You seem a little off to me."

"It's been a long day, I'm just tired."

"I'm sorry. I should have called you first before I came over here but I was so excited, I had to see you."

"What's going on?" He gave me a hint of a smile. It was another thing that I loved about Merlin. Even when he wasn't his best, he always tried to make me feel special.

"I had so much to tell you, I didn't want to do it over the phone. Mother and I went shopping and I found a dress for our wedding."

"A dress? I thought we were going to keep this thing small."

I pulled back in shock. We hadn't really discussed our plans in detail and now that the date was coming closer it was high time that we did get on the same page.

"I can't very well walk down the aisle naked can I?"

"Aisle? I was think more like going to the courthouse."

"Merlin, no. My mother would have a fit if I didn't have a church wedding."

Merlin frowned. "How are we going to swing this in such a short amount of time? I don't even have a church."

"I can talk to the father at our church, it shouldn't be a problem."

"That's gonna cost money and I don't think it's all that practical given our time constraints. We still have to find an apartment and all."

"I will work on the church."

"How many people are you planning on inviting?"

"Only a few besides my family. What about you?"

"There's only Braxton and maybe Gina. My circle is small. That is why I thought the courthouse would be the best way to go."

"Every girl dreams about her wedding day. I don't want mine in front of an impartial judge. Please, can we just do this one thing? I promise I will keep it small. I just want my white dress and an aisle to walk down. That's all I want."

Merlin didn't look all that convinced, but he slowly smiled letting me know things were going to be as I wanted.

"I have something else I need to talk to you about."

"Why am I getting a bad feeling? Is everything okay?"

"Everything is good but I met with a recruiter today and he really had some interesting things to say."

"A job recruiter?"

"That's great. Oh, I forgot to mention that I got a job today too."

"That's wonderful Cojo. I'm happy for you."

"It's not just for me, it's for us! We've about to become one."

Merlin cleared his throat. "This wasn't a job recruiter, it was for the Army. Well, technically, it is a job."

This was so far out in left field I couldn't even speak for several seconds.

"I don't understand. Why would you be talking to a recruiter?"

"He came to our class in school and he had some good things to say. He told us about the reserves. Hell, the signing bonus alone would be enough for us to get an apartment and some furniture. After boot camp, it's just one weekend a month."

"Are you really considering this? I've lived Army all my life, so you don't have to try to sell me on the benefits. But this isn't the life that I had envisioned for myself."

"It makes sense, Cojo. I have some money saved up, but it's not nearly enough to start living off of."

"You have your job and I have mine. We'll be okay."

"If I do this thing with the reserves, I could have a career not just a job. Not to mention the medical benefits. And, they even pay for school. It's a win win situation and one I think we should seriously consider."

I wanted to cry. "I don't know. I am going to have to think about this."

"Me too. It's a big decision but in the long run I think it will be the best decision. I could even delay my start date for a couple of months while we get settled. I just want to make a better life for us."

The fact that Merlin was willing to sacrifice his freedom for us said a lot about his character. This would also endear him to my mother who had just expressed concern about how we would be able to survive. "If you feel it's the right thing to do, I'm behind you one hundred percent."

Merlin opened his arms and I leaned into him with my head on his shoulders. Listening to his steady heart beat soothed me. "Good, then we can start looking for apartments tomorrow and I guess I'll need a suit or tux."

"Tux. I want my baby to look as good as I am going to look." Even though we still had a few details to work out, things were slowly falling into place.

34 GINA MEADOWS

Two months later

A white envelope was propped up on the kitchen table amidst my other mail when I got in from work. It was the first sign that I had all week that Merlin had been by the house. He had been keeping his distance from me ever since I failed to show up at his graduation.

I was proud of the boy, but I had a fucked up way of showing it. The entire week leading up to the gradation I had been pumping myself up about it. I cut back on my drinking and I was looking forward to seeing him walk across the stage. Even though Merlin spent most of his time over at his friend's house, we were still communicating. He called me at least twice a week to check up on me which made me very happy.

For the occasion, I got my hair done and had even brought a new dress for the ceremony. But the biggest surprise came from Ronald. He came in town the night before graduation. I was surprised to find him home when I got back from the hair dresser.

"How come you didn't tell me you were coming?" I felt self-conscious even though I knew I was looking good. It never ceased to amaze me how easily Ronald could get me worked even after all the years that we were together.

"It's my son's high school graduation, why wouldn't I be here?"

I had to swallow my words. Ronald hadn't attended anything else in Merlin's life, I almost didn't want him there. I certainly didn't tell him about it. I looked at Merlin's graduation as evidence of a job well done. Ronald showing up to take credit for it irked me since he had little to do with Merlin's rearing. "How did you find out about it? You never answered the phone when I called you."

"My son told me."

I was stunned. I didn't even realize that Merlin spoke to his father like that. Then again, Merlin was keeping to himself a lot these days. His relationship with that girl was still a bone of contention between us.

"Oh, that's nice."

"I bought the boy a car. I hope he likes it." Ronald boasted.

I was ashamed of the jealousy I felt. Ronald never bought me a car. The most I got out of him was some money to pay my bills. Hell, I needed a car more than Merlin did. I tried not to allow my true feelings to show. "Oh, that's nice. What did you get him?"

"A Toyota hybrid. It's parked out front. I'm going to need for you to take me to the dealers so I can pick up my ride."

"Can't you get Merlin to do it? I just got home from work and I'm tired."

"Damn, Gina. Why do you have to make a big deal out of everything? I was trying to surprise Merlin at graduation. I was going to put a big red bow on the car and everything."

"Ain't that special. How was I supposed to know the car was a secret if you parked in front of the damn house?" I could not hold my resentment inside. Ronald's generous gift made my paltry fifty dollar Amazon gift card a joke even though it was the best I could do.

"Because I was under the impression that he wasn't staying with your evil ass."

I felt like I had been punched and I wanted to hurt Ronald as much as he had just hurt me. "Well, the only reason why he's staying over there is because he didn't want to be here when you came by."

"We both know I haven't been by in a minute. Are you sure he ain't staying away because of flashbacks of seeing you with your pants down around your ankles and a dildo sticking out your twat?"

I could have dropped through the floor with embarrassment. It was bad enough that I did those things but it was even worse that Merlin talked to his dad about it.

"You know what, I have apologized about that six ways to Sunday. I'm not going to apologize for it again. And you can go fuck yourself because I wouldn't have been doing it if you had been handling your business in the first place."

"Don't blame that shit on me."

"Did he tell you that he was getting married too?" I was hoping to shock him just like he had done me.

"Yeah, I signed his permission slip. Are you going to take me to get my car or what?"

I was outdone. How could he have signed the form without even discussing it with me? I was more of a parent than he ever was. "Nope. I'm not."

Fine, I will get one of my other bitches to take me." Ronald stormed out taking my heart with him. I couldn't explain to Ronald what his indecision was doing to me. The back and forth was destroying me.

I reached for one of the bottles of vodka from under the sink and cracked the seal. Opening that bottle was not the reason why I missed his graduation. Drinking the entire fifth was. I was so sick the following morning, I just couldn't drag myself to the civic center for the ceremony. Other than working, the only thing that I had been successfully doing was drinking. As a tribute to my drunkenness, I had amassed a pile of empty bottles which were rapidly taking over my bedroom. I had gone through so many bottles, I was ashamed to throw them out for fear of the garbage man judging me.

I gingerly picked up the envelope off the table and examined it. There was no writing or personalization on the front of the sealed envelope. I already knew what was inside before I opened it. The fact that I was even invited to his wedding in the first place was enough to start my tears flowing. In spite of everything that I had done, Merlin still invited me to his wedding. Even though I appreciated the gesture, I had no intentions of going to a wedding I didn't support. I couldn't in good conscious show up for something I didn't believe in. If Merlin really wanted me to attend, he would have timed it so he could extend the invitation to me in person. So I really didn't feel bad about not going.

I opened the invitation anyway, just to see if he had enclosed a note or something but aside from the invitation the envelope was empty. The invitation announced the wedding was in less than twenty-four hours. I felt sick to my stomach as I tossed it on the table. It was a courtesy offer at best and I was going to treat it as such!

I woke up with an enormous headache and sour stomach. Had it not been for my full bladder, I wouldn't have gotten out of the bed. It was the weekend. I had no place I needed to be. I was going to hide amongst my covers until I felt better.

I took a swig from one of the ever present bottles by my nightstand. The alcohol burned my throat but I immediately started to feel better. With any luck, I could be back asleep within the hour. Several swallows later, I was still wide awake and trying to convince myself that I needed to do something to stop this disastrous wedding from happening. Doing nothing meant I condoned it. I couldn't have that.

I stuffed my bottle in my purse and grabbed the keys off the kitchen table. I had sat idle too long in this whole farce and it was time for me to act like a mother in this situation since it appeared as if Cojo's mother wasn't doing her duty.

When I got to the church, I started having second thoughts about going inside. I knew my advice and interference would be unwelcomed. It was a small church which I had driven by at least one hundred times but I had never gone inside. I was hoping to catch Merlin before he went inside but the doors to the church were closed. He obviously wasn't operating on colored people time today.

I lurched up the stairs holding onto the rail for balance. Even though I swore I wouldn't attend the wedding, liquor has a way of making you do stupid shit. "If I could just get him to listen to me, I'm sure I could make him change his mind," I muttered out loud.

The church was darker inside than it was out so I couldn't make out the faces in the room that turned when I opened the door. I help up my finger in the air signaling them to carry on with their business. "Shush," I whispered amidst some giggles.

"Who is that?" someone whispered.

I looked around to see who they were talking about. The sudden movement almost made me fall. I grabbed hold of the pew to steady myself. I walked past a few more rows before I slid into an empty one in the rear of the church. I would have walked up closer, but I wasn't sure my legs were going to support me. The exertion winded me and I took a few minutes with my chin resting on my chest to get myself together. To some, it might even have looked like I was sleeping.

From my vantage point, I couldn't really tell the exact number of people inside the church. Needless to say, I didn't recognize any of their faces. I assumed they were students who Merlin and Cojo went to school with. This woman, with a white veiled hat slid into the pew in front of me.

"Honey, can I help you?"

What are we in a drive in? "To do what?" I didn't know who this lady was but I was quite sure she shouldn't be talking in church.

"You appear like you're lost or something."

"I ain't lost. I know perfectly well where I'm at." I looked down for my purse and realized that I must have left it in the car. I picked up the hymn book and flipped through the pages hoping the lady would go away.

"Then you know this is a wedding?"

"Well I didn't think it was a funeral." My patience was running thin with this lady. I looked up to see if anyone else was watching her make a spectacle of herself. To my chagrin, some of them were.

"Are you a member of this church?"

"Are you taking a fucking survey?"

"Oh, my God," someone else whispered.

I was ashamed of myself for cussing in church. Even though I didn't regularly attend, I knew how to act in one.

"I beg your pardon."

"Well, I beg yours too. Ain't nobody ask you to come over here and sit near me."

"I think I'm going to find someone to escort you out of here."

"I don't need an escort. I am clever enough to get out the same way that I got in."

This lady was really starting to get on my nerves. Who goes up to a total stranger and starts talking to them? Granted, she might be someone's friend in the church but she wasn't any friend of mine so she could go back where she came from.

The woman got up and walked back toward the front of the church and out the side door. Periodically a few people would turn around and stare at me, but most minded their business while someone softly played the piano.

I don't even remember how I got to the church. I was so drunk. I looked around to see if Ronald was there, but I didn't see him. I wasn't surprised though because I was beginning to believe that Ronald didn't believe in marriage. As the piano player stopped playing, I started to doze off. It was so peacefully quiet, I couldn't help it.

I missed the entrance of the groom and the priest. They snuck in while I was sleeping. I was alerted to their presence by the mummers of the small crowd. I wanted them to shut up so I could get a few more winks in. I sat up in my seat and searched the faces in hopes of seeing Ronald. He owed me an explanation as to why he was going behind my back.

When I first noticed the groom, I was immediately drawn to his sex appeal. The black tux that he wore looked like it was tailor made for him. To me, there wasn't anything sexier on a man than a good fitting tuxedo. With his standing there, there was no way I could go back to sleep. I sat up even straighter in my chair hoping that he would look to the back of the church and notice me.

As I concentrated more on his facial features recognition filtered into my brain. "This is some bullshit." I was getting angrier by the second. The man I had been staring at facing the alter was Merlin. He stood next to the priest and was apparently waiting for his bride. The crowd in the church was buzzing with anticipation as they appeared to twitch in their seats. He turned around and looked to the door at the back of church, and I saw the eagerness on his face. I was trying to figure out how to get his attention so I could get him alone to talk but he would not look in my direction.

I was focusing so hard, my eyes appeared to cross. The feeling was much like when you concentrated on one spot long enough you began to see multiples. Suddenly, Merlin didn't look like to Merlin to me, he was Ronald. I shook my head in confusion. That couldn't be right. Ronald wouldn't be up at the alter unless he was waiting for me.

"Ronald," I tentatively called out to him. No wonder he was standing there looking all lost. He was waiting for me. I licked my lips in anticipation. They were as dry as the Sahara Dessert. I looked around for my purse again and uttered, "shit." My lipstick was in my purse.

I struggled to get out of the pew as the entire congregation got to their feet. I could not believe that my dream was finally going to come true. I was about to get married, chapped lips and all. I rushed down the aisle to get to him. "I'm coming Ronald," I whispered. My voice cracked with emotion as tears spilled down my face. Ronald was about to make me the happiest woman in the world. I only wished I had washed my face.

I didn't see Cojo walk up the aisle until she joined hands with Ronald. I didn't know whether she came out the side or if I was so focused on him, I didn't see her. Whichever way it went, she was there trying to steal my joy.

"No!" I yelled with everything in me.

All eyes were on the front of the church, so no one was really paying me any attention. She looked lovely but there was something wrong. Cojo was wearing my dress! *That bitch!* I looked down to see what I was wearing and I was appalled to see I was wearing blue jeans and my tattered robe with slippers on my feet. Not only had she somehow taken my dress, she took my shoes as well.

"This isn't right." I looked up to see if Ronald noticed that she was wearing my dress. He wasn't even looking at me. He was staring at Cojo with this stupid ass smile on his face as she tried to take my place.

I was able to run all the way to the alter without being detected. My face was fixed in a grimace and I could feel the snot running down my nose. "Bitch, how did you get my dress?" I reached for Cojo, but she jumped back behind Merlin.

"Oh my God! Miss Meadows? What are you doing?" Her face was twisted up into an awful grimace and she kept turning her head as if she smelt something foul.

Merlin's eyes grew wide as his smile turned into a frown. "Mom? What are you doing?" Still always the gentlemen, he did not raise his voice unlike that harlot that was hiding behind him.

"She's trying to steal you away from me, Ronald." I reached out to Cojo again, but Merlin guarded her well.

"Let go of that heifer and let's get married." I saw the ring that he was about to place on her finger and I grabbed it from him. "Give me my damn ring." I tried to jam the ring on my finger but it would not go past the knuckle. Leave it to Ronald to buy a ring for me and it not even fit. I slipped the ring on my pinky finger.

"You're drunk." He turned his nose up at me as he pulled Cojo to his side.

Pandemonium broke out in the church as several people rushed the alter. One of those people was that lady with the stupid veil on her hat. She reached out and grabbed Cojo from Merlin's arms. Out of everything that was happening, that was the best thing that I could have seen. Finally someone other than me understood what was going on here. But I wasn't done with Cojo yet. I looked around the room at all the angry faces.

"Who is that?" someone in the crowd asked loudly.

"I think that's Merlin's mother," answered another.

"Get out of here."

"What the hell is she wearing?"

"I think she's drunk. I heard she wasn't wrapped too tight. I believe it has something to do with Merlin's father."

"Who is this Ronald she is talking about?"

"That's Merlin's father."

I held up my hand so that Ronald could see the ring. "It fits Ronald. She tried to ruin things for you and me, but I'm not going to let her." I pointed at Cojo.

Cojo started to cry into the woman's shoulder. "You cow, you're ruining my wedding!"

I reached for her again, but only managed to grab the flowers out of her hand. "Let's do this, Ronald. I've been waiting all my life to be your wife."

"Mother!" Merlin yelled as he tried to grab my shoulders.

I didn't understand why he was yelling at me on the day that I was finally marrying his father. I reached for Cojo again and managed to grab the bodice of her dress. I yanked it hard, trying to get the dress so I could at least look the part of the bride. I felt the fabric tear and I yelled out in frustration. "Give me my dress bitch." I had lost all rational thought. The woman standing next to Cojo slapped me hard across the face. I fell back onto the pew as Merlin restrained me.

I could see the anger on Merlin's face. I struggled to get free and Merlin struck me too. I never thought I would live to see the day he'd hit me but he did. He slapped me across the other cheek, breaking me out of the trance that I was in.

"Merlin?" My head started spinning. I looked around at all the open mouthed faces in the church as the reality of what I'd done rushed back to me. "Oh, God."

Merlin let me go. I started walking down the aisle as the spinning inside my head grew. I began to fall to the floor, but Merlin caught me under my arm before I could hit the ground.

"I just wanted to say *I do*..."

Cojo rushed up beside me and grabbed my other arm. I turned to her to apologize for my behavior. The bile in my stomach rose to my mouth and before I could stop myself, I puked all over Cojo's beautiful dress.

35 COJO WINFREY

While the Father helped Merlin carry his mother to the rectory, my mother went with me to the bathroom to clean up. I was sobbing uncontrollably as I struggled to get out of my puke soaked gown.

"Mother look at my gown!" I screeched. My false eyelashes were hanging from my lashes. My makeup was ruined.

"Terrible. Simply terrible. Pull your arm through here." She helped me step out of the gown while I stood shivering in the cold rectory bathroom.

"I can't believe she did this to me. To us! Did you see Merlin's face? He's devastated."

"And he should be. That woman is nuts and should be locked away somewhere."

"Merlin told me his daddy drove her batty. He was her undoing. As much as I love her son, I can't see myself loving to the point of destruction."

"I can't believe you are offering excuses for that woman. If we weren't in this church, I would have dragged that bitch all over these floors."

"Momma, please. We're still on church grounds."

"Sweet Jesus, forgive me. I swear, this was what I was talking about when I told you when you marry, you marry their families too. Aren't you glad you found out about it before you actually married him."

I stopped wiping the vomit off of my skin with some paper towels. "What are you saying?"

"You aren't still going to marry this man after all that has happened are you?"

"Of course I'm going to marry him. As soon as I finish putting on my other dress I'm going to find the Father and have him continue the ceremony."

"Baby, no. This is surely a sign from God. You can't ignore it. Why else would He let it happen in His house?"

My mother was a big believer in signs. She was into having her tea leaves read and psychic readers too. I didn't put much stock on either of those beliefs. I put my faith in God. I was of the firm opinion that if those practices worked so well, why were all the readers scratching to make ends meet.

"I'm not going to give up on Merlin for the mistakes of his mother.

"But if she's acting this way now, can you imagine how she will be down the road. She is only going to get worse."

"Merlin doesn't spend much time with her anymore. He practically lived with his best friend all year this year and now that we have our own apartment, he won't have to see her at all unless he wants to."

"I don't think he is going to leave her as easily as you think. Even when she was wilding out he didn't lose his cool with her except maybe when he slapped her."

"That just goes to prove that he is a respectful man and isn't prone to violence. You should be happy that I am marrying such a man."

"I wish I could be happy but I'm afraid that she is going to bring you nothing but misery."

"I'm not going to have anything to do with her unless she gives me a complete apology." I finished wiping up as best I could and I put on the dress that I had brought to wear after the wedding. I was actually glad that I had brought it with me.

"I wish your father was here. He would be able to talk some sense into you. You don't know the heartache family can bring you."

"Can you go please tell the Father that I will be ready in about ten minutes. And if you see Merlin could you ask him to come in here please?"

My mother threw her arms up in the air. "Okay, I give up. I hope you know what you're doing." She left the room shaking her head, closing the door behind her.

I saw down on the couch to touch up my makeup. My hands were still shaking when Merlin knocked on the door. I rushed to him.

"Baby, are you okay?"

"I'm fine. I should be asking you that question." He pushed me away so he could look me up and down.

"What about your mother? Where is she?"

"She's sleeping it off. I can't believe she actually thought I was my father. I know we look alike but that shit was crazy."

"Hey, don't forget where you are."

"Darn. I'm sorry. I did for a moment, didn't I?"

"What are you going to do about her?"

"She can sleep it off here. If I were to take her home she would just get more liquored up. She's right where she needs to be."

"What about tomorrow? What will you do then?"

"Once we leave here, I'm done. She's embarrassed me for the last time. I don't want to have anything to do with her until she gets her act together."

"Then are you ready to make an honest woman of me? I don't imagine those people out there will sit around much longer."

"You still want to marry me after all the stuff that went down here today?"

"Are you kidding me? Now, more so than ever!" I pulled Merlin to me for a big kiss.

We walked back into the church arm and arm to a standing ovation. Merlin's friend Braxton and my mother approached the alter with us as witnesses.

"Dearly beloved, we are gathered here today to witness the union of Merlin Mills to Cojo Winfrey. Who gives this woman to this man?"

"Her mother," My mother said as she placed my hand in Merlin's. She kissed me on the cheek. The only person in the room that knew she wasn't that excited about our union was me. She never let on to her misgivings.

The Father continued with the ceremony and other than reciting our vows, I didn't hear most of it.

"I now pronounce you man and wife. You may kiss your bride."

"Finally." Merlin said as he bent me over and gave me the best kiss of my life. His kiss signified the end of a total dysfunctional relationship and the beginning of the greatest love ever.

I was looking forward to the day when we would have a family of our own and break the cycle. I was determined to show Merlin what a real family looked like. I could only hope my kiss gave him all those promises and more.

THE END

It ain't over!
Are you ready for the next installment?

Outdone

This story can't end just yet. There's still too many things hanging in the balance. What happened to Gina? Will she ever find love? What about Gavin? Is he out of jail yet?

Will Cojo and Merlin live happily ever after?

EXCERPT FROM
OUTDONE

1 COJO MILLS

Normally, I'm the last person to give up in a fight. I'm the one who wants to have the last say, or in some cases the last punch. However, in this fight with my new husband's mother, there would be no winners. Either way, we all lost. I lost out on a potential mother figure now that my own mom had moved away, and Merlin lost the only person who had shown him love other than me.

I didn't want him to have to make a choice. I knew he had enough love in his heart for both of us, but after the way she showed her ass at our wedding, I understood his decision to disassociate himself from his stepmother. He didn't seem at all upset about it either, which really surprised me given his loving persona.

"What's got your face all frowned up, wife? We just got married and I can't get a smile?"

"Honey, don't mind me. My mind was a million miles away."

"You're bored with me already?"

"Stop playing. I could never be bored with you. Do you even know how long I've been waiting to get my husband alone?" I leaned over and kissed Merlin on his cheek. I would have done more, but I didn't want to interfere with his driving.

"Well, you got me, for life. How do you like them apples?"

"I think I like it very much, and I plan to wear it well."

"That's good to know because it's too late to trade me in on another model. I've got the paperwork that says you're mine."

"Like property? Oh no, sweetheart. We ain't rolling like that. We're mated for life because we belong together."

"Okay, I'll take that but I still got paperwork." Merlin laughed wholeheartedly. I loved to hear his laugh.

"Then the same goes for me; I've got papers on you too buddy, so don't go getting any bright ideas."

"About what? You made me the happiest man alive today. Your mom really went all out with the reception, too. I think everyone had a good time after…"

Merlin didn't have to finish his sentence because I already knew what he was going to say. A feeling of sadness came over me. My wedding day would always be paled by Gina's behavior. "I know you don't want to talk about this, but don't you think you should go by the rectory and see about getting Gina home?"

"You're right, I don't want to talk about it. Not tonight."

"But babe, her car is there. What if she gets up and decides to drive it somewhere? Or if she wants to act the fool in the rectory?"

"You don't believe God can handle it? I thought we were supposed to bring him our problems and drop them in his lap."

"I doubt it was meant literally. Like in give us your weak and hungry. That's a liberty speech, not God's creed, at least I don't think it is."

"I disagree with you there. God is a fixer and Gina needs fixing."

"What about the rest of the rectory? Do you plan on punishing them in the process?" I was getting a little irritated with the conversation. I didn't want our marriage to be riddled with regrets. If handled correctly, we might be able to salvage something of a relationship with his mother. I didn't see that happening if we just left her in the church like we didn't give a damn.

"Cojo, what do you want me to do? She has already ruined our wedding day. Do we let her screw up our night too?"

I could tell he was frustrated and so was I. "We've got the rest of our lives together. So I don't mind giving Gina a few more hours of it if it will make things better between the three of us.

"You would go with me to check on her?" He seemed genuinely surprised.

"Of course I would. I would never ask you to do something that I wasn't willing to do myself. Wrong or not, she's still the only mother you've known, and it's our duty to check on her."

"Cojo Mills, you are an amazing woman, and I am so happy to call you my wife."

"I'm sure you would do the same thing for me if the show were on the other foot."

"I'm not so sure about that. The whole thing in the church was very intense. I thought I was going to have to punch my mother out."

"You wouldn't do that! I know you better than that. Is there someone you could call who would come and sit with her?"

"I would call my dad if I thought he actually gave a shit about her. She has this one friend named Tabatha who has been around forever, but I really don't want to embarrass Gina any more than she's feeling right now. Tabatha would ride her ass bareback."

"Ouch, would she be that hard on her?"

"Absolutely. Tabatha believes in tough love. She's there when you need her, but she doesn't tolerate a lot of foolishness, and she doesn't cosign either. Those two fight like star-crossed lovers but they really care for each other."

We pulled up in front of the rectory, and Merlin made a big production of turning off the car without making a move to get out. I could tell he really didn't want to go in.

"Do you think she's still here? I don't see her car."

Merlin's face brightened with a smile. "You're right. It was parked right here when we left."

"You don't think she tried to drive or fought with the priest? Do you?

"With Gina, I never know what to think. Just when I think she couldn't possibly do something worse, she does."

"Should I go inside just to make sure everybody is still alive in there?" My joke was in extremely bad taste.

"As far as I know, she hasn't killed anyone yet. Knowing her, she's at the house having cocktail hour." Merlin turned on the car, and we drove in silence to Gina's house. Luckily, we didn't have any concrete plans for our first night as husband and wife. If we were going to be able to enjoy it, Merlin had to see this through.

I started to open the door, but Merlin stopped me.

"I love that you want to do this with me, but I think I should do this alone. Heaven knows what I will be walking into."

"Okay, I understand." I was secretly relieved. I didn't want a repeat of the last time that I had been in their house.

"I won't be long. I promise."

"Take your time, baby. I know how important this is."

"Did I tell you that I loved you today?"

"I think it was somewhere in those vows."

"Be right back."

ABOUT THE AUTHOR

Tina Brooks McKinney began her writing career as a dare. As an avid reader, writing was the next step for her. Armed with a very active imagination and a story to tell, Tina penned her first novel All That Drama. Readers fell in love with Tina's no-nonsense characters and her comedic style of weaving a story. Since then, Tina has written ten novels and two novellas. Her titles include, All That Drama, Lawd, Mo' Drama, Fool, Stop Trippin', Dubious, Deep Deception, Snapped, Got Me Twisted, Deep Deception 2, Snapped 2: The Redemption, Betta Not Tell and Catch Fire and Catch Fire 2. Her next book Outdone should be released in the coming months.

A wife and mother of two, Tina uses real life situations to both entertain and inspire her readers. You can find out more information about her by visiting her website.www.tinamckinney.com or drop her an email at tybrooks2@yahoo.com. She would love to hear from you.